Peckover Joins
The Choir

Peckover Joins
The Choir

Michael Kenyon

St. Martin's Press
New York

Library of Congress Cataloging-in-Publication Data

Kenyon, Michael.
    Peckover joins the choir / Michael Kenyon.
        p.   cm.
    "A Thomas Dunne book."
    ISBN 0-312-10523-1
    1. Peckover, Henry (Fictitious character)—Fiction.   2. Art
thefts—Europe—Fiction.   3. British—Europe—
Fiction.   4. Police—Europe—Fiction.   I. Title.
PR6061.E675P464   1994
823'.914—dc20   93-43656
                                                                CIP

First published in Great Britain by MACMILLAN LONDON LIMITED.

First U.S. Edition: March 1994
10 9 8 7 6 5 4 3 2 1

Peckover Joins
The Choir

ONE

Chief Superintendent Frank Veal, Criminal Investigation Department, said, 'Can you carry a tune?'

'Carry it where?' asked Peckover.

Veal, in his office at Scotland Yard, in his power chair that could rock, swivel, and would emit an explosive gasp when sat on, fished a paper from the file in front of him.

He said, 'Ghent, Gap, Bra, and Andorra.'

'Pretty obscure places.'

'It's an obscure choir. Amateurs. The Sealeigh Choral Society. Heard of them?'

'Heard of Sealeigh. Dover way, Folkestone. Somewhere down there. Chunnel territory.'

'The Sealeigh choir's been on TV seven times.'

'Thought you said they were obscure. Anyway, I missed them. I'd 'ave been watching the Epilogue.'

'Obscure compared with the Vienna Boys' Choir. Mormon Tabernacle. King's College, Cambridge. Sealeigh's good, though. They tour the Continent. This next programme, the one you're in, is Mozart—'

'What did you say?'

'Mozart. You've heard of Mozart. Wolfgang Amadeus—'

'You said the one I'm in.'

'Let me finish. Mozart's *Regina Coeli*, pardon the pronunciation, couple of songs by Brahms, some good old Gilbert and Sullivan, Schütz—'

'Who?'

'Heinrich Schütz.' Veal, after some scrabbling in the file, read aloud. 'Fifteen eighty-five to sixteen seventy-two. Born Saxony, working life Dresden . . . and such and so forth. He's German.

7

You're doing his Psalm 150. I think I saw somewhere it has some other title. *Lobet den Herren*?'

'You asking me?'

'Then a bunch of English folk stuff to send them away humming.'

'Send who away?'

'The music lovers you'll be singing to. First in Sealeigh, then on the Continent, the Easter tour. You leave for Ghent in two weeks. Third of April. You a bass or a tenor?'

'No one's ever told me.'

'What about Twitty?'

'What about 'im?'

'Does he sing?'

'Gawd, you're enlisting Twitty?'

'Mrs Coulter?' called Veal to the only other occupant of the office. 'Was Detective Constable Twitty my idea or yours?'

'Yours, Mr Veal.'

Screens, keyboards, terminals and telephones besieged Mrs Coulter at her array of desks and side desks at the distant end of the office. To judge from her composure she had the measure of them. The butterfly fingers of Mrs Coulter, administrative assistant, without whose diligence and discretion the CID would have long since fallen apart, fluttered over the keys of a word processor. When Frank Veal had been promoted and acquired Mrs Coulter, he had addressed her by her first name – once. The twitch of her nostrils had made it plain that this was a familiarity not to be countenanced. Veal could no longer have said with certainty what her first name was.

He said, 'Henry, why don't we get comfortable in the Feathers. You're likely going to be needing a pint.'

'Likely I am. Tell me, this Schütz, is he in German?'

'How d'you mean?'

'Do we sing, that's to say, does this misbegotten throng of warblers sing, what was it you said, his lobets and herring, in German?'

'We'll bring the file, it's all in there. I can't understand what you're getting so sweaty about. If you can sing 'Knees Up, Mother Brown' you can sing Schütz. Dammit, singing's singing. Like flying Concorde, doing a heart transplant. A spot of practice, any idiot can do it.'

* * *

Not for the first time that week, drizzle grizzled on Scotland Yard and environs, moistening St James's Park, dampening Petty France, and veiling Buckingham Palace in murk. Five number eleven buses bound for Chelsea and either Richmond or Shepherd's Bush spattered in convoy along Victoria Street, eliminating all possibility of further number elevens arriving for another fifty minutes.

Head down, scurrying through the gloom, watching for a gap in the traffic, Detective Chief Inspector Peckover said, 'Look, Frank, I don't sing. Get Sergeant Flynn. He sings. Hums, anyway.'

'Watch it.' Veal grabbed Peckover's arm, stopping him stepping off the pavement into a cyclist.

'I don't know a word of German. *Gemütlich. Angst. Himmel.* That's it. I don't know what they mean.'

In the Feathers the policemen took their pints of Bass to an umbrageous corner table and removed their coats. At this hour they had the pub much to themselves. Macaroni cheese in a dish on the food counter had congealed, and the last of the sausages, after three hours of slow heat, had shrunk to brittle, hollow tubes, like items from a plumber's kit.

'Good health,' Veal said, and lifted his glass.

'*Auf wiedersehen.*' Peckover took a swallow of flat, malty, room-temperature bitter. 'Presumably there's an audition. Have you thought about that? You know what they say – "Don't call us, we'll call you."'

'It's all arranged.'

'I bet it is. What you're holding back, what you 'aven't dared let on about, it's me does the solo in Mozart's *Regina* whatsit. What language is that in – Latin?'

'How about shutting up. Moan, moan, you're a tedious old woman.' Beads of beer glistened on the underside of Veal's handlebar moustache. 'Do you want to hear what all this is about or not?'

'I know what it's about. It's me standing up there in my angel gown in front of a concert hall of foreigners and the first sound that comes out of my mouth will be something nobody's heard before and they'll have to stop the concert.'

'Don't be so swollen-headed. What makes you think the spotlight's on you? This is a big choir. You're a face in the crowd. No one will hear you unless you shout.'

'I won't shout.'

'The Sealeigh Choral Society has sixty-five or so members plus instrumentalists like a string quartet or trumpets, depending on what they're singing, and a regular pianist and organist. That's around seventy in all, give or take a half dozen depending on who's down with a virus, who's on holiday, random newcomers—'

'Random is me and Twitty, right?'

'—and sometimes ringers.' Veal waited. 'Go on, then, ask.'

'What's a ringer? Apart from a horse of a different colour substituted for the real thing at Ascot, and a felony.'

'These ringers aren't a felony. They're professionals the conductor brings in to strengthen the choir if it's not up to snuff. They're hauled in at the last minute, and with Sealeigh usually not at all.'

'I'll be a ringer.'

'They're not to be confused with leaners.'

'I would 'ope not.'

'Leaners, I gather, are the weaker singers who're unsure of the notes and tempo and everything so they lean towards their neighbour to pick it up from him, or her.'

'What if the neighbour's a leaner, what then, Mr Know-all?'

'As you may have divined, or would have if you weren't so busy being anxious—'

'Frank, you still haven't got it. I am anxious. Therefore I'm not your man. Lower me into a nest of vipers, face me against Scotsmen with claymores and bagpipes, I'm yours. Sing I do not. True, I've trilled "The Road to Mandalay" in the bath. Miriam belts up the stairs to shut the door and Sam and Mary come out in hives. Frank, I do not sing in public.'

'As I was saying,' Veal said. Before going on to say it he took a swallow from his glass, patted his moustache, and opened the Sealeigh file. 'You will have guessed that one of the choir, but we don't know who, happens to be a public enemy.'

'Me. Wait till they hear me.'

'When I say one, could be two, or a gang for all we know. Stuff's been going missing from where they hold their concerts. Serious stuff. Not ashtrays.'

'It'll be the sopranos. Light voices, light fingers.'

'Gold, icons, holy relics. The sort of treasures that once would

10

have sparked off a crusade. Like a sixth-century black madonna missing from Amiens cathedral since the choir performed there in October.'

'Mary was black?'

'Mary was a virgin is all I know. Black here seems to describe the wood. There are black madonnas all over. One in France at Rocamadour. Plenty in Spain and Italy. Famous one in Poland at a monastery is a painting by St Luke. Three hundred thousand pilgrims every August.'

'How d'you know all this?'

'Done my homework, haven't I?'

Veal riffled through papers in the file. Computer printouts, lists of choir members, balance sheets, concert programmes, flyers for shop windows and telegraph poles advertising bygone Sealeigh Choral Society concerts, messages from police departments on the Continent and faxes from Interpol, translations attached, memos from the assistant commissioner, and a calendar.

Questing, Veal said, 'What do you mean by sopranos being light? They're not light at all. Light is how you sing a note, it's quality, not the register. Sopranos can pierce like a laser and some of them weigh in at three hundred pounds.'

'You know so much about it, you join the choir.'

'Oh, matey, if only. Those sweet harmonies, that soaring sound, the teamwork and fellowship—'

'You all right?'

'—the controlled tumult, the abrupt pianissimo, the pulsing rhythms, the profundities, the froth. No, I'm not all right, I'm jealous. Stop worrying. Pick out the notes on your piano and learn them. You got a piano?'

'No.'

'Thought you'd bought one.'

Peckover and Miriam had bought a piano for £30 from a junk shop in the hope their children might grow up to be Paderewskis. One day they would get round to finding a teacher. They hadn't had the piano tuned yet. Miriam had taken piano lessons as a child. Her excuse for not sitting down at their piano and seeing if she had retained anything was that it was out of tune.

Veal said, 'Here, one black madonna. Missing.'

11

He slid a ten-by-eight-inch photograph through the table's beer rings. Peckover held it close to his eyes, then away, and wondered when he would make an appointment with an optician. No big deal, everybody wore glasses, and Miriam would at least stop badgering him.

He said, 'This is a madonna? You've got the right photo?'

'Hot from Amiens Police Judiciaire.'

'This is a lump of charred timber.'

'Walnut.'

'Could be from the Louvre, the modernist wing.'

'Right, it's old, weathered, and probably been lost and looted and buried and dug up and shot at and used as a doorstop and carried as a banner and clobbered a thousand heathens, like Samson's ass's jawbone. It's also been nicked from a chapel in Amiens cathedral, the day the Sealeigh choir sang there, and it's priceless. Don't even ask.'

'Am I allowed to ask could you put it in your pocket or do you need a block and tackle? This is the most useless photo I ever saw.'

'Dimensions on the back. Forty centimetres. About fourteen inches? You could put it in a shopping bag if you were sauntering round the cathedral at a quiet time, no one else about, and you jimmied open the brick and glass under the altar, as someone did.' He was reading a slip of paper gummed to the back of a second photograph. 'This is a chalice from St Mary of the Angels in Padua – Chiesa di Santa Maria degli Angioli – lifted four days later, same day our choristers happened to be there. They didn't perform in the church, they sang in somewhere called the Villa Favorita, but they have leisure time for shopping and sightseeing.'

'And filching?'

'That's what you're going to find out.'

'A religious nut?'

'Possibly.'

Peckover studied the black-and-white photograph of a goblet carbuncled with what he assumed to be gems. Capacity about three-quarters of a pint.

'Ought to fetch a fiver or two on the Portobello Road.'

'This one's not priceless, the Padua polizia have priced it,' Veal said. 'On the back. Whatever it says in lira comes to sixty thousand quid. It isn't the Holy Grail. But enough for a small swimming pool and getting the roof fixed. Here's the next and last. So far.'

Raising and lowering beer glasses had created new beer circles through which Veal, deskman, workaholic, and lecher when he allowed himself the time, slid towards Peckover a third photograph.

Peckover peered sceptically at a tiny spike, or splinter, or perhaps an exquisitely delicate dab from a Japanese paintbrush.

'So what's this?'

'That, Henry, is a thorn from Jesus's crown of thorns.'

'Ah.'

'Stolen from the Bruder Klausenkirche in Basel, where, by happenstance, the Sealeigh lot gave their final performance on their last tour of the Continent.'

'A thorn, eh?' Peckover refused to allow his mouth to fall open. 'From the crown.'

'In fact, it's not. It's a fake. Makes no difference, it's still beyond price, and Basel apparently has crusaders who'll kill to get it back. The thorn's a sham, a counterfeit, it's been proved to be a counterfeit by carbon dating and microanalysis, six years ago, same as the shroud of Turin. It's also drawn a zillion pilgrims for six hundred years, and they're still coming because the current crop, nineteen-nineties pilgrims, have more faith in this thorn than in microanalysis. Basel says they kneel in front of the empty space under the altar.'

'Thought it was the madonna that was lifted from under the altar.'

'And the thorn. Relics are often on show under the altar. A painting might hang over the altar or close by. All you do, Henry, is get the thorn back. Watch who's thieving this stuff on the upcoming Sealeigh tour, and when you're back, recover it from under his bed in Acacia Avenue, Sealeigh. Basel will give you the freedom of the city.'

'What can you do with that?'

'You'd have to go to Basel, find out.'

Five cheerful builders with plaster on their boots were among the few remaining customers in the Feathers. They stood with their pints at the far end of the bar, sometimes in discussion, sometimes erupting in laughter.

13

Peckover said, 'This Sealeigh thief, this warbler purloining priceless relics, I don't quite believe it. It's like stealing a Van Gogh. What do you do with it? Where's your market?'

'Most of these thefts are done on contract. The buyer's there before the stuff is nicked. A mad Texan? A Japanese electronics mogul? A third world dictator who's beheaded the opposition and plundered his country and hopes the relics will bring him salvation?'

'How about an investment for the wife and bairns?' mooted Peckover. 'Like that American soldier at the end of World War Two who looted a treasure trove from some church in Germany—'

'Quedlinburg.'

'—and 'alf a century later 'e's dead but Germany gives his family a million quid to get the stuff back. Amazing. Any ransom demanded for our thorn?'

'Not so far.'

'Has to be a religious maniac. It's so amateurish it can't be true. Every place the Sealeigh lot stop and sing something goes missing. How long have we known?'

'Sunday. There was no reason to suspect the Sealeigh lot. It's only on the last tour stuff went missing, and I told you, the choir's obscure, they don't get police outriders and the red carpet. No one knows they exist except concert-goers. The press hasn't made the connection yet and the longer it stays that way the better our chances. The thefts have been written up but no mention of Sealeigh.'

'Don't tell me the choir doesn't know.'

'The choir's the last who'll know. By the time the story's out they're in the next country singing their shanties, and if they saw it on television news in Reggio they wouldn't understand it. Well, some might. Oscar Thomas has his ear to the ground and he's convinced nobody in the choir's aware of any link. Except now, of course, himself.'

'Who's Oscar Thomas?'

'The choir's director. He runs it. Give credit to our colleagues on the other side of the Channel, say I. They've been brisk making the connection.'

'All I'm saying, our songbird ain't no professional. If he exists. It's like he wants to be collared.'

'So collar him, Henry. Sing, snoop, enjoy yourself, and nab him.'

14

'Who are the suspects?'

'Except for a few who weren't on the last tour, we haven't counted out anyone.'

'Come on, pull the other. Seventy of them and we've no hint? You're telling me they're all equally suspect?'

'Probably not Mrs Green. She's in her seventies, wife of Alderman Green, the mayor.' Veal delved in the file and came up with stapled lists. 'Alderman Philip Green, tenor, mayor of Sealeigh. He's seventy-four. Half the choir are senior citizens.'

'Prime suspects. Religious kleptomania among the sunset folk.'

'They're a mixed bag of jobs and professions. One has an antiques shop. There's even a copper—'

'It's 'im. Case solved.'

'—Superintendent Day, Sealeigh Constabulary.'

'Anyone with form?'

'Two. Let's see.' Veal found the sheet. 'Peter Witherspoon, a peeper, nine years ago. No details. He was bound over. Age forty-one, lecturer in fine arts at Folkestone College of Further Education. The other's Clemency Axelrod, drunk driving, three months' suspended. New Year's Eve two years ago. She drove her Toyota along Brighton promenade and down eighteen steps on to the beach. Six hundred quid's worth of damage to benches, bollards and railings.'

'Singing as she went?'

'Singing what?'

'I don't know what. Just singing.'

'She's a mezzo-soprano. Or alto. It's not clear.' Veal frowned at Clemency Axelrod's unclear record. 'Anyway, lower than soprano but not as low as contralto. She'd have been singing contralto by the time she hit the beach, all those steps. She has a glass eye.'

'Before or after?'

'Before or after what?'

'The beach.'

'Doesn't say. She's the one with the antiques shop. Curiouser and Curiouser: Curios, Antiques, Bric-à-Brac. Beach Terrace, Sealeigh. Your round, I think.'

Peckover went to the bar. He returned with two pints and peanuts.

15

'I don't like amateurs,' he said.

'Villains or choirs?'

'Villains. They don't have rules or routine or tradition. You can't predict them. They can be lucky and get away with murder. Frank, I'm flattered, and a free holly-wolly on the Continong thrown in. You mean well but I can't do it. Sergeant Flynn's your man. Have you heard what 'e does with 'Ol' Man River'? Paul Robeson, move over.'

'You've missed a week's rehearsals but you'll catch up – they were probably only handing out the music and collecting subscriptions. Ten rehearsals in all – leaves you and Twitty with six, or is it five, and a dress rehearsal – Monday, Wednesday and Friday nights, seven o'clock at the Presbyterian church—'

'Methodist. Could be Congregationalist. Even Church of England. Not Presbyterian. Scotland has the Presbyterians.'

'Try the Presbyterian church first. Wycliffe Way. You start tomorrow. Rehearsals are over by ten so you can catch a train back, be in bed by midnight, or you could drive. Up to you. Cheaper if you and Twitty share a car. If you don't and you miss the last train you'll have to stay over but not at any fancy five-star job. We've had another directive from the Home Office. You'd think we were living off caviar. The principle is you're in Sealeigh only for rehearsals. You keep your head down. No drawing attention to yourself. There's not much you can do until the tour starts, anyway. That's two weeks from today, the fourth, a Tuesday. First you give two performances in the church, Sunday. The local press and TV will be there to laud you with the usual raves, so I gather, because the mayor and his lady are in the choir. You'll need an alias. Your name could be familiar to addicts of the poesy page in the public prints. Twitty could be Twitty. I suggest you're Bill Smith in some job so boring no one's going to ask, like household cleansers, and you moved to the area only a couple of months ago. Nobody will bother you, they're too busy getting their singing right. The only character in the choir knows you're a copper is the director, Oscar Thomas. He sounds like a pain in the arse. I've talked with him, but he had to know to get you in. If he happens to be our looter we're up the creek, we can all go home, because he's hardly going to swing into action with Scotland Yard on board. Though you never know. Questions?'

16

'I 'aven't time to rehearse. I'm round the clock on the Tooting Bec bank job.'

'Not any more. I'm doing some reshuffling. The choir rehearsals are work, natch, the line of duty, so you can spend the next morning in bed.'

'Resting my voice?'

'Exercising it. Learning your notes. Reading *The Life and Times of Ludwig van Beethoven.* Miriam well?'

'She was this morning. Dunno what she'll say about this.'

Peckover took a long swallow of beer. Veal straightened the Sealeigh papers, closed the folder, and pushed it towards Peckover.

'Yours,' he said. To his damp moustache adhered a sizeable peanut crumb, indeed, close on half the actual peanut. 'Oscar Thomas, the director, he's not your conductor. He runs the show, him and his committee, and they bring in guest conductors, professionals. Yours is Robin Goodfellow. Evidently he's young and telegenic and sought after and leads the City of London Chorale. He'll be a Sir one day, so his fan club says. You'll be in good hands.'

'He's about to become the most terrifying person in my life. Tell me this, if there's an angel-gowned chorister—'

'The men wear dinner jackets, black tie.'

'—if there's a bloke in a black tie up there among the warblers with his mouth open like a cave but no sound coming out, because if there were it'd be the end of the concert – all you'd hear would be police sirens and fire engines swarming in to assist the maimed and bereaved – will Sir Goodfellow know? What I'm asking, what's 'is eyesight like? Any chance he 'as a glass eye? Two glass eyes?'

Veal finished his pint, taking his time, swamping the lower reaches of his moustache. When he set the glass down the half peanut had gone. He put on his coat.

'Good luck, Henry, you lucky dog. Since you're agreeable, I'll pass a copy of the file to Twitty.'

'Twitty, oy vey,' sighed Peckover, who was not a Jew, but was a regular at the remaining bagel shop on Whitechapel's Brick Lane, close to where he had grown up. Once an animated enclave of the Diaspora, Brick Lane was now an equally lively outpost of Asia.

Veal left, back to his desk and a score of chores more urgent than Sealeigh. Fact was, he had heard Our 'Enry sing, albeit at

17

parties. If he knuckled down he'd add resonance to the Sealeigh lot.

Peckover eyed the file but did not open it. What if it included music? Schütz? English folk music even? Fa la la and a hey nonny nonny.

He had never heard Twitty sing, not beyond 'Ten Green Bottles' and 'I've Got a Lovely Bunch of Coconuts' when everyone was plastered, except Twitty, whose customary tipple was pineapple juice. But he had seen him hefting a ghetto blaster and snapping his fingers. The lad would be home and dry if the Sealeigh concert included some heavy metal and a few calypsos.

TWO

Detective Constable Twitty had one bare black limber leg in his harlequin pants and was inserting the other when the telephone rang.

'It'll be the Queen,' he told the woman in his bed. 'She usually phones about now.'

Bent-kneed, hobbled, one trouser leg trailing, Twitty lurched towards the telephone at the other end of his bedsitter. He passed white walls, a kitchen alcove with done-for cans of chilli awaiting recycling, a door to the bathroom, jumbo cushions serving as chairs – chez Twitty, guests needed supple knees – bookcases, a shelf of records, tapes and compact discs, and an adjacent space-age edifice with switches, speakers, dancing lights, and a tray that opened and closed at the touch of a button on a distant magic wand. One almost expected to see olives or a bar of Cadbury's on the opening tray, but it was for playing CDs until dawn, which was about when he had returned from the disco with Alice, unless she was Amy. A huntin' and fishin' gel, anyway. Blank windows looked down on cars and red double-deckers splashing along Lavender Hill.

Twitty was content with his pad. It cost him more than his housing allowance but it was private, which could not be said for the police barracks he had started out in. This afternoon, his first day off in nine days, not that much was left of it, he had a spring in his step – or might have had but for the dragging trouser leg, not to mention the person in his bed. Anna? Hannah?

He hoped she would depart happily and soon back to the shires.

If the phone wasn't Alex with a spare ticket for the film festival, or his mum needing to know if he was eating his greens, it was a wrong number.

Curriculum vitae, Jason Twitty: twenty-five, bachelor, of Jamaican

19

immigrant parents, copper, and prior to that scholarship boy at Harrow, acquiring the rudiments of Latin, Greek, computer science, cricket, and pals among the nobs, not that it was easy thinking of them as nobs when you had known them in extremis with their noses runny, eyes watery from homesickness, knees bloody after football, defeated by algebra, bullied and bullying, and performing private acts with their pants round their ankles.

He picked up the phone, pinched his nose, and said, 'Jockey Club, Captain Carruthers speaking. Fearfully sorry but we don't take bets.'

Twitty then crossed himself and said, 'Sorry, sir, I was expecting someone else.'

Listening, he bowed his head and kept bowing it in brisk, servile jolts like a houseboy in the days of the Raj. He replaced the phone when there was nothing further to bow to, Chief Superintendent Veal having hung up.

A choir? Sealeigh? Where was Sealeigh? Singing on the Continent in black tie and dinner jacket? Collect the file and contact Mr Peckover apropos of transport to Sealeigh tomorrow?

Our 'Enry. Yes, yes, he would do all that.

Clothing, yes, he'd do that too. Twitty, lover of finery, pondered the bizarre commands. For the rehearsals, a low profile, the super had said. Grey, sombre, choral. Get your hair cut.

Twitty touched the roof of his hair, several wiry cylindrical inches above his skull. If it had to go, it had to go. The fashion wouldn't last for ever anyway. Would he dare put in an expenses chit for the lopping off? It'd cost twenty quid.

Mr Peckover, Bard of the Yard? Henry was a bit odd but he saw you through, more or less.

Twitty lurched gracefully back through the sitting room, harlequin pants in place, and plucked from a closet a fluorescent blouse of abstract design.

'Work, you know how it is, the call of duty,' he whispered to the woman in his bed. He avoided risking giving her a name. 'All you do is close the door behind you. It locks itself.' Was she listening? Her eyes were shut. She sighed and stirred. The door locked itself if you didn't fiddle with the lock. 'Don't fiddle with it, just close it.' Dearest Sophie, he would have liked to add, demonstrating that he

20

was on her side, but she might have been Clarissa. He whispered, 'Goodnight.'

Goodnight? It was mid-afternoon.

Twitty sprinted in balloon-soled sneakers through the murk of Lavender Hill, on to Wandsworth Road, onward over Vauxhall Bridge, and, thereafter, by way of Rochester Row and various alleys, to Victoria Street and the Factory. He sprinted not because of eagerness for the Sealeigh file but because he burst with energy and would arrive quicker and cheaper on his bouncy joggers. Several congested miles and marvellous.

Miriam Peckover had taken off her shoes, tights and skirt and lay on her back in paradise. She heard the front door open, the pause, then close. Henry never got home this early.

She didn't stir because it had to be Henry. Perhaps he had a fever. Something had to have happened. Nothing she was about to leap up for, though.

She lay with the *Independent* on the sitting-room sofa lamenting her ignorance, though not so much as to wreck the heaven of being supine. Where exactly was Eritrea and why was it always in trouble? Was an undervalued dollar good or bad for her British housekeeping? Her ignorance discomforted her less than her feet, and they were repairing. She had been on them for five hours preparing deep-fried calf's head à la piémontaise for her darlings at the Royal Archaeological Society, baked cod for those with delicate tummies, and the usual starters, soup, veg, rice pudding, fruit barquettes, and, though she said it herself, a very dashing mocha parfait with chocolate sticks and whipped-cream rosettes. She hoped Henry would be wild about the calf's head. She had brought home a ton of leftovers.

Sam and Mary were in the debris-strewn playroom in front of Bugs Bunny, that maniacal sadist. That wouldn't last long with Henry home, or not for Mary, whose Bugs Bunny attention span was short. Sam's was of sturdier stuff. It didn't have to be Bugs Bunny, either, it could be 'Business World' or the news in Welsh. Miriam heard Mary whooping into the hall. Then trumpetings and screams.

Peckover came in holding a folder between his teeth like a

21

golden retriever and twirling squealing Mary above his head. She was wearing her princess's gown, an old slip with holes cut for the arms.

Miriam said, 'For heaven's sake put her down, you'll make her sick.'

He did so. Mary began climbing up his leg for more. The situation was saved by Sam shouting for her from the nursery, Bugs Bunny having surpassed himself in atrocity. Mary rushed from the room.

'Don't just lie there,' Peckover commanded. 'Sit up. I want your full attention.'

'You've been demoted again.'

'Worse. I am a chorister with the Sealeigh Choral Society. Undercover. One of the choir steals as well as sings. We are to sing on the Continent.'

Miriam sat up. 'Wonderful! When? Where?'

'It's all in there.' He handed her the file. 'Except the music. We have to buy that. Schütz. And English folk ballads, you know, "I was opening my veins one merry May morn, When a maid I chanced to meet." 'Ow can you say it's wonderful? This is singing with a proper choir.'

'You have a very nice voice.'   .

'I 'ave?'

'I'm not saying it's trained. You'll have to practise.'

'I start practising tomorrow night. Three nights a week in Sealeigh. I'll not be 'ome till midnight.'

'I'll leave something in the oven. Don't wake us up. We've been through Sealeigh, haven't we, off the ferry? It's all ribbon development. Bungalows and pensioners.'

'Exactly, that's us, pensioners. Choirboys and chorines of mature age. One of 'em has a glass eye. Correction – our leader's a sprig. Robin Goodfellow. Heard of 'im? He's going to be a Sir one day.'

'Isn't Robin Goodfellow somebody in *A Midsummer Night's Dream*?'

'He'll wish he was when he hears the new recruits. My partner's Twitty.'

'Better and better! You can practise together, help each other. Where do you tour? Is it dangerous?'

22

'Course it's dangerous! You let loose an F sharp or a B major, and what it should be is a G flat, they throw things at you.'

'Who does?'

'Robin Goodfellow for one. Throws his baton. He can pierce a voicebox at twenty paces. Oh, Miriam!' Peckover sat beside her on the sofa, put his head in her lap, and howled, 'Miriam! Miriam!'

'Stop that, you'll frighten the children!' She pushed him away. 'Aren't F sharp and G flat the same?'

'Same what?'

'Same note.'

'Not when I sing them.'

'I'm going to find them on the piano,' Miriam said, starting to get up.

Peckover held her arm. 'See what I mean? Everyone knows about music except me.'

'And Twitty, I expect.'

'Twitty plays a mean ghetto blaster.' He put a hand between Miriam's legs. 'Get the children to bed. I need succour.'

She removed the hand. 'You try getting them to bed. If it works, you deal with them when they wake up at four.'

'I'm unloved and I'm getting laryngitis. Hysterical laryngitis, it's called, same as our finest opera stars suffer from. Pavarotti. Melba. What's for supper?'

'Surprise.'

'Ah. What did they reject today? Eel mousse with sauerkraut? Those diggers and shovellers don't deserve you.' He stood up. 'I'm taking a shower. I may then guide you to the piano where you will instruct me in arpeggios and crotchets. I may also attempt to sing the one in the middle. Middle C?'

'I'd be delighted.'

'One other request. You're not to listen.'

At the Service Régional de Police Judiciaire, Amiens, the co-ordinator of the French end of the Sealeigh affair, Frank Veal's deskbound counterpart, was Divisional Commissaire Mouton. The name when conjoined with Veal's would arouse mirth on both sides of the Channel among the more witless clerks and dogsbodies who were to have dealings with the case. Commissaire Mouton bit into the *pan bagna* that had arrived for him from the bistro on the rue Chapeau-des-Violettes.

He accepted that someone had to lead the inquiries. He also accepted, having no choice, that the directorate in Paris should farm the job out to the provinces, the provinces being where the looting was going on. That the task should have fallen on him caused him unease. He had considered delegating as no one had ever delegated but who else could be guaranteed to bring home the bacon? He himself was actually going to have to work and be brilliant. The case's cosmopolitan flavour brought every opportunity for *la gloire* and equally for disaster. The only reason Amiens had been put in charge was that its cathedral happened to have, had once had, the first relic to have gone missing.

Now that Scotland Yard had moved, the commissaire felt easier, even encouraged. They hadn't let the grass grow. Together, Amiens and the Yard might chalk up a success on this one, nab the thief, as long as the thief kept at it. If and when the mess was cleared up he would see to it that all possible kudos would be his, no question of that. Meanwhile, he could not see much that he could do beyond the obvious.

'Here's the itinerary, the dates, and the composition of the choir,' he told Sergeant Pépin. 'Understand that these two, Chief Inspector Peckover and Constable Twitty' – he pronounced the names Peckovair and Tweety – 'are incognito. You will contact them only as absolutely necessary. You will reveal their identities at your peril. Evidently this Peckover will have an assumed name but we have not received it. So what is the first thing you do?'

'Advise the criminal brigade in the towns of the dates when the choir will perform so that all possible targets for theft may be staked out, every precaution taken against their removal, and the criminal apprehended, Monsieur le Commissaire.'

The commissaire gestured with the hand holding the *pan bagna*. 'What will be your approach?' The hand and the sandwich emphasised each noun with a stabbing movement. 'Your advice, if you will, should the authorities on the itinerary require guidance?'

'Discretion, Commissaire, if we are to take the pig English perpetrator in the act.'

A strip of anchovy slid out of Commissaire Mouton's *pan bagna* and on to the fax from Chief Superintendent Veal. Half a black olive followed the anchovy, next a wedge of tomato which missed the fax and dropped on the commissaire's fly. *'Merde,'* he said. He retrieved the morsels, popped them into his mouth, dabbed his wrist on the olive oil smears on the fax, licked his wrist, soused a handkerchief with Kronenbourg, and sponged his fly.

What was not obvious, he reflected, was whether he had picked the right man as his agent in the field. The sergeant's fair hair was shorn to within an inch of his skull and his eyebrows were so pale that he didn't seem to have any. To the commissaire he looked like a member of the Foreign Legion, though not the one in Edith Piaf's 'Mon Légionnaire', who smelled of hot desert sand, had 'unseen, uncaught' tattooed on his neck and 'no one' over his heart. That légionnaire broke women's hearts, loving and leaving them. Sergeant Pépin would be more likely to break an immigrant's legs. He was a chauvinist and a racist. His 'pig English perpetrator' spoke worlds. Fair enough, he was entitled to his opinion, except that the Sealeigh case with its cargo of Brits required diplomacy. Nothing but grief would result from going in head down and trampling on the precious sensibilities of the English.

On the other hand, Sergeant Pépin often achieved results, and if someone in the choir was robbing France blind of her sacred relics he might be the man to put a stop to it.

'You will need to exercise your widely admired and most enviable tact, Sergeant.' Commissaire Mouton, an armchair psychologist, believed that to flatter someone with virtues he or she demonstrably lacked would be to assist that person in acquiring those virtues. 'We do not want an international incident.'

'J'enfoncerais une baguette dans le cul de cette espèce de rosbif et puis j'y mettrais le feu, comptez sur moi, Commissaire!'

The commissaire flinched. He handed across his desk a copy of the file. Sergeant Pépin took it, clicked his heels, and departed.

In Sealeigh and its neighbourhood the majority of members of the Sealeigh Choral Society were at home minding their business, this not being a rehearsal evening.

They read, knitted, ironed, puzzled over income tax forms, worried about the garden, ate insipid, meagre, overpriced, microwaved television dinners, in some cases, and in others, such as Joseph Golightly, baritone, bachelor, and plumber, a two-pound pork pie, chips, and peas with Colman's mustard, Worcestershire sauce, HP sauce, and pickled onions.

Dr Willis, GP, mezzo-soprano, and treasurer of the Sealeigh Bridge Club, helped her younger daughter with her geometry homework.

Angus McCurdle, farmer, a Scot among Sassenachs, had the unyielding look of a seventeenth-century Protestant dissenter, and spiky thickets of eyebrows. Wielding tweezers, he made progress on his mighty model of the Royal Pavilion, Brighton, built entirely from matchsticks and glue. He had so far used twenty-one thousand matchsticks and judged he had another nine thousand to go. As long as the kine were milked and the apples harvested, nothing thereafter was a waste of time that was well accomplished.

Oscar Thomas, the choir's director, sat in his study brooding on a) the economy, and b) the matter of two undercover policemen joining the chorus. Apart from anything else the rule was that no choir member be permitted to miss more than two rehearsals. These bluebottles had missed four before they had started. The more he brooded the less happy he was. But to have protested would have been to obstruct the course of justice, so the superintendent fellow had hinted.

Clemency Axelrod, on the wagon since her car ride down the steps from the prom and on to the beach, lay in the bath in her flat above Curiouser and Curiouser: Curios, Antiques, Bric-à-Brac, turning the pages of *Connoisseur*. Her artificial eye lay in a saucer on the window ledge.

Eleanor Sandwich, a Presbyterian and a contralto, embroidered a cushion cover while reading the First Epistle General of Peter, which she had doubts about. *All flesh is as grass, and all the glory of man as the flower of grass* was demonstrably true – Peter had stolen it from Isaiah and it came in the Brahms Requiem, *Denn alles Fleisch es ist wie Gras*, and heaven knew how many other requiems – but unhelpful. *Abstain from fleshly lusts, which war against the soul* was even less helpful. Easy to say it. *Be sober, be vigilant; because your adversary the devil, as a roaring lion, walketh about, seeking whom he might devour.* She could go along with that all right. Not that the devil had to be a roaring lion. The devil could be a silent snake. She turned to Genesis, chapter three.

Bahama O'Toole, daughter of tuneful immigrants – one from the Caribbean, the other from County Kerry – and youngest driver for Southland Express Coaches, sat at a table in her bedroom taking notes from Paul Tillich's *The Courage To Be.* Her essay for her Open University psychology instructor was due on Friday.

Alderman Philip Green, mayor of Sealeigh, chairman of SCAT (Sealeigh Campaign Against the Tunnel), and substantial shareholder in CHAFAHS (Channel Ferry & Hovercraft Services Ltd), hunched forward in his armchair as the video of the second SCAT annual general meeting and reception came on the screen. 'Watch this, Gladys,' he said, chuckling and already enraptured with himself, though his speech to the meeting was not for another thirteen minutes.

Gladys Green murmured, 'Yes, dear,' and closed her eyes. Of late she had found difficulty in keeping her eyes open, also in talking, swallowing, or holding a knife and fork. The tests would tell. At least Philip was so often out of the house that she could get to the infirmary without him knowing. Never would she burden him with what after all might turn out to be nothing much. Even had she felt lively as a kitten she believed she would have closed her eyes. She had sat through the performance on the video, and indistinguishable performances, more times than she could count. The horn had blown so now the meeting would be standing. Now it was applauding the arrival on stage of the SCAT chairman and officers. Now the hooligan in the audience would shout, 'Blow up the bloody tunnel!' – there he was shouting it. Now everyone was going to do that frightful chant. So coarse, so unnecessary.

> 'SCAT! SCAT! Froggies, SCAT!
> We don't want no rabid rat!
> Kick the Froggies up the pants!
> SCAT, Froggies, back to France!'

Here was Philip now. 'Ladies, gentlemen, members of SCAT . . . ' Gladys mouthed along with the mouth of her husband on the screen. 'No rabid rat, no rabid anything – no Tunnel!' Applause, whistling, stamping. 'But no violence either.' The mayor's voice had dropped to a passionate rumble. 'Those who talk of bombing are not welcome in this assembly. We of SCAT are a peaceful protest and shall win by peaceful means as have others before us. Jesus Christ, Gandhi, Martin Luther King . . . '

Most statesmanlike, most Churchillian, thought Gladys, and her drooping eyelids closed.

Only two of all the Sealeigh stay-at-homes took time to study the music for the next concert, the rest being either lazy or satisfied that ten three-hour rehearsals were adequate to bring themselves and the chorus to its customary standard of excellence.

Fleur Whistler, assistant at Curiouser and Curiouser, and part-time aerobics instructor at Shape Up, considered the rehearsal time sufficient but fled to the piano and opened the Mozart because her awful husband and the excruciating snooker on their grossly oversized TV screen overwhelmed the sitting-room.

Peter Witherspoon, retired peeper (he hoped he had retired – urges still sometimes welled) turned up the volume of the Salisbury Cathedral Choir's recording of *Psalm 150*, by Heinrich Schütz, and followed the boomingly catchy result in the score. He was aware he was not one of the more proficient members of the choir. His sight singing in particular was weak. At least he knew it, which was more than he could say of a ululating tenor or two he might mention, and a couple of quavery sopranos.

From the back of a cupboard, from a Selfridge's shirt box behind the paint tins, brushes, and rolled ends of wallpaper, from the crêpe paper inside the box, and from individual Kleenex wrappings within the crêpe, one of the Sealeigh Choral Society laid bare a weathered stick which was a madonna, a chalice, and a thorn.

Had Chief Inspector Peckover been a fly on the wall, preferably with a camcorder, he would have done the necessary: called Frank Veal, collared the culprit, and the Sealeigh nonsense would have been over, and Our 'Enry back on the Tooting Bec bank robbery.

Not a fly on the wall, Peckover sat at an untuned piano depressing Middle C over and over and singing, 'Doh, doh, doh.'

Actually, it didn't sound too bad. He believed he might be ready to move on. He consulted *How To Read Music* which lay open on the lower end of the keyboard, craning to bring the instructions and little black and white notes into focus. The page bore much ancient pencilling. Miriam had dug it from a box of her mementos in the attic.

He didn't care for Veal's Bill Smith as an alias. Sounded like a burglar. Bill Brown, though, that had resonance. Bill Brown, the famous baritone. If baritone was what he was.

He pressed the key one up from Middle C, eliciting from the joanna's innards a stifled sound, but none the less a sound higher than Middle C, though not by much. The key's ivory, indeed the entire keyboard, was stained a delicate nicotine brown. Perhaps the piano's previous home had been a saloon bar.

'Re!' Peckover sang, striking the note with vigour. 'Re, re, re!'

Up another notch.

'Mi, mi, mi!'

Sealeigh Choral Society would appoint him chief soloist in no time.

THREE

Sealeigh Presbyterian Church on Wycliffe Way was a capacious brick edifice of Gothic revival design from the pen and calipers of Sir Reginald 'Blaze Away' Blaze (1811–86), a church architect who came to popular notice when at the age of sixty-eight he married Mrs Peg Satterthwaite, madame of the Dover Rover, a brocaded establishment with sea views offering petits fours and the services of ladies from the Midlands and industrial North named Yvette, Ginette, Babette, and Marie.

Today a Tesco assaulted it on one side, a Sainsbury on the other, concrete malls of boutiques crowded at the rear, and in front rumbled buses and lorries, spewing fumes at the stained-glass windows. In the tenebrous interior the air was musty and mushroomy. Every Sabbath a century ago the pews were filled. In spite of a twentyfold increase in the population of Sealeigh, this was no longer the case, and, far from attracting a new generation of churchgoers, melancholy experiments with guitars and translations of the Bible into jarring contemporary English had served merely to alienate the regulars. The church was now filled solely at Christmas and for the Sealeigh Choral Society sell-outs.

As Henry Peckover had correctly understood, Scotland and Northern Ireland were the home of Presbyterianism in Britain. Only one of the choir was a committed Presbyterian who attended services here. The rest were a mix of Anglicans and other Protestant persuasions, Roman Catholics, Jews, agnostics, and atheists. If there existed among the singers a Christian Scientist, Buddhist, nuclear disarmer, or flat earther, the choir at large was unaware and indifferent. Surprisingly, perhaps, many members having sung together for twenty years, few were close friends. The majority met only for choir purposes. Probably no one but Oscar Thomas and

30

one or two of his committee could have named every member of the chorus. Certainly no one but Mr Thomas would have been able to name Bill Brown. And while apprised of the name, as from that Wednesday morning, he would have been utterly unable to recognise him.

Keeping his profile literally low, Bill Brown, alias Chief Inspector Peckover, pretended to study a headstone in the churchyard. The clock on the tower said ten to seven. He might have trouble with newspaper print but he could read the great white clock even in this shroud of twilight.

Where was Twitty? If the lad swanned in late and drew attention to himself he'd wring his neck.

He might have been on the commuter train from Waterloo but they had chosen not to travel together or be seen together. From his vantage point as inspector of graves, Peckover watched the church's side entrance. He had arrived early, reconnoitred, and here, up five steps, seemed to be the only unlocked entrance. Along the path in ones and twos, carrying music, the singers were trickling in.

Five to seven. Damn Twitty.

The white-haired couple, the bloke with an important tilt to his chin, the woman with a cane and a hand on his arm, might they be the mayor, Alderman Green, and his wife, the one Frank Veal had said was probably not a suspect? He couldn't see either of these two prying open a relic case under an altar. On the other hand, people of their years would be pretty sure they'd not be suspected. One of them could jimmy, the other distract the sexton with questions about the reredos. If he knew anything about this case it was that the thief or thieves were beginners and born lucky. So far.

'Evening, Guv.'

Peckover looked round. Twitty stepped cheerfully over a grave and held out his hand.

'Where did you come from?' Peckover took the hand grudgingly and let it go. 'What've you done to your hair?'

'Like it? Cost an arm and a leg. Trudy's in Shepherd Market.'

'You look as if you've been got ready for brain surgery. Listen, you're going to blow it before we've started. We don't know each other or 'ad you forgotten?'

'We don't know each other. We just met. We're new boys

getting the lay of things. Never been here before. Which way's the sea?'

'How do I know?' Peckover sniffed the air for sea smells. 'That way? Get into the church and find the bloke who doles out the music. I'll follow. Where did you get that suit? This is a choir rehearsal, not a Bank of England directors' meeting.'

'Would you stop finding fault – sir.' Twitty's suit was a subfusc pinstripe. His tie was pearl grey with a pin in it. 'Mr Veal said to dress sombrely.'

'He meant you don't wear your gaucho hat and sequins and Sinbad pants. Where's the funeral?'

'They'd not let you in. Look at your poofter shoes.'

'Poofter? That's honest suede.'

'Poofter shoes, burgundy slacks, and Alpine ski-guide sweater. You look like a scriptwriter. You might, if you didn't have the snappy hat. Off to the races, are we? Guv, can we sing next to each other, help each other along?'

'We spread ourselves out, get to know as many of the choir as we can, then pool results. Miriam says we'll all likely be with our own section. You're a tenor, I 'ope?'

'I am?'

'That's what I'm asking.'

'No idea, Guv. I could free float, go where I'm needed.'

The blind leading the blind, Peckover thought. At least the lad hadn't brought his ghetto blaster. 'You can't go in there not knowing whether you're a bass or a tenor. Sing me a line. Keep it quiet.'

'I couldn't.'

'Why?'

'I'm shy.'

'Just do it.'

'What would you like?'

'I don't care. "Rule, Britannia!". Quietly.'

Twitty tapped his foot, swayed his hips, clicked his fingers, and sang in a whisper, 'Rule, Britannia—'

'You're a tenor. Take off that tie and get in the church.'

Seven o'clock. The choir was still drifting in. Peckover watched skinny six-feet-six Twitty lope towards the church, snapping his fingers. Up the steps, at the door, he stood aside – bowing, overdoing the gallantry, in Peckover's opinion – to allow a stout woman through first. Now they stood in conversation. Twitty had his hand on her arm and she was not screaming for help. They were both laughing. Twitty, comedian and charmer. He had made his first acquaintance. He could be telling lightbulb jokes to a relics thief. He followed the stout woman into the church.

Peckover realised his hands were clammy, and not because a criminal element might be in the church. 'Mi, mi, mi,' he sang experimentally. He had missed two-fifths of rehearsals. If he opened his mouth all would be lost. If he didn't open it, people would wonder why. His only hope would be to hide under a pew. He set off between the graves, clearing his throat and practising, *sotto voce*, 'Do, re, mi, mi, mi. Fa, la, la, jug, jug, hey nonny nonny.'

On a wall of a vestibule hung a rack holding tracts. To a notice board were pinned children's crayonings, invitations to Bible study, and lists of guest preachers. From behind a curtain heavy with dust issued an unspiritual hubbub and trills on a piano.

Half the Sealeigh Choral Society lounged in a dozen pews at the front of the church. The other half leaned against the end of pews, stood in groups on the worn red carpet, or wandered in the aisles, taking off their coats and seeking or avoiding acquaintances. One huddle talked with each other on the stage, though Peckover doubted that stage was the right word here, even though that is what it was. His irregular childhood attendance at eleven o'cock Sunday service, and subsequent wedding and funerals, had been Church of England, mainly at St Anne's, Stepney, where the vicar's throttled striving after a posh accent had moved a despairing group of the cockney faithful to petition that he be replaced by someone they could understand. Peckover believed this might be the first time he had entered a Presbyterian church. It smelled of hay and there was no communion rail. Presbyterians took communion, didn't they? Centre stage (dais, rostrum, podium, yet it was still a stage) stood a communion table. No crucifix. Peckover looked about him. No bleeding hearts, no statuary. There was a gallery and a pulpit with fancy ironwork in need of dusting, as did everywhere, except perhaps the shiny piano which four hale males were manhandling into position between the stage and the front pew. At the edge of the stage, above the piano, a woman was setting up a music stand.

He was aware of several gazes turned in his direction, which was to be expected. His was an unfamiliar face, object of curiosity. For all anyone knew he was an off-duty traffic warden arrived to warn about an illegally parked hatchback.

He spotted Twitty in conversation with a bald man and a woman in tweeds. Having removed his tie, Twitty looked like a chairman of the board who had removed his tie. He held a wad of minutes and company reports which he had not been holding in the churchyard. Everyone seemed to be in possession of similar, if not identical, papers.

Everyone except Bill Brown, singer without songsheets.

So who in this stew of unknowns was his contact, Director Oscar Thomas? Peckover wiped his damp palms on his trousers. He tried to catch Twitty's eye but the lad was locked in discourse, not actually speaking but earnestly nodding his head, the good listener, absorbing whatever the tweedy woman was telling him. Behind the music stand a tall, handsome bloke with effulgent red wavy hair like a rough sea at sunrise was opening a music score. The conductor? He didn't look like the Robin Goodfellow in *A Midsummer Night's Dream*, who was a sprite. He had a prize-fighter's torso to which loosely clung a lacy pink shirt of the sort Twitty might have been wearing if he hadn't been ordered to dress sombrely. Thirtyish, thirty-five.

'Mr Brown?' said a voice at his side.

'Mr Thomas?'

This bloke wore a bow tie. Paisley. Peckover wasn't sure when he'd last seen a bow tie. Medium build, medium everything, except for the bow tie. Age fifty, according to the file. Single. Rich. Made it in property in the seventies when he'd have been a mere go-getting lad. Owned property companies, still go-getting. What was he doing running the Sealeigh Choral Society? Why wasn't he standing for Parliament? He liked to sing? Liked to run things?

'Here's your music,' Thomas said. 'Six pounds. The subscription's another ten. I can't waive it, it'd confuse the accounts. I wouldn't if I could.'

'Sorry?'

'Damned awkward, all this. I told your superintendent chappie – Veal, is it? – I wasn't happy.'

'I can understand.'

'Might as well be straight about it. Nothing personal, not yet. I'd sooner you weren't with us.'

'Mutual.' Peckover brought out his wallet. 'Change for a twenty? So as not to confuse the accounts. And a receipt. Later will do.'

'Sign your name in your section.' Thomas produced a sheet of foolscap with four columns of signatures. 'Bass, are you?'

'Bass will do.' Peckover signed his name. William Brown. The last entry under the tenors was J. Twitty. 'This is everyone who's singing?'

'Yes.'

'I'd like a copy.'

'I'll let you have it at the next rehearsal.'

One rehearsal at a time was Peckover's view. The sooner this one got started and done with the better. Would it begin with new members having to stand up to be introduced and be applauded or was that Baptists? He reminded himself that this was a choir, not a congregation. How could he have forgotten? He flipped through his music. Mozart. Psalm 150 by Heinrich Schütz, the *Lobet den Herren* one, thick as a ledger. Then a wedge of flimsy stuff. 'April Is In My Mistress' Face'. 'Blow the Candles Out'. 'What Is Our Life?' More, too much more. How was he going to learn all this and would the concert last all night?

Director Thomas had gone, taking his straight talking and sixteen quid of taxpayers' money with him. Peckover spotted the woman in tweeds but not Twitty. The fine redheaded brute on the stage clapped his hands once and called out, 'Places, please! Let's get started!' The stage emptied unhurriedly, leaving the redhead in splendid isolation beside the music stand. People were stepping behind and in front of each other murmuring, 'Excuse me,' and finding places in pews.

Where was Bill Brown's place and where was a kind face who would enlighten him? Perhaps there was spillage and seepage of one section into another. All appeared to be disorder, like slowed-down footage of rush-hour at Paddington Station.

Where, Peckover wanted to cry aloud, is my place, Lord? Where the basses, Almighty and Everlasting God?

They weren't, he judged, on the far side of the aisle where mainly women seemed to be gathering. Except there were men, too. A gaunt lady in an enveloping tartan shawl sat at the piano. He wanted his place to be on the back pew half a deserted mile away. They might think his voice was so powerful that he had to distance himself in order not to upset the textural balance of the harmonics. He homed in on a passably vacant male face who would tell him, if there were love and sympathy in the world, 'Welcome, sit by me, and don't worry about a thing.'

Twitty aimed nimbly for a still unfilled pew, stepped into it, and halted at the blank space beside a black woman.

She was one of the only three or four blacks he had noticed in the throng and she was a knockout. Not only stunning but not too stunning, not Hollywood fodder and void. Nose infinitesimally convex at the bridge, oh, a nose for kissing! Quite a chin, too, bespeaking resolve. Great cheekbones. High brow crammed with brains. Hair short, not as short as his own, not shorn virtually to the scalp, but honest, unmessed with. Dainty feminine hands – actually quite muscular now he looked more closely, with a callus or two, but fingers and thumbs all in place, not a wedding ring in sight, and turning the pages of music. Happy pages to be held by such capable hands! He couldn't see her eyes, cast down to the music, but they would be aglow with tenderness and wit, no question about it. Yellow jersey, brown skirt, all of astonishing tastefulness, though he would be able to help her with dress, expand her horizons, once they knew each other. She'd be twenty, thereabouts. And a singer, a nightingale! He'd be seeing her three evenings a week! Then, oh golly, the Continent! A familiar tingle entered the soul of Constable Twitty. When she glanced up he bestowed on her the smile that devastates, and with his most dulcet articulation said, 'All right if I sit here?'

She smiled back. 'Fine, if you've had your balls cut off. We're the sopranos.'

That's diminished his ardour, mused Bahama O'Toole, watching the Romeo's retreating back. She hadn't time for involvements. She was not even sure she should be in this concert. But driving one of the coaches across the Continent was a free trip that was hard to pass up. She would get her brother to video the Open University lectures she would miss.

Farther along the pew, Dr Willis, medical practitioner and bridge champion, explained to Fleur Whistler that however rapidly society was changing for the worse, Euclidean geometry remained pure and immutable, no small solace when one had teenage daughters. Fleur Whistler did not give a parson's piss for Euclidean geometry or for Dr Willis's daughters. She was on the brink of leaving her husband. She wondered about two new faces in the choir, one black, the other battered, bothered, and frowning.

In a pew behind the sopranos, Mr McCurdle, tenor, model-builder extraordinary, peeled dried wood glue from his fingertips, always a pleasingly sensuous procedure, the glue peeling free in silvery strips. Phil Green was giving him figures on the cubic volume of pollution that would be generated by traffic through the Chunnel. Mr McCurdle uttered gasps of disbelief in appropriate places. He considered the mayor to be certifiably mad.

Twitty found a place with the tenors. He furled his music into a cylinder and eyed the back of the head of the soprano in the yellow jersey. If someone in this choir had been pocketing relics it wasn't her. Never. What class, what wit!

Across the aisle and in front of the basses sat the altos. Clemency Axelrod prattled to Eleanor Sandwich, narrating in frame-by-frame detail the plot of a Meryl Streep film she had seen at the Odeon. The faster she prattled the more stiffly Eleanor Sandwich smiled. Clemency could not stop herself. She believed that Eleanor had disapproved of her ever since the incident with the car and the beach, not that the matter had ever been mentioned. There had been a time when Eleanor would drop in at Curiouser and Curiouser, but not since the incident. Eager for Eleanor's approval, or at worst a truce, on and on Clemency babbled.

Three pews behind, Joe Golightly, plumber, said to Oscar Thomas, 'Say what you like, a shake of Worcestershire does the trick every time. You don't catch me flitting off to these foreign places without my Worcestershire.'

The man with the adequately friendly face in whom Peckover had put his trust slid along a pew, making room. He was not as tall as Twitty, but tall enough, and to accommodate his knees he had to slide at an angle. His long, meagre hair flopped over his ears. His jersey was an elaborately patterned turtleneck.

'Welcome,' he said. 'Peter Witherspoon. First time, is it? I don't think I've seen you before.'

'Bill Brown,' Peckover said.

He was sitting beside the peeper. The fellow had a proper height for peeping. Lecturer in fine arts. Might have knitted the jersey himself.

The nicked stuff from Amiens and Padua and Basel was art. Artefacts, anyway. A fine arts lecturer would know what was worth nicking.

'You've missed a few rehearsals,' Witherspoon said.

Peckover hoped this was an observation, not an accusation. He said, 'Have to work hard, catch up.'

'How was your audition?'

'Not so bad, considering.'

'Robin's reasonable, knows he's with amateurs. But there's no fooling him. Get the pitch wrong, or your cut-offs, or breeze along allegro when we should be slowing it, allegretto, he'll know, even if you're the only one. Especially if you're the only one. He doesn't single you out or anything but he gives you a look.'

'Sounds reasonable.'

'He knows if you're not singing, just opening your mouth and faking it. That can happen in the first rehearsals before we've got the hang of it.'

'So he gives the look.'

Peckover expected he might soon find out. Robin Goodfellow raised both arms in a balletic gesture as if scattering flowers to the wind. He waited for the coughing and sneezing to cease. 'Stand, please,' he called out. The woman at the piano banged chords up and down the scale.

She repeated the first chord, whereupon Sealeigh Choral Society, now standing, burst out singing.

FOUR

'Ah ah ah ah ah ah ah ah,' briskly sang the choir up and down the scale. Without a pause they were off again, a tone higher. 'Ah ah ah ah ah ah ah ah.'

Peckover could cope with this. This wasn't Mozart, this was tuning up. He didn't have to fake it, either. He let the sound roll out. Not that he could hear too well whether he was hitting the notes correctly, his voice being submerged beneath sixty or seventy rival voices. Up and down the scale rollicked the choir, skipping every other note in the scale and each time starting higher and mounting higher. Peckover found that reaching the top notes became increasingly a strain. He was content not to be able to hear himself, though for whatever reason he was hearing himself more and more clearly.

'Ah ah ah ah ah ah ah ah.'

He was also glad not to be able to see himself. His eyes would be bulging, veins hopping in his temples, his visage a grimace, as if the commandant of the security police were beating the soles of his feet. He realised that the basses around him had thrown in the sponge and ceased singing.

The pianist banged out a fresh set of chords, almost a tune. 'Ha ha ha ha-ha ha ha ha,' sang the chorus, this time down the scale, repeating the line over and over, each time lower and lower until only the basses, it seemed to Peckover, were staying the course, ha-haing in their boots.

The next exercise was more complex. Peckover guessed the pianist had just invented it. Over the tops of the heads in front of him he could see only the back of her head and a swatch of shawl. '*Ah* ah-ah ah ah *aah* ah-ah ah *aaah*,' sang the obedient choir on an' array of notes. Then again higher, and higher again. For the first

39

but not the last time, Peckover, for the greater good, permitted no sound to leave his mouth.

He would have defied Robin Goodfellow to have known that issuing forth from his mouth was a grand silence. Not only did the mouth gape and twitch but his head jigged rhythmically. As it happened, Goodfellow was not watching the choir. He had disassociated himself and stood sideways on, studying a music score. Peckover thought him perfectly correct to leave the warm-up to the pianist. A conductor who one day would be a Sir should not have to concern himself with scales.

'Red leather yellow leather red leather yellow leather,' sang the choir over and over and fast, up the scale then down.

An articulation exercise, Peckover supposed. Loosens the lips and tongue. The pianist trilled frivolous notes in the uppermost register. The choir and Peckover sat gasping.

'He ought to start with the Schütz, it's pretty difficult, but we divide up for it and we're not in our right places,' Peter Witherspoon said.

'Right,' agreed Peckover.

Seeking Twitty, he leaned forward, then back. In the row behind sat more basses. Round faces, lean faces, an Arran jersey, Oscar Thomas in his bow tie, someone with a pencil-line moustache which must have needed constant attention, someone else fairly formal in a jacket and tie. Strangers all. Apart from Twitty, the only people in the church Peckover knew were Oscar Thomas, Witherspoon, and, by sight, Robin Goodfellow. How was he going to keep track of them all? What had been the trick of that memory expert on telly? Somehow attaching each item to be remembered to a finger joint? Oscar Thomas would be the top joint of his little finger, right hand. Witherspoon the middle joint, same finger. That would cover thirty – no, twenty-eight. Why didn't thumbs have three joints? The Arran jersey extended a hand and said, 'Joe Golightly.'

'Bill Brown.'

'Good to have you, Bill. The basses could use some reinforcing.'

Joe Golightly looked darkly along the pew at inadequate basses. Peckover flexed his little finger. Third joint, Joe Golightly.

Robin Goodfellow stood with a hand holding a music score raised high for hush.

Peckover thought Goodfellow, as conductor, warranted a thumb joint. Or no joint at all, thereby saving one, because he was not going to forget Goodfellow. How about joints of the right hand for men, left hand for women?

'The Morley,' Goodfellow announced. '"April Is In My Mistress' Face."'

'We haven't looked at this yet,' Witherspoon whispered.

Everyone sorted through music in search of 'April Is In My Mistress' Face', Madrigal for SATB, by Thomas Morley (1557–1603).

'Quiet, please.' Goodfellow set his music on the music stand and walked away from it. 'Sopranos, you have a C sharp. Altos, A natural. Tenors, third measure, you have the A natural, and basses an F sharp.' He hummed notes. 'No introduction. Straight into it. We are a swain lamenting his beloved's cruelty. In her heart is cold December. Mezzo piano.'

What, Peckover would have liked to know, was he talking about?

Hunched like a redheaded Richard Crookback about to pounce, eyes shuttling from sopranos to altos and back until he had their breathless attention, Goodfellow lifted both hands, held them steady for a millisecond, then tapped the air.

'"April is in–"' sang the sopranos and altos to piano accompaniment, and stopped short before they had completed the first bar. Robin Goodfellow was waving his arms, not conducting but cancelling.

Again his poised hands, the pause for attention, then the jabbing the air.

'"April is in my—"'

The hands waved like a referee's signalling full time. Sopranos nil, altos nil. Voices which had hardly got started trailed to silence.

'Kate, can we hear the first two measures?'

The shawled pianist was evidently Kate. Peckover allotted her his left first finger, third joint. She played the first two bars. They sounded straightforward to Peckover. On the other hand, he didn't have to sing them. The basses were the bottom part, marked Bass, and they came in with the tenors after the women had finished with the mistress's face. Pretty damn quick after, from what he could see, because there wasn't much of a gap between the altos' white note with the tail sticking up and the basses' black note with the tail sticking down.

He wasn't going to worry because he wouldn't be coming in with the basses, not tonight, and probably not this week. He'd pick it up some distance along in a loud passage, once he'd got the tune. No way, José, as his son Sam kept saying, he would ever get that first note right, not its spot-on timing, or where it came in any scale invented by man – the pitch, that was the word – or whether it would emerge loud, soft, mezzo-piano, with or without brio, or *tremolo con carne e formaggio*.

The ladies were off again. Peckover thought they sounded terrific.

'April is in my mistress' face . . . '

Now for the tenors and basses. Good luck, chaps.

'April is— . . . '

Robin Goodfellow was waving his arms.

' . . . in my mistress' . . . ' sang a bass and tenor or two, loath to give up.

'Your entry is the second beat of the third measure, tenors and basses.' The conductor's voice had resonance. 'Wake up. Take responsibility. It's not difficult. It's in front of you, it's written in the music. Basses, pick up your F sharp from the altos. Nothing simpler. Tenors, you're a minor third from the F sharp but you have no A natural anywhere near so you've just got to hear the F sharp. We'll go through to the end. This may be the last as well as the first time we shall do it to the end because if it's as difficult as you insist on making it I shall withdraw it and replace it with "Three Blind Mice". Ready?'

'He doesn't want us to get over-confident,' Peter Witherspoon whispered.

Peckover nodded.

Sealeigh Choral Society sang 'April Is In My Mistress' Face' without a stop. Peckover joined in on page five where the singing grew louder and seemed to repeat itself. 'But in her hea-a-art . . . ' pom pom pom pom . . .

He sensed Witherspoon casting a glance his way. Prior to joining in he had had three choices: opening his mouth and voicelessly faking it, holding his music in front of his face, or having the music on his knees and bending his head to it so that all Goodfellow would see would be his scalp. He had tried all three. He was surprised to discover he much preferred singing the song, or he would when he knew it.

' . . . a cold Dece-e-embe-er.'

He was sorry when it ended. He thought the choir sounded stunning.

Whatever Goodfellow thought, he wasn't saying. He said, 'Now we'll take it apart. Top of page four, third measure. "Within her bosom." Pianissimo, if you please.'

Twenty minutes later when Peckover was beginning to sing along about his mistress's eyes, bosom and cold heart with a degree of confidence, the conductor switched to Brahms. Bill Brown, new boy, stared at the little white and black circles with tails dotted about his music and mouthed noiselessly, relying as best he could on the robust vibrations of Joe Golightly in the pew behind.

Schütz was a disaster. Even Peckover, who had never heard of Schütz and had missed four rehearsals, thought the choir's version was probably not as Schütz had intended it. The language was the least of it, being all much the same or variations on the same. *Lobet den Herren! Lobet Ihn mit Pauken und Reigen!* But each section had split in two, there had been milling and switching of seats, and when everyone was settled and singing, and Robin Goodfellow had charged down from the stage and into the aisle to be in the thick of things, the new groupings tossed the Lobet Ihns back and forth at each other quicker than Peckover could turn the page, and he was sunk, and he believed he wasn't the only one.

Ignorant of which half of the divided basses he should be with, he had thought he would not stay with Witherspoon. He would keep close to Mr Golightly. Witherspoon had in any case already upped and left. Perhaps fled was the word. With nobody telling him he should be somewhere else, Peckover remained put, leaning back and trying to tune in to the resolute braying of Joe Golightly. *'Lobet Ihn mit Saiten und Pfeifen!'* crashed the basses. *'Lobet Ihn mit Psaltern und Harfen!'* rippled the sopranos.

Schütz swarmed and echoed, bouncing off the roof and reverberating round the Presbyterian walls.

Once, when Peckover believed he had almost caught up with his

Lobet Ihns, and had given voice to several, then glanced up, Robin Goodfellow was observing him from the aisle. Was this The Look? The conductor's expression was more of puzzlement than of anger. Peckover, shocked, hiked his music in front of his face. He believed he might have been singing his Lobet Ihns with the sopranos.

If the Goodfellow bleeder gave him any grief he'd take him in for questioning.

Calm, calm, it could be worse, Peckover advised himself. He and Twitty had not been called on to stand and be applauded. Where was the lad anyway and was he behaving himself?

Which was the Sealeigh copper, Superintendent Day? Was he a bass or a tenor?

At a quarter to nine Robin Goodfellow announced a five-minute break.

Two sopranos and a tenor rushed from the church to smoke. People stretched themselves, meandered about, and resumed coughing. At the end of the break Oscar Thomas mounted the stage with announcements.

He announced that the choir's deficit was four hundred and sixteen pounds. This was not at all bad, he said. Down from last year due to generous contributions from two new benefactors, Barton's Leather Goods, and the Phyllida Hump Shape Up Health & Fitness Clinic, the latter donation being in part due to encouragement from one of the choir. 'Thank you, Fleur.' (Applause.) But would all members make a special effort to seek out sponsors and underwriters, impressing on them that their names would appear in the programme, and they would receive advance notice of concerts plus priority for tickets, except for the Christmas concert.

Some incentive, thought Peckover and waited for a brave soul to stand and point out that four hundred and sixteen pounds being not at all bad as a deficit, Oscar Thomas, being a millionaire, could make up the shortfall out of his own pocket and be done with it.

Meanwhile, warming to his role, Oscar Thomas rambled on. 'Proceeds from our television appearances constitute a healthy source of revenue but these appearances can't be guaranteed and once again the Arts Council in its infinite unwisdom has turned down our request for a grant.'

'So change the government, vote the philistines out!' someone called out.

Heads turned, Peckover's among them. He failed to find the heckler. At least it hadn't been Twitty.

'They're a sight better than your lot!' objected a woman's voice. 'Look what you did to education!'

Peckover spotted a flushed young woman in a blue corduroy dress.

'Look what you did to the whole miserable economy!' hit back the heckler.

'We got our priorities right is what we did!' The blue corduroy. 'Call yourselves housekeepers? Spare me!'

'Why spare you? You never spared the country! You and your lefty butch sisterhood should go float out to sea on an iceberg and play with yourselves!'

Strong stuff. Peckover located the pest. He was one of the younger choristers, plump and pinkish in a pink-and-white striped executive shirt of the kind found in Jermyn Street, and unnecessary red braces. He looked plump enough for his trousers to have stayed up without braces. Though his heckling had sounded seriously vexed his expression was amused. He lolled in a pew with his arms resting along the back.

Peckover spotted Twitty too, standing intimately with a group of warblers for all the world as if he'd been their pal since childhood.

'Your people would send us to hell in a handcart!' called out the amused red braces. 'Make that a tumbril! *Vive la guillotine!*'

'Charming!' inadequately riposted the blue corduroy.

'Please, gentlemen, ladies!' Oscar Thomas requested, muddling the etiquette of precedence.

A jest, a defusing quip, was what was required, in Peckover's view. Thomas failed the test. Flustered, the director rabbited on about finances.

'The downside of the equation is rising costs, especially for our tour of the Continent. We are fortunate that Bahama has agreed to drive one of our coaches again. This, as you know, is in return for free accommodation, but let me say that the Choral Society comes out ahead. Gus, our other driver, must be paid the union rate, and we might wind up in court if the European Community decides that employing one of our own members as a driver, gratis—'

'Let Clemency drive Gus's coach,' loudly suggested the man in red braces. 'Clemency knows about courts.'

Someone sniggered. Someone else said, 'Shame!'

Clemency Axelrod. Peckover strove to remember names from the Sealeigh file. The one with the antiques shop and glass eye who had driven her car down steps on to the beach. He wondered if the red braces had been drinking.

Oscar Thomas said, 'This year as you know we're travelling by ferry, but we must look to the future, and always be thinking of ways to reduce costs. It's never too early.'

In Peckover's opinion he was really flustered now. 'When the Channel Tunnel opens we shall have to ask ourselves, do we go with this Tunnel, with progress, as we hear it called, or do we stay with the ferry? The bottom line is finance. But there is a matter of loyalty. I put it to you that the ferry has never let us down.'

Peckover was tempted to raise his hand and move that the choir resume the rehearsal. Not that he would have done, but a booming voice forestalled him anyway.

'Damn right the ferry has never let us down!' boomed the voice. 'May I have members' attention?'

He had it, though Peckover, craning and searching, detected yawns. This was not the red braces. It was the white-haired cove he had seen arriving with the woman with the cane. The mayor?

'Friends, choir members, good people of Sealeigh!' The portly gent had climbed up on to a pew. 'This so-called Chunnel, this aberration, this abortion of all we hold dear, this abomination to our island race, our blessed plot, this England – we don't want the Chunnel, right?'

'Wrong,' someone said. Mixed murmurings. Somebody else called out, 'Bit late, mate!'

The man on the pew stood with both arms raised. A ham, an actual politician, Peckover opined. He felt a mild pang of sympathy for Oscar Thomas, who had no charisma, who in a bid for votes would sway no one.

'Never too late!' exhorted the white-haired rabble-rouser, standing sacrilegiously on the pew. 'Join SCAT!'

46

Applause. Scattered booing.

'Our own home-grown Sealeigh Campaign Against the Tunnel! Away with it, we say!'

Peckover wondered if Oscar Thomas had to put up with this at every rehearsal. Why didn't he simply tell the Goodfellow conductor, no five-minute break? The break had lasted ten minutes already. In a way Thomas had started it all with his jabber about costs and the ferry and loyalty. Maybe he enjoyed the disruption.

'As mayor of Sealeigh,' proclaimed portly Pericles on the pew, 'I must inform you that once the Chunnel opens – if it opens,' he added with an air of mystery, 'the price of visits to the Continent will rocket . . . '

Peckover was not listening, he was concentrating on his finger joints. Second finger, first joint, the mayor, Alderman Philip Green.

' . . . and our Sealeigh economy will be down the plug!'

'You mean your ferry shares will be down the plug!'

'A low blow! Withdraw!'

'Sink the ferry!'

'Gentlemen, ladies!'

'Sealeigh could become a ghost town!'

Somebody blew a powerful raspberry.

'As Mark Antony might have said,' boomed the mayor, 'we come to praise Sealeigh, not to bury it!'

'Thought we'd come to a choir rehearsal!' Joe Golightly shouted.

'Let SCAT be our hope and our salvation!' exhorted Alderman Green, pugnacious on the pew. 'Our estimable director and loyal ally, Oscar, tells us of benefactions from Barton's Leather Goods and the Shape Up Health and Fitness Clinic. I say to you, where will Leather Goods and Shape Up be, and all our businesses, built out of our blood, sweat, and tears, and you and I and our dear families, good friends, should this Channel Tunnel come to pass, and our dear Sealeigh be forsaken, as it will be, of visitors, all of them buggering straight on to London without stopping for so much as a cuppa or a picture postcard!'

Desultory applause, tentative hissing. 'Poppycock,' said somebody. Peckover had anticipated mild pandemonium, but mistakenly. Many of the choir were chatting among themselves and not listening.

47

Having seen who had said 'Poppycock', six feet away, Peckover sat beside her.

'Bill Brown. A new boy. Incredible choir. Evenin'.'

'Good evening. Eleanor Sandwich.'

Second finger, second joint. A motherly soul, comfortable and comforting, observed Peckover. Not a sort one would have expected to hear 'Poppycock' from. He judged that if her hands had not held music they would have been knitting rompers for a grandchild.

'Great choir, really. I mean . . .' Bill Brown said.

'I'm so glad we come up to expectations. The Schütz is quite tricky. You mustn't judge us on that.'

'My word, no, I wouldn't. Always like this, is it?'

'The Gilbert and Sullivan is tuneful but perhaps a little bland.'

'What about the politics?'

'What politics?'

'The last ten minutes. The discussion.'

'It's the mayor.' Eleanor Sandwich, leaning towards Peckover, spoke in a hushed voice. 'A bee in his bonnet, I'm afraid. I take no notice.'

'You said "Poppycock",' Peckover teased.

She was thrilled, or pretended to be. 'Oh my goodness, did I?' She gave a gleeful shudder. 'The campaign makes good points but of course the members are interested only in their pockets. They don't make nearly enough of the risk of rabies, mad dogs and rats scuttling through the Tunnel from France, you understand. Some go too far with their bomb threats.'

'The one in the red braces, he seems to have a bee in his bonnet too.'

'Archy Newby. Very sad.'

'I can imagine.' Second finger, third joint.

'Fortunately his parents have been gathered.'

'Gone beyond?'

'To their reward.'

Peckover bowed his head. There followed a moment of mourning.

He said, 'The singer in the blue dress, the corduroy, she doesn't get on exactly famously with him.'

'My dear, who does?'

'Absolutely. Who's she?'

'Fleur Whistler. She helps Clemency in her antiques shop. I believe she also teaches some sort of fitness class.' Eleanor Sandwich leaned closer. 'It's rumoured she had an affair, but of course it's over.'

Middle finger. Wait, shouldn't we have shifted to the left hand for the women?

He said, 'An affair with Clemency?'

'Gracious me, I don't believe so. With Archy.'

'Naturally.'

'I'm not saying it's true.'

'No, no.'

'Though rumours of that kind almost invariably are.'

'Yes.'

'Sealeigh, these tight little communities, you understand.'

'No smoke without fire.'

'"As a jewel of gold in a swine's snout, so is a fair woman which is without discretion."'

'Golly, yes.'

Whose side was she on? Archy's? Peckover smiled at her winningly. Kate at the keyboard trilled high notes. Robin Goodfellow was on stage holding aloft new music.

Eleanor Sandwich said, 'It's the Mozart, everyone's favourite.'

Not Lucky Jim Dixon's favourite with his 'filthy Mozart', nor mine either, Peckover sourly thought. He was surfeited with music. He sagged into a place beside the bass with the pencil moustache. With luck he would escape introductions. He had just assigned three more finger-joints and couldn't handle any more this evening. Further along the row was Joe Golightly, saviour of weak basses. Peter Witherspoon sat in the row in front.

Witherspoon. Golightly. Oscar Thomas. Alderman Green, mayor and anti-Chunnel activist. Archy Newby in red braces. Fleur Whistler in blue corduroy. Eleanor Sandwich. Robin Goodfellow and Keyboard Kate. Peckover stared at his hands, trying to remember which finger joint was assigned to which. This device wasn't going to work, he decided.

'"*Regina coeli!*"' erupted the chorus in earthquaking unison. '"*Regina coeli! Regina coeli lae-ta-a-re!*"'

Goodfellow's energy may have been on the wane. He interrupted less than hitherto, allowing the chorus to drive on for two pages before flagging them into the pits. The stoppage was something to do with tempo, overall dynamics, flabby entries, taking responsibility, some straining among the sopranos for the high G, and a conflict of opinion over pronunciation of the Latin. To Peckover's mind the Latin was less trying than the Schütz. Alleluias looked to be abundant, not that they had got to them yet. How could you go wrong with alleluias? An alto put up her hand and asked if the first syllable of laetare rhymed with light or with late. Goodfellow said, '*Late! Late-are-y! Regina coeli lae-tar-e!* Praise the Queen of heaven!' Flipping the pages he roundly articulated the rest of the score's Latin, not that there was a lot once you took away the alleluias. Goodfellow said, 'We'll speak it through.'

Led by their conductor, the chorus mouthed in a monotone through *Regina Coeli*, omitting the solo passages. They sounded like Catholics at prayer before the vernacular took over.

'That's how the Romans pronounced it and what was good enough for them is good enough for us,' Goodfellow said. 'Problems? Off we go, then!'

He lifted his hands for the off.

'Not a problem, but it depends which Romans,' somebody said. 'If we're talking about the Classical Latin of Virgil, Horace, Catullus, Cicero, et alia, the g and c would be hard, not soft. Re-*gina*. Coeli.' The voice emphasised the hard classical g and c. Peckover was not listening, he was counting alleluias. '*Laetare*, the first syllable, that would be rhymed with light, not late. The i in *regina* would have been long as in feet. *Coeli*, which we're pronouncing *chelly*, like a Tuscan dessert, or a skin disease, that first syllable would be almost two syllables, *co-e-li,* though this is debatable, we've only the literary evidence. But Classical Latin preferred pure vowels to the diphthongs we're pronouncing, which would have been considered trashy. What we're singing is vulgar Latin. That's vulgar in the sense of popular – not rude and lewd – but none the less a corruption which got under way around the third century, after the Augustan Age, and evolved into the Romance languages and, most directly, Italian, the language of Verdi and Neapolitan fig-sellers. Virgil and Cicero wouldn't have recognised it. After all, in Classical Latin Cicero was Kikero.'

Mouth open, Peckover was certainly listening now. The Sealeigh

Choral Society listened. Robin Goodfellow, hunched and listening, watched the source of the lecture intently, his expression flitting between uncertain smile and scowl.

'Just thought I'd mention it,' the voice from the choir said cheerfully. 'Look, it's Mozart. Our corrupt version probably sings better.'

Peckover was aghast. He craned and half stood, knees bent, the better to locate the lecturer, though he didn't need to see him to know that it was Twitty.

He'd kill 'im.

FIVE

At ten on the dot, after eight inadequate minutes of Gilbert and Sullivan, Goodfellow sang out, 'Goodnight!' Sealeigh's choir gathered up their music, put on their coats, and drifted for the exit.

Constable Twitty drifted with them. He felt alert and satisfied. Having broken the ice with his discourse, or one might say smashed it with a hammer, he found himself approached by several of the curious, introducing themselves and welcoming him. One of these was Alderman Green. 'Join SCAT, young fellow,' he said. 'You'll find no racial prejudice with us. We take all sorts.'

A Mr McCurdle said, 'It's many years since I opened my *Aeneid* but I'm not sure you're correct about the diphthong. I shall look it up.'

A fluttery woman, too nervous to offer her name, but who blinked at him with one eye, said, 'Such a nice speech, so helpful.' Clemency Axelrod?

She was not the only one who welcomed him with passing words of small talk without asking his name or offering his or her own. Very British, Twitty thought. Others introduced themselves as Mrs Judd, Mr Charlesworth, Ms Belcher, with no first name. Betty Belcher? Bonnie Belcher? Nothing wrong with that. Their first names were on the members' list. Soon as possible he would have to write all this down, match names against an identifying feature – a mole, dimples, lorgnettes – or he'd forget and the whole getting-to-know-you exercise would have been futile.

Nothing to write down about quite a few who made a point of not meeting him, who avoided his eye and detoured three or four pews out of their way. The lambkin in the yellow jersey for one. Bahama O'Toole, soprano and castrator. And the boss man, Oscar

Thomas. Another – there he went now with the sprightly waddle – was Archy Newby.

Twitty, thoughtful, watched the waddling red braces. He was nosier about Archy Newby than Archy Newby evidently was about Jason Twitty.

'You're new too, aren't you? How nice.' She was a comfortable lady he had noticed talking with the guv. 'I so enjoyed your little dissertation on the Latin. I'm Eleanor Sandwich.'

'Jason Twitty. Fantastic choir. Great honour to be one of you. More political than I'd expected.'

'Oh, most of us are not very excited.'

'Alderman Green just told me I should join SCAT.'

'My dear, do think twice. Some of them would like to bomb the Tunnel, or so they say. I'm positively terrified.' She gave a shiver. 'The most dangerous don't belong to SCAT, they're too independent, but the SCAT people are mad enough. The police ought to take them very seriously. Of course, that's only my opinion. The campaign does have plenty of sensible, Christian members.'

'Like Alderman Green?'

'I certainly hope so.'

Twitty watched out for the guv'nor but didn't see him. He listened to two men in front of him evidently agreeing about Mahler.

'The symphonies all last three hours.'

'It's not the length so much as they're on one note, sometimes two.'

'He's always making you think he's about to finish but he never does.'

Twitty didn't see the guv outside the church or in Wycliffe Way. Henry might have been one of almost any of the shadowy figures heading away into the night, but the night was moonless and the lighting along Wycliffe Way miserly. The mayor would have purloined the town's electricity fund and diverted it to SCAT.

Twitty jogged along Wycliffe Way in his pinstripes, hoping this was the direction he had arrived in from the railway station. Then he sprinted because his legs ached for a workout. He caught up with Peckover in King Street, a street decently lit, the Boots, W. H. Smith's, Computer World, Gap, Ralph Lauren, Sock Shop, Moti Mahal, McDonald's, Kentucky Fried Chicken, Jolly Sailor, Duke of Cumberland, Video Arcade – hey, lookee, Barton's Leather Goods! – and every window having cranked up its lights to fullest wattage, making the most of life before the warnings from SCAT's pamphlets and mobile loudspeakers came to pass, the Tunnel opened, and Sealeigh's retailers went up in flames, crumbled to dust, or otherwise became agonisingly defunct, French arrows through their hearts. Peckover stood in the glare of a window filled with shoes, writing in his notebook.

'Guv!' hailed Twitty.

Henry must have had his skates on to have got this far before stopping.

'No rush, Guv.' Twitty pulled up panting. He was tempted to peer at the notebook, see what gems of detection were being noted down, which choristers' names. 'Train's not till ten-thirty. How did you get on? The Schütz, isn't that a blast?'

Pecover put his notebook in his pocket and strode on.

Twitty padded alongside. 'Something the matter?'

Peckover was silent.

'Guv?'

'What?'

'What's the matter?'

'Nothing. Thought for a moment there might be, back there, your sermon. Thought I just might break your legs and leave you in the graveyard for the bats and owls. But it's all right. You've done me a favour. That's the last of Sealeigh for us and good riddance. Ever you and me meet again, which with luck we won't, I'll buy you a drink. Still pineapple juice, is it?'

'What d'you mean, the last of Sealeigh?'

'Don't be innocent. You made a public impression, mate, not to say a spectacle of yourself. You lifted your profile so high it took off over the organ loft.'

'So?'

'So you've blown it. There's seventy warblers got you marked down as a motormouth new boy who gives sermons. Our brief was discretion, far as I recall. Lay low, blend in, ears and eyes open. Ears and eyes, not mouth. Now everybody's off 'ome chattering about the black beanpole in the undertaker's suit who tells the conductor his Latin's corrupt.'

54

'So it is. Now I've given them an excuse they come up to me, some of them – they might if I'm there – because they're inquisitive. I don't need to seek them out and watch their eyes and tick them off the list or put them on it. Among those who're not going to say hello, who don't want to be sociable, could be a guilty party who nicks relics.'

'Poppycock.'

'Thanks.'

'You believe that? That what prompted your little homily to the nation?'

'Matter of fact I just thought of it. Something in it all the same. Half a dozen came forward and declared themselves. We'll know better next rehearsal.'

'Forget next rehearsal.'

'That's barmy, Guv. I know you're not serious. This way, unless you're walking to Folkestone.' Twitty veered into Drake Street. 'I've got a possible suspect, I think.'

'I've got five. Who's yours, the mayor? You two should team up, open an Academy for Uninvited Speech-Makers.'

Drake Street was ill lit. Shops and bright windows petered out abruptly. Here were a car park, closed offices, an anonymous chrome factory for microchips or canned peas. A hundred yards ahead twinkled the lights of the railway station.

Twitty said, 'Aren't you even going to ask? Honestly, Guv, but you make life difficult.'

'You think you make it easy?'

Peckover forged ahead past semi-detached houses with trim lawns and herbaceous borders in shadow. From behind drawn curtains in living rooms glowed television screens.

'Go on, then, who's your suspect?' Peckover said. 'Just don't sulk.'

'Thank you, sir. I think I had in mind a kind of test. If the black beanpole in the undertaker's suit—'

'Don't be cheeky, either.'

'No, right. If this new choirboy started sounding off on some topic, didn't matter what, and somebody seized up or behaved oddly, that might be of interest. I couldn't be much aware of anyone except the tenors around me because I had to be talking to Goodfellow, but it was one of the tenors who interested me.'

'Double poppycock. You're the odd one. You pipe up to test the reaction of one of the tenors?'

'I may have piped up because of Goodfellow's Latin. Somebody had to put him right. But the tenor bloke was part of it. And making myself known, which I still say makes sense. Don't think I'm urging you to do the same.'

'I'll keep it in mind.'

'The test may have worked. Everybody seemed to be paying attention except this one tenor who had his eyes shut and his chin on his chest as if he were asleep.'

'I was asleep. 'Alf of us were asleep.'

'He wasn't asleep. But he wasn't applauding or being insulting either, like he was with that woman—'

'Fleur Whistler.'

'Don't know, is she? But he's that sort, he has to be the centre of attention, unless he's changed. If he's changed, it has to be for the worse.'

'You know 'im?'

'During the break I'd said hello, and he said, "Do I know you?" That withering way some people put you down? It's twelve years ago and we never really met or spoke to each other but I know him and he knows me. I was over six feet when I was thirteen and black. There weren't many of us.'

'This is Algy Newby you're talking about.'

'Archy.'

'The same. Get to the point.'

They trod down stone steps.

'We were at school together,' Twitty said. 'Only for a year. Less than a year because he left suddenly. He was four or five years older. Far as I remember, the full name is the Seventh Marquess, Archy, Nineteenth Earl of Newby and Eleventh Earl of Grapenuts. I don't have it dead right – I made up Grapenuts – but he inherited two earldoms, if that's possible. Gaveston, perhaps, or Grammercy. You need evening classes to fathom peerages, unless you're a peer. Prince Charles would know. You could look him up in *Burke* or *Debrett*.'

'Wrong. You could look him up.'

'He left under a cloud. Damn!'

56

Twitty had stepped in a puddle. More than probably a puddle of piddle. They had entered a dark, smelly subway to the platform for the up train to London. No one was about. Perfect for muggers.

'Cloud of what?' Peckover said.

'Stuff had been going missing. It was recovered from Archy Newby's room. I don't say he was expelled but one day he was there and the next he was gone. Asked to leave, presumably.'

Their shoes echoed along the subway. Peckover watched the light ahead. No footpads so far.

'What sort of stuff? Missing from where?'

'Exactly. From the church. No black madonnas, we didn't have any, not that I know of. There was a sketch by Canaletto of a chapel in Westminster Abbey. A nativity scene by Holman Hunt – pretty awful, everyone said. Churchill's prayer book, the one he had at Harrow. And some of the brass of the founder, John Lyon, must have been four hundred years old. May have been more bits and pieces but that's what I remember.'

They surfaced from the subway to find the train waiting and the platform empty except for a guard.

'Get the lead out, dawdlers!' called the guard. 'All aboard for the metropolis and all its wonders and 'orrible muck and litter!'

Peckover and Twitty scampered. The guard peeped his whistle.

This late at night, midweek and out of season, no one wanted to go to London. The train was almost empty. The policemen found seats in a coach occupied only by a young couple with a baby and a plenitude of luggage. Peckover put his hat on the rack, and they sat across from each other, a table in between. Through the window was darkness dotted with lights which passed at increasing speed and grew fewer. Already they were deep in the Kent countryside, not that they could see it. Twitty took out his notebook and a ballpoint.

He said, 'Anyway, it's a start. Archy Newby nicked collectibles at Harrow and he could be nicking them on the Continent twelve years on.'

Peckover said, 'What's the chance of refreshments on this train?'

'Slim. If it fills up towards Easter we'll go first class, right?'

'I'll go first class because I'm a chief inspector. You will stand in the corridor with the refugees.'

Twitty grinned. 'Told you. I said you weren't serious about this being our last rehearsal.'

Twitty wrote notes. Peckover opened his own notebook. He said, 'You meet the local copper, Day, Superintendent Day?'

Twitty shook his head.

'I didn't either. Probably best stay clear. Coppers can smell each other out.'

'Everybody can smell coppers out.'

'They think they can. I was once at the zoo in uniform and a load of tourists took me for the geezer in charge of the elephants.'

'When I was in uniform at Heathrow there was a family of Nigerians thought I was their pilot. Couldn't convince them otherwise. They wanted to know about the weather over the Sahara and if the simoon was blowing.'

'We'll stay clear of Superintendent Day, though it'd be easier if we knew what he looked like.'

Peckover yawned. He stared out of the window. He opened music and began tapping the table with his fingertips. '"But in her hea-a-art . . . "'

Twitty looked up.

'" . . . a cold Dece-e-embuurrr,"', Peckover sang with grim, quiet intensity, drumming with his fingers, his voice sliding about in search of the pitch. 'What're you looking at?'

'I was trying to write.'

'Thought I 'ad this April one but it's gone. Seemed simple enough when everyone was singing it. Hurry it up, then. I've a question.'

'Archy?'

'Who's Archy? This.' Peckover stabbed the score with a forefinger and slid it in front of Twitty. 'What's it mean? *Poco rit.*'

'A little retarded.'

'You taking the mickey?' Peckover recovered the music and scowled at it. 'Actually, this one about April and my mistress's face and bosom could be my favourite. Schütz, on the other 'and, should never have been born. Gawd, it's all so exhausting. You exhausted?'

'Among other things.'

'What makes you so sure Archy would only have changed for the worse?'

'Got a chip. Must have. He's come down in the world.'

'Come down to what? From where?'

'Come down from being Archy, Seventh Marquess – in full he'll be something like Archibald Edward Rochester St Oriface Fortescue Dubois – Earl of Newby. He's too humiliated to use his title because he's got nothing to back it up. No stately home, no Chippendale, no salmon river.'

'Where've they gone?'

'Wherever they go when a nob of the *ancien régime* suddenly finds himself a *nouveau pauvre*.'

'You speak French?'

'Only in England, Guv. It'll have gone on inheritance taxes, investments, who knows? I doubt he gave it to charity. I've a feeling the father squandered most of it. Archy inherited an earldom and debts.'

'But he might be trying to recoup by filching relics and flogging 'em to Texas and Japan. That it? What's 'e do for a living?'

'You've read the file.'

'I've read it, I 'aven't learned it by 'eart. Don't be impudent.'

'Apologies.'

'Accepted. It's the Schütz, lad. We're worn to shreds.'

'What he does, he's assistant manager of the Sealeigh Odeon Sexplex. That probably means he stands by the popcorn tearing tickets in two. If he doesn't tell the peasants he hopes they enjoy the film, someone will complain he's a surly ape and he'll be shown the door. Assistant cinema managers can't be hard to replace. Bet he makes half what I do and none of the benefits. Your lucky day, Guv.'

'What's lucky about it?'

'Here comes supper.'

A youth in a whiteish jacket trundled a laden chariot along the aisle.

Peckover asked for two cans of Worthington, and as an afterthought a third, because last year or some years ago had been Mozart's anniversary and he hadn't celebrated it yet. Twitty chose a wrapped sardine sandwich, a cheese and chutney sandwich, a packet of chocolate biscuits, an apple, and a tomato juice. Peckover told him to put his money away, this was on him, and he gave the youth a five pound note, telling him to keep the change. The youth said it was another one pound thirty-five. Baffled, Peckover handed over two further pounds and waved the charioteer on to the couple with the baby and the luggage.

Twitty said, 'Where's your appetite? Dieting, are you?'

'There'll be something waiting at 'ome.' Peckover popped his first beer can and drank. He would have been happy to have had waiting at home what Twitty was delicately unwrapping, but it would be medallions of ham Polignac on celeriac mousse, or sweetbreads Florentine with Swiss chard fritters. 'You think Archy recognised you?'

'Yes. But he probably doesn't remember my name.'

'He can find out. He could ask you. Does he know you're a copper?'

'No reason why he would.'

'If he does and he's our relics bandit we've lost 'im.'

'Not my fault he's in the choir.'

'When you've cleaned the sardine off your fingers you can write down, "Archy Newby, possible affair with Fleur Whistler. Source, Eleanor Sandwich."'

'I met her. She thinks the police should keep an eye on SCAT. Does Fleur Whistler have money?'

'Archy as fortune hunter? If she has it doesn't show. She's the antiques shop help and a gymnast.' Peckover swallowed too much Worthington and gasped. 'Did you 'ave an affair with Archy?'

'Me?'

'Behind the squash courts. We all know about the public schools. "Rum, sodomy, and the lash."'

'That was the Royal Navy.' Twitty's mouth was filled with sardine sandwich. 'Archy didn't turn me on. Too old. And I didn't play squash. Ask me about Jeremy Gould.'

'I'd as soon not.'

'Pale and melancholy, my age, played the flute.'

'Stop looking wistful, you grotesque pervert. Show me your notes.'

Peckover held out a hand. Twitty pushed over his notebook.

'They're not finished,' said Twitty. 'Guess why.'

'You've got terrible 'andwriting, you know that?'

'I had to work at it. There was a time I wanted to be a doctor.'
'Can't read it. Bahama O'Toole? What's this roach liver?' Purée of
roach liver, sounded like a delicacy rejected by the archaeologists and
fetching up on his own dinner plate. 'Roach diver? Beach rover?'
'Coach driver. May I?'

Twitty reached for Peckover's notebook. Peckover grabbed his
wrist.

'Nothing there, lad, not yet.' Releasing the wrist, he tapped his
temple. 'It's all up 'ere.' He thought he wouldn't mention his
finger-joint device. 'And don't say there's plenty of room.'

'What were you writing in the street?'

'Personal stuff.'

Come to think of it, thought Peckover, the lad knew Latin,
French if he wasn't in France, possibly *poco rit*, unless he'd been
being cheeky. He knew words. He might have a halfway helpful
comment.

''Elp yourself. Mind, I want no comment.'

He watched through the window the hurtling dark and hummed
his version of 'April Is In My Mistress' Face'. Twitty sat back with
the notebook. All that was in it was on the first page.

> Of two kinds of bass
> The one I prefer
> Is the Bass that is beer
>   Not the one sung at Mass.
>
> Of the tenor's two sorts
> The one that makes sense
> Is the tenner that's pence
>   With one thousand noughts.
>
> But of altos, sopranos
> I'd hug every one
> For the sheer bloody fun
>   Of their circles and hollows.
>
> Goodfellow, Goodfellow,
> Don't interrupt;
>   Schütz is kaputz
> And your Latin's corrupt.

'Great!' Twitty enthused. 'It's so stupid! I don't even have to read it twice. Is it finished? Light verse, is it? You could be anthologised.'

'Give it 'ere,' Peckover said, reaching.

'Wait.' Twitty, perusing, withdrew the verses from reach. 'I'm not missing anything, am I? It's not a metaphor, choral music as the male libido? Or an allegory? Goodfellow as Satan?'

'At least it's legible.'

A lame riposte, but he was weary. The reasons for weariness were five per cent the beer, five per cent the sleuthing, and ninety per cent the singing. Singing was draining. He could see that singing should have been, might yet become, exhilarating. But it knocked the stuffing out of you, getting all that Mozart and Schütz and April in my mistress's face straight when you were too far from Joe Golightly to hear him, and the Look from Maestro Goodfellow might at any moment cleave you in two.

He who had faced up to villains with bludgeons, with shooters, and foolishly given chase across rooftops in Bermondsey, across Greenwich in a car with a flat tyre, on Northumbrian grouse moors, and once with his breaststroke in the Serpentine, he'd almost sooner that than the Sealeigh Choral Society. One solo bray in a silent bit and you'd never again hold your head high.

Tomorrow he would write his report, naming names, and Twitty's names. Frank Veal would despatch the report on the computer link to Interpol. Best outside bet to date, really the only bet, was Archy Newby. Someone was going to have to get the details from Harrow. There remained getting on for a mere three score unknown choristers, a honeycomb of mouths in the void.

Eleanor Sandwich, rumourmonger, he would not forget. But was the blue corduroy Fleur Whistler or Clemency Axelrod? Elbow on the table, hand in front of his eyes, he flexed his second finger, first joint.

'Rheumatism?' inquired Twitty, concerned.

In the oven were exotically messed-about sausages and on the side a verdigris-flecked mould and pencilled directions from Miriam. The 1982 Calvet Reserve was what he was to have with it.

Not bad, the supper. It never was. Never less than a quarter ton of it, either. Peckover munched, toyed, faded, and finally, furtively, jettisoned sausage and mould down the disposal unit. One day he would acquire a dog or a compost heap.

He performed as rigorous a toilet as he was capable of, considering his post-choral fatigue. Should he gargle? Should he buy, first thing tomorrow, throat spray and lozenges? Enveloped in his polka-dotted nightshirt, a birthday present from Sam and Mary, he looked in on them then slid into bed.

'G'night, Caruso,' mumbled Miriam.

SIX

At noon Chief Inspector Peckover brought his preliminary report on the Sealeigh Choral Society to Chief Superintendent Veal, who took it and said, 'So what have you learned?'

'Read it, you'll find out.'

'Not this. I've too much on my plate for this. The music.'

Peckover, who had just sat, stood. He looked behind him. Mrs Colter's dispiritingly neat desk was unoccupied. Out to lunch, or her back was troubling her again. He wondered if she permitted an osteopath or chiropractor, any of those magicians, to touch her back. Mrs Coulter was very particular.

He clasped the lapels of his Donegal tweed jacket, took a deep breath, and sang, '"April is in my mistress' fa-a-ace,"' and kept singing with volume and feeling. He became muddled in the passage where July hath her place but soldiered on, louder if anything – the acoustics were splendid, like an indoor swimming pool – and recovered for September within her bosom. He finished passionately pianissimo, out of breath, and off key, with not two, as written by Thomas Morley, but three 'But in her heart, but in her heart a cold Dece-e-ember.'

Frank Veal massaged his moustache, playing for time. This was an error.

'Like to 'ear the Mozart?' Peckover said.

'Very much, but not now. That was truly soulful, Henry. Can we—'

'I don't know it all. There are thirty-two pages. But lots of alleluias.'

'Another time—'

'*Regina coeli!*' burst forth Peckover. He'd fix Frank. '*Regina coeli! Regina coeli lae-ta-a-re!*'

Then from the corner of his eye Peckover noticed that the door into the office had opened. Mrs Coulter stood in the doorway holding a box file.

Peckover, still holding his lapels, said, 'Good afternoon. Decent weather. For the time of year.'

Anything Mrs Coulter might have said Peckover would have preferred to her saying nothing. She walked to her desk, very stately and finishing-school, sat, and opened the box file. He also thought he might have coped if her appearance had been severely headmistressy, pitiless spectacles and enamelled hair done in a bun, but she didn't have spectacles and her curly hair always gave off a lemony whiff of shampoo, and you'd have been happy to have buried your nose in it and inhaled if she hadn't been Mrs Coulter. She was dressed fetchingly in a Capri blue suit cut in the current mode, which this season was a couple of inches below the knee. Peckover had to accept that he was more nervous of Mrs Coulter than anyone in the world, after Robin Goodfellow.

'Tomorrow, two o'clock sharp, lecture room B,' Veal told him. 'Inform Twitty, would you? Art instruction on likely targets for our relics bandit in Ghent, Gap, Bra, and Andorra.'

'Art instruction? Do we wear berets?'

'Berets are compulsory. Not obligatory but recommended are an easel, turpentine, and a goatee.'

With a look in Mrs Coulter's direction in case she was waving him goodbye (she wasn't), Peckover departed.

The directions PNC Hendon Immediate and Interpol (Lyons) Immediate appended, copies of Peckover's modest report travelled from Frank Veal in C department to the police national computer in Hendon for storage, and, closer to home, eight floors below the CID and a step along the corridor from the message switch office, to the Interpol (UK) radio station. Constable Dottie Blenkiron in a short-sleeved white shirt with blue Metropolitan Police epaulettes transmitted the report on the scrambler to Lyons. She took off her headphones and turned to Sharon at her radio teleprinter. Between rushes of activity Sharon manicured her nails and dreamed of a prince on a white horse, or he could be a hairy goblin with missing teeth, she didn't mind so long as he kept himself clean and had masses of money.

'Sharon! Our 'Enry's singing in a choir!'

'Our 'Enry?'

'Undercover. Singing.'

'Is it a rock group?'

'It's posh. Mozart. And people nobody's heard of.'

'Can we get it on a CD?'

'I expect so. It's Sealeigh Choral Society. They're on telly.'

'My nan goes to Sealeigh, day trips, she says it's not so commercial as Brighton.'

'Honest, Our 'Enry singing, undercover. If he sang near me I'd go under the covers with earplugs.'

'I'd take him under the covers with me.'

'He's married!'

'Aren't they all?'

While little could have been less Immediate, Priority, Urgent Priority, Priority Confidential, Secret, or Secret Priority Immediate, within forty minutes of Peckover bringing his Sealeigh report to Chief Superintendent Veal it lay, translated, on the desk of Commissaire Mouton in Amiens.

There it languished for two hours until the commissaire returned from lunch.

Commissaire Mouton first missed then found and pushed a button on his intercom. Too late he attempted to stifle a belch.

'*Pardon.*'

'*Oui*, Commissaire?'

'I would like to see Sergeant Pépin.'

'*Oui*, Commissaire.'

Commissaire Mouton focused again on the report from Scotland Yard. It had gained nothing since the first focusing. The sergeant could deal with it. If Scotland Yard was going to start deluging him with paper because they had two men in the Sealeigh Choir – *ma foi*! There came a point where efficiency numbed the brain.

Lunch, now that had been something else, the barely warmed-over pressed Rouen duckling which the chef had carved at the table – there was efficiency! – swimming in its own blood, juices, pounded liver, butter, brandy, and, if he were not mistaken, a surprising vin de Cahors. How many bottles of Beaune had they tested before

66

the Krug? Four? And the songs after Madame le Juge had left! Three senior policemen serene in harmony, harmoniously vivace, and André always knowing the words. '"*Sous les ponts de vieux Paris*,"' sang the commissaire at his office desk. They'd have had more singing if the Juge d'Instruction had left sooner, but she was André's sister-in-law and entitled to her dessert. '"*Il y avait un beau navire*,"' sang Commissaire Mouton, tears and childhood welling. He looked to make sure he had switched off the intercom. He had not. He turned from it to clear his throat, leaned towards it, and pronounced in a voice unnaturally low, 'Madame Rouvier?'

'*Oui*, Commissaire.'

'Sergeant Pépin?'

'*Il arrive*, Commissaire.'

The commissaire switched off the intercom and shuddered. Other than the proposition that a woman's place was either in the kitchen or between the sheets he shared none of the sergeant's opinions. Sergeant Pépin unsettled him. Chauvinism had its place. After all, what other country was as glorious as France? Everyone agreed on that. But as for the parades and salutes and bashing of immigrants, that was unacceptable. His eyelids drooped, his chin sank. '*C'est moi*, Commissaire,' he thought he heard someone say, a voice both servile and bullying, through a dream of not one but two grisettes, nubile working girls with pouty lips and satiny bare boobies jiggling towards his face.

Commissaire Mouton came to attention in his chair. 'We have a report from Scotland Yard.'

'I am apprised.'

'You've seen it?'

'It came my way.'

I bet it did, thought the commissaire. You've made arrangements. Come the revolution, first twenty minutes of it, you'll defenestrate me and take over.

'Your appraisal?' said the commissaire.

'The Peckover is a fool, Commissaire. The Twitty is not to be countenanced.'

'Why not?'

'He is a Negro.'

'He is? How do we know?'

'I have made inquiries.'

'Where?'

'I have my sources.'

Britain's National Party, supposed the commissaire. A toejam rabble with steel-capped boots, same as France's.

'You are in touch with our colleagues in' – the commissaire had to hunt through papers – 'Ghent, Gap, Bra, and Andorra?'

'Yes, Commissaire.'

'You have spoken with them?'

'I have.'

'By telephone?'

'Yes.'

'But you have not met them face to face, greeted their wives and families, wined and dined with them, and won their confidence?'

'No.'

'You should, you will This is not a nothing matter, Sergeant. This is bald thievery of the very heritage of Western civilisation, to say nothing of a crucial tes of European Community co-operation and amity. Understand?'

'The Sealeigh rosbifs do not arrive in our country for another two weeks.'

'Twelve days,' corrected the commissaire, consulting the calendar. 'Twelve days pass fleetingly. *Où sont les neiges d'antan?* You must meet and personally advise your counterparts in the Police Judiciaire in Ghent, Gap, Bra, and Andorra, of the threat to come. You will assist them with security. They are provincials and they need you.' To the commissaire his beloved Amiens was only technically the provinces. In spirit and nobility she was the luminous queen of cities, unmatched in France or on the face of the earth. 'You will leave tomorrow. You will travel by train.' In *Le Monde* he had read of renewed threats of a rail strike for more money and less work. Should the strike come to pass and the sergeant be marooned for a few days in a siding at Didier-sur-Dildo, population four hundred, well and good. The longer he was far away the better. 'Present yourself to Madame Rouvier at eight o'clock for documentation. Questions?'

'No, Commissaire.'

'So, till we meet again.'

Sergeant Pépin clicked his heels and departed.

"'*Au clair de la lune*,'" crooned the commissaire, soggy with regret for his childhood and lost innocence.

The combination of Pépin and alcohol always had this effect on him.

Meanwhile, back in out-of-season Sealeigh, on this Thursday of the second and penultimate week of rehearsals, the town's choristers pursued what it pleased them to think of as their humdrum lives. With a cheery pessimism which only a psychologist of rare insight could have begun to plumb, they almost all subscribed to the theory that nothing happened in Sealeigh, whatever happened.

Oscar Thomas sacked two managers and a secretary and closed the Farringham office of Oscar Thomas Estates Ltd. Recession was recession. It was also the contemporary word for slump, stagnation, bust.

Angus McCurdle telephoned the vet, the police, the National Farmers' Union, and the regional office of the Ministry of Agriculture, after observing what he had little doubt was bovine spongiform encephalopathy among his Herefords. Awaiting the arrival of officials, he pressed on with his matchstick Royal Pavilion.

Joe Golightly, drilling into the wall behind a leaking toilet in a mansion on Laburnam Avenue, drilled into a feeder circuit cable. He had not committed such an error in twenty years. True, the cable ought not to have been there, but he should have guessed it might have been, every iota of evidence demonstrating that the last renovations had been performed by cowboys. He blamed himself as there came a flash, a bang, and he was thrown backwards with both arms jarred to the shoulders and rockets criss-crossing in his head.

Alderman Green took his place at a board meeting of CHAFAHS. Later, at Sealeigh Town Hall, he put on his gold chain and rose grandly from behind the mayoral desk to receive two tourists from Sealeigh, Maine, USA. He had not known Maine, USA, had a Sealeigh. Somebody should have briefed him. Then he prepared his forthcoming address to SCAT.

Gladys Green, the mayor's consort, received confirmation that her trouble was myasthenia gravis. She was not told much more. Young victims were sometimes helped by removal of the thymus gland but apparently this was not advisable in her case. She resolved to keep the news from her husband until the end, if possible, and it would be possible. If he noticed at all, he would remark that she was under the weather, she had been overdoing it. Feeling more than ever useless she pottered about the substantial lawns and shrubberies of her home in west Sealeigh. She would have written letters to her boys, one in New Zealand, one in Toronto, but she had written only three days ago and did not want to burden them.

Clemency Axelrod placed her eye in its Wedgwood saucer – the socket was more comfortable with the eye out than in and she was expecting no visitors. Below, in Curiouser and Curiouser, no customers for Fleur either, it being that slow time of year, one of several slow times. She settled on the sofa with travel guides. Andorra looked to be nothing but sheep and mountains. Gap, in the French Alps, and Bra, in Italy, looked hardly more promising. Ghent, old capital of Flanders, was a different proposition, however. Museums, art galleries, medieval and Renaissance churches . . .

For Fleur Whistler, in the stuffed barn of rubbish that was Curiouser and Curiouser, the question was not why she had left her husband but why it had taken her so long. He wouldn't notice that she had left, not as long as there were billiards on television, or any game where men struck, kicked, coaxed, or threw balls. Much good his balls had ever done her.

Dr Willis, whose husband had left her eleven years earlier, endured a mixed day which started well with word that Chloe, her elder daughter, had won a scholarship to Newnham College, Cambridge. Decline set in when Gladys Green reacted so maddeningly to the facts of her condition, neither screaming nor praying to God, either of which would have been understandable – she might after all have another year or more of life – but concerned only that her husband should never know, that he should be shielded. Her husband, the mayor! That brimming tub of megalomania! The day reached its nadir when she went an unheard-of five down doubled for inexplicably failing to finesse the knave of clubs.

Bahama O'Toole was involved in her first traffic accident. Witnesses, police, and every word of testimony pronounced her blameless. She had been driving her Southland Express coach at fifteen miles an hour through a green light on Bexhill Esplanade when a Ford Escort crunched into her offside luggage compartment, causing no worse than startlement among her passengers, and minor shock and brushing to the Ford escort driver, Derek Eversham, fitter for Kustom Kitchens, and his shoeless, knickerless co-driver, whom he had encountered two hours earlier in the lounge bar of the George Hotel, and who slammed on her shoes, grabbed her knickers, and high-heeled away before the Bexhill plods could discover her name. After conferring with a sympathetic Southland Express inspector, faintly nauseous Bahama drove onward to the Brighton depot.

Archy Newby tore tickets in two at the Sealeigh Odeon Sexplex and smiled like a viper. When he had proposed that a student might be engaged for this task, or one of the homeless who disfigured the promenade and pounced from doorways with doffed cap and open palm, he had been told the idea was interesting and if implemented he would be free to leave for Hollywood and become head of Paramount. Tearing and smiling, he fantasised the deporting of the entire Odeon management to Australia in chains, with maggoty sea biscuits and slime water for sustenance, and for the Odeon customers, the sweaty populace – this punish- ment didn't amount to much, he would dream up something better – a glob of Tate & Lyle's Golden Syrup on each cinema seat.

Peter Witherspoon did famously throughout the day, lecturing to appreciative classes on Picasso as Chameleon; Ruskin's Art Criticism; Mannerism in High Renaissance Italy; Burchardt and the Cultural Environment; and Abstract Expressionism, Dead End or Way Ahead? He fell from grace when darkness fell. Fatigued by lecturing, he sidled along the fenced lane behind Lime Terrace, peering at curtained windows, smelling wildflower smells, then, oh, uncurtained and lit up, he touching her, she touching him, nude as an Ingres, shameless, and, oh, the stench of wildflowers, the reek of creosoted fence, the dribbling of his armpits! 'Oi!' shouted a voice from some other window. 'Oi, yes, you!' Witherspoon raced stumbling and sobbing along the fenced lane pursued by 'Oi!' and 'Oi!'

* * *

71

Whether the relics thief was among the aforementioned choristers or the sixty still to be met, neither Peckover nor Twitty would have had the least notion. Today, being in London, they were in no position to become acquainted with more of the choir. Of those so far encountered, Archy Newby headed Twitty's list. For this reason Peckover put Archy Newby at the bottom of his own list, or he would have done had he had one. His instinct was that the case was not going to be simple.

Alternatively, it could be easy as pie. All that was required was for the police and curators and clerics in Ghent, Gap, Bra, and Andorra to stake out their precious relics, assuming they had any, hide in the clerestory with a big net, and bingo. If, that was to say, the thief planned to carry on nicking.

What still puzzled Peckover was the amateurishness, as if the thief had put all his faith, her faith, in luck. Either that or he didn't care if he were nabbed, or he might want to be nabbed. Prison-wish syndrome, home to the cosy womb and no ringing telephone and no junk mail. Lifting one relic the thief might have got away with, but three at three consecutive concert stops? The police hadn't cottoned on immediately but they had cottoned on. At work here was either a mind-boggling beginner or a genius, and geniuses, genii, in Peckover's experience, were thin on the ground.

All he knew, courtesy of Constable Twitty, was that the g was hard if Ciceronian, and soft if Goodfellowian and foully corrupt.

Amateur or genius, the Sealeigh thief was in the process of deciding that a trip to London might be necessary.

Keeping the relics at home was stupid. Also lacking appeal were burying them under an oak, depositing them at Charing Cross left luggage office, or posting them with remorse to the Archbishop of Canterbury. A bank safe deposit box seemed as tidy a solution as any.

Not in Sealeigh among the High Street NatWests and Barclays where everybody knew everybody. Somewhere obscure, anonymous. Bank of China, Bank of Lebanon, Crédit Suisse, Credit Bank of Djakarta. That meant London. The City. Gracechurch

Street, Leadenhall Street, Poultry, Threadneedle, that area, where the anonymous vaults would be in return for a fee.

If they asked questions, wanted to know about the Selfridge's shirt box, the shirt box would move to the next bank on the street, and the next if necessary, until it found a nest.

Then back to Sealeigh in time for rehearsal.

SEVEN

'The bronze lamps which hung in early Christian churches,' lectured Fiona Macrae, assistant professor of aesthetics at Birkbeck College, University of London, 'were designed in a variety of symbolic shapes, though never, I should add, the phallus, which was largely the province of Greek, Etruscan, and Egyptian ornamentation and worship. The lamp we see here is a thirteenth-century Coptic import in the church of the Holy Sepulchre at Gap. A tempting target for your thief, I'd have thought. Next.'

Peckover and Twitty, in adjacent chairs at the front of the darkened lecture room, waited while Inspector Ruggles, head of the arts and antiques squad, fumbled with the projector. The chairs had a wide right-hand arm-rest for note taking, if you were right-handed and the light was sufficient for taking notes, which it was not. Not that either Peckover or Twitty was prurient beyond the normal, but both rather hoped the next slide might be of an ornamental phallus. It would make a change from lamps and crucifixes.

On the screen arrived a disappointing book: open, decorated, and the right way up, which elicited an audible sigh of relief from the projectionist.

Inspector Ruggles regretted having volunteered to work the projector when he might have been off with the rest of the squad. Apart from it being Japanese and more state-of-the-art than a projector needed to be, he had not checked the professor's slides and two had already come on the screen upside-down. Only a matter of time before there'd be a ribald comment from Our 'Enry.

'The painted word, the printed word,' announced Ms Macrae to her audience of two; three with Ruggles. 'This magnificent psalter is in the museum in Andorra. Let us hope it stays there.'

Twitty watched shadowy Ms Macrae, who wasn't young any more, she'd be over thirty, but she hadn't dieted herself to scrag and sharp edges and her mouth was this hearty ladleful of a helping which laughed when she made a joke, and made him laugh too, though he didn't understand the jokes. He wondered if she gave private tutorials in aesthetics and would he be able to claim on expenses?

'Illuminated manuscripts, Books of Hours, some with ivory covers, manuscripts of every kind, and early printed documents such as the fifteenth-century tax register from Gutenberg's hand press, stolen in December from the Cologne city archives, these are increasingly a target for thieves. Next.'

Inspector Ruggles pressed the button. This time a painting of a painter seated at an easel, heavily clothed women grouped around, and correct way up.

'Every detail in this painting pertains to the Flanders of six hundred years ago,' Ms Macrae said, 'yet it pretends, with painterly licence, to illustrate Cicero's version, in his *Rhetoric*, of the story of Zeuxis, the Greek artist whose grapes were said to have deceived the birds. Here we find Zeuxis painting the most beautiful woman in the world – any offers?'

'Helen of Troy,' Twitty called out.

'Quiet,' whispered Peckover, and jabbed Twitty with his elbow.

'The fair Helen, thank you,' Ms Macrae said. '"What were all the world's alarms – To mighty Paris when he found – Sleep upon a golden bed – That first dawn in Helen's arms?"'

'Yeats,' loudly offered Peckover.

'Top of the class,' acknowledged Ms Macrae.

'Cor,' said Twitty.

'Zeuxis,' informed Ms Macrae, 'as we can see, is painting Helen not from one model but from five, combining the finest feature of each into one idealised portrait. The work we see here is a miniature in a fifteenth-century book in the Centrale Bibliotheek der Rijksuniversiteit in Ghent. Next.'

The next slide was of candlesticks in the cathedral of St Bavon, Ghent. The slide that followed jammed like misshapen toast in a toaster. Berating beneath his breath the female professor and her incompetent sloppy slides, Inspector Ruggles eventually prised free the slide with his Bic, the inky point of which skidded in the process, pierced the celluloid, and gouged in it a hole three-eighths of an inch in diameter. From the rear of the classroom sounded treadings and tramplings. The projectionist slid the sundered slide into his pocket. She'd lost that one. No one was going to miss it whatever it was.

'Mr Peckover,' a voice, not Twitty's, said in Peckover's ear.

Bernie Bright, oldest copper in London, if not the nation. Mild conniving and turning of blind eyes in high places – a nephew in the Home Office had been no disadvantage – had kept devoted Sergeant Bright in uniform for many years after he had been due to retire, there being agreement that quickly after he was retired he would pine and expire, and nobody wanted his blood on their hands. For twenty years past retirement age he had stood on foyer duty in the main entrance to Scotland Yard with its blue Metropolitan Police flag and the yellow flame burning for London police dead in wars. He had fielded questions, directed visitors, looked in the bags of those permitted beyond the foyer, but he had begun to make errors. After telling the Chief Constable of Derbyshire, 'Stalls to your left, curtain up in eight minutes,' he had been withdrawn from public view and put to running errands along the corridors of the inner sanctums. Walking them, anyway.

He whispered, 'What's the slide show, Henry? Girls?'

'What can I do for you, Bernie?'

A pause. Sergeant Bright searched his memory.

'Got it,' he said. 'Geezer calling himself Thomas Oscar or someone on the blower for you. He said you'd want to know.'

'Peckover?'

'Bill Brown. 'Old on a moment.'

Sergeant Bright, wheezing somewhat, had positioned himself a yard away as if eager to be the one to raise the alarm if Peckover tried to steal the telephone.

'I can manage, Bernie. Get yourself a cuppa.'

'I remember you when you were demoted for those limericks,' Bernie said, and traipsed away.

'Yes.'

'The Andorra concert is off,' Oscar Thomas said. 'The hall's being renovated, they don't have the facilities, or so they say. My guess is they can't be bothered. Suits me. Andorra was going to be a totally unwarranted expense.'

Peckover's first reaction was to scuttle back to the lecture room to tell Ms Macrae she could skip the Andorra slides. Otherwise the news failed to gobsmack him one way or another.

He said, 'Is that it?'

'No. One of the tenors has been asking about you. Bob Day. Superintendent Bob Day. You might say conducting inquiries.'

'What kind of inquiries?'

'Who Bill Brown and J. Twitty are, where you're from, what you do, and how you manage to breeze into the chorus after missing four rehearsals.'

'He asked you?'

'Rang me this morning. I don't like it.'

'What did you tell him?'

'Told him I didn't have the particulars with me but you were experienced singers, very keen, and the men's voices needed strengthening. He's not satisfied. I think he should be told.'

'Was he on your last concert tour?'

'Yes.'

'I'd sooner we told him nothing yet.'

'What if he asks Robin Goodfellow about the auditions you didn't have?'

'Think 'e might?'

'Sure to. He's learned nothing from me except I'm probably keeping something from him. He might not reach Robin today but he can buttonhole him tomorrow at rehearsal, then where are we? Either Bob Day or Goodfellow has to be told, preferably both. How long do you imagine we can get away with this nonsense?'

Not too long now Nosey Bob was sniffing about, Peckover feared. He said, 'Let's wait and see. Each person we let in on it is one more chance we've tipped off our thief. I'll let you know. What department is Day?'

'How do you mean?'

'Drugs, vice, firearms training, catering, admin?' How d'you mean, 'ow d'you mean? Gawd's sake. 'Community relations, illegal immigration, flying squad, dogs, 'orses, beach patrol?'

'I think he deals with traffic.'

'Stands on the prom directing it, does 'e?' asked Peckover and wished he hadn't. He needed Thomas on his side.

'Bob Day, for your information, is a respected senior officer,' said Thomas. 'You still haven't grasped it. He's asking about you and I've had to lie to him. I've lied to the police. I don't care for lying. It's one thing I do poorly and I'm not going to keep on doing it.' Peckover felt dazed. A self-made property tycoon and he didn't care for lying? Not even the eentsiest fib about the true value of the seafront site he was buying and the office block he was selling? Sanctimonious berk.

Peckover said, 'But you're learning to lie, sir. I 'ope you see it as serving the cause of justice. See you at rehearsal.'

Twenty-four hours later Peckover squeezed on to a train which set off crowded, shed passengers at Croydon, lost more at Sevenoaks, and debouched the rest at Tonbridge. Nobody went the whole route to Sealeigh except coppers masquerading as choristers and similarly lost souls. He had four seats and a table to himself and nothing to do except learn the words and music of pieces by Mozart, Schütz, Brahms, assorted hey-nonny madrigals, and selections from G&S.

That morning he had peered through lenses slotted in front of first one eye then the other and announced his findings to the lady slotter, herself adorned with bold spectacles in hexagonal tortoiseshell. He had had to announce 'Now!' when two parallel lines moving towards each other merged into a single line. She had known he was a copper so when the lines became one he had cried 'Freeze!' to amuse her. She hadn't been amused.

He had telephoned Twitty, interrupting heaven knew what riotings the lad was up to in unsuitable company in his Lavender Hill pad. Whatever the music he had had on, it wasn't Mozart. He had advised the lad that one Bob Day, tenor and Sealeigh police superintendent, was asking questions, so stay away from him, don't give him the chance. First they would need to know which was Bob Day so as to be able to stay away from him.

Here he came now, Twitty in a sombre track suit, jaunting along the aisle with music, and hoisting an arm in salutation.

'Evenin', Guv. Choral Society Special, this train.'

'We shouldn't—'

'Be seen travelling together. Honestly, I can't see it matters. Could be too late, anyway. I'm passing right along, not stopping, but we've a couple of other members towards the rear.'

'Who?'

'Our director and the woman with the glass eye and the Curiouser and Curiouser shop.'

'Sit down. I can't see it matters either. Did they recognise you?'

'I don't think they saw me.' Twitty slid into the seat opposite Peckover. 'Thomas is buried in papers and a lap computer. The woman—'

'Clemency Axelrod.'

'—is asleep. They're not together, they're in different coaches.'

'Might have been together and not want to be seen together.'

The music in front of him was Heinrich Schütz, Psalm 150: for Double Chorus, Double Brass, Choir with Organ. As newcomer, Wednesday, he had been let off. Tonight he might be asked to stand and sing the last seventy-eight measures of Psalterns and Harfens and Earlobes and Herring because someone was botching it and it was imperative to discover who.

He said, 'How many of this choir are keen on art?'

'Peter Witherspoon teaches it. He might know Ms Macrae.'

'Who else?'

'This, who did you say, Clemency Axelrod has a shop, and Fleur Whistler helps her in it. They ought to be keen. I mean, we shouldn't assume, they might loathe art and antiques. Then there could be another twenty or fifty we don't know about.'

'Hard to see those two bringing holy thorns and madonnas back from the Continent and setting 'em up for sale in their shop.'

Twitty the Sage nodded.

'Still and all,' Peckover said, 'we'd look a couple of regal idiots if there the relics were among the bedwarmers and pewter pots and old postcards from Morecambe.'

'You're suggesting we should check it out?'

'Suggesting you should. Tomorrow. I can't, happy to, but you understand, family man, children, commitments. The shop should be open Saturday. Have yourself a spell by the briny. Breathe the ozone.'

'Thanks,' said Twitty, who had been looking forward to the Chabrol retrospective at the National Film Theatre. If he stayed a night in Sealeigh, looked in on Curiouser and Curiouser at nine or whenever it opened, he should be back in London in time to catch as much of it as he could take. 'I'll spend the night.'

'Bed and breakfast, lad. Mrs Mulligan's behind the gasworks. Not the Sealeigh Ritz.'

In Amiens, Commissaire Mouton received word from Interpol that Andorra had been cancelled.

He would not confuse Sergeant Pépin with the information. The sergeant would be on his way there when? The commissaire sifted through papers in pursuit of dates. Day after tomorrow. No train strike so far but a fool's errand to Andorra would serve equally well.

The longer Sergeant Pépin was out there in the field, the farther out the better, the happier the commissaire would be.

'"*Lobet den Herren, lobet den Herren!*"' exploded the Sealeigh Choral Society in a tumultuous outpouring of praise to God which shivered the church's timbers, loosened the stained glass, buckled the lead on the roof, raised the hairs on Peckover's arms, and dwindled to silence as flame-headed Robin Goodfellow, agonised eyes lifted to heaven, arms waving all over the place, shouted 'No!'

Hunched yet towering on the edge of the stage, the conductor addressed the choir on the subject of taking responsibility. He was Lucifer, Prince of Darkness, his exquisitely articulated sentences and honeyed voice the more terrifying for being hushed. Released, his baton would have become magically a pitchfork, skewering at one toss sundry of the doomed, damned denizens of Pandemonium in the pews.

'Again, you dogs' dinners!' he cried, raising his baton and having to wait for the laughter to cease.

Most of the laughter was nervous but some was heartily amused and went on too long, as if the insult had been the pinnacle of wit.

The baton twitched.

'"*Lobet den Herren!*"' eructed the choir, berserk.

Goodfellow bounded from the stage and along the centre aisle, swatting the air, watching everyone at once, and singing all eight parts in support. Peckover believed there were eight. Taking responsibility and singing like a fool, he was too occupied with his words, notes, and those petrifying traps where he was not to utter a squeak, to work out whether Herr Schütz had eight parts going or eighty.

"*Lobet Ihn mit Saiten und Pfeifen!*"

This second bash by the choir at the lobets seemed to Peckover no different from the first but Goodfellow allowed it to continue. "*Alleluia! Alleluia! A-a-allelu-u-uia!*" Pages and pages of it, raging and ranting. Keyboard Kate thrashed the ivories, possessed Robin lunged and plunged. "*A-a-allelu-u-uia!*"

There followed milling as normal seating patterns were resumed for something completely different, G&S as it turned out.

"'And so do his sisters, and his cousins, and his aunts!'" gabbled the choir. "'His sisters and his cousins, whom he reckons up by dozens, and his a-a-a-aunts!'"

This might have been manageable sung at funeral speed by a maximum of three voices but Goodfellow wanted all sixty plus choristers going at it lickety-split. The result would have been unintelligible to any English audience which was not hearing-impaired – the deaf might have got something from the lip movements – so prospects for the Continent were not bright. Those burghers of Ghent who had believed they had a decent command of English would be discouraged.

The other G&S ditty Peckover had music for was from *The Pirates of Penzance*, the policeman song about constabulary duty, but it was not to be, not now, anyway. Goodfellow called out, 'Take five.'

The smokers sprinted for the exit.

'Hello,' somebody in a khaki safari jacket said to Peckover before he had a chance to leave his pew, shuffle about a bit, seek out familiar faces – Oscar Thomas, Archy, Alderman Green, Fleur, Eleanor, Clemency, Witherspoon, Joe Golightly (God save his larynx) – and take evasive action should a Sealeigh police superintendent named Bob Day bear down on him.

'My name's Bob Day,' the man said. 'A policeman's lot is not a happy one, eh?'

EIGHT

'Great to have new blood in the choir,' Bob Day said. 'Bill Brown, isn't it? Robin's a stickler when it comes to auditions. What did you give him?'

Give him? Like chocolates? All Peckover knew was that he was going to be grilled unless he ran. He felt fingers between his shoulders, a mere touch.

'Pardon,' said the bass with the pencil moustache. He had the ferrety face of a 1950s barrow boy.

Peckover took a pace to the end of the pew and sloped backwards, allowing the barrow boy to pass. Nobody could leave the pew because the superintendent geezer blocked the end, but he stepped aside, permitting the barrow boy to walk to freedom. Then he stepped forward, closing off the pew as effectively as a portcullis. Peckover looked for escape at the other end of the pew. Its exit was clogged with women sitting, lolling, chatting.

'We all give him something,' Day said.

Youngish for a superintendent, mid to late thirties, must have had something going for him beyond passing exams, perhaps he'd seen the chief constable doing something he should not have been doing, or the chief constable's daughter was in love with him. He was an early Robert Redford women might fall in love with, searingly blue-eyed and Aryan. Alternatively, he could be a straight-up Sealeigh copper, underpaid, overworked, wife and two kids, car in need of new tyres, and curious to know how a couple of unknowns had managed to muscle in on the choir after missing four rehearsals, and, more to the point, why? His belted safari jacket was smothered in patch pockets and epaulettes.

'Well,' Peckover said because he couldn't say nothing, Day

82

standing there eight inches away. 'Give 'im, right. Much the usual, I'd say. Nothing out of the ordinary.'

'Robin sets great store by it, it's really a getting-to-know-you thing. Not that he fails anyone, not unless they're tone deaf, but after the sight-singing it's the personal choice that lights him up, or fails to. Most give him something grand like "Vesti la giubba" or "Liebestod" but Dennis Hurley gave him "Waltzing Matilda". He loved that.'

The bloke wasn't going to go away. On the other hand, Oscar Thomas was stepping up on stage. Move, Oscar, find your notes, get cracking.

'"The Road to Mandalay",' Peckover said.

'An old favourite. Joe Golightly gave him that. What about Twitty? John Twitty, is it? Jeremy?'

'No idea. Who?'

'You were auditioned together, surely?'

'"Rule, Britannia!". Excuse me, an announcement from our director, we have to hear this. I'm going closer.'

A weak exit line, but Thomas on stage had a hand raised for quiet, and those who had noticed were becoming sibilant. There being no getting past Nosey Bob without a battering ram, Peckover strolled along the pew in the direction of the blockade of women, hooked a leg over the back of the pew, and nimbly a second leg, carefully making no eye contact anywhere. He wove between knots of gossipers in the centre aisle, and sat, all the while watching the director intently, thereby encouraging others to watch him too, rather than himself. Pew-hopping was probably disapproved of.

'Friends, I'll not keep you a moment,' Oscar Thomas announced. He looked solemn, as far as anyone wearing a bow tie was capable of looking solemn. 'Many of you will have heard that the Andorra leg of the tour has been cancelled.'

From those who had not heard came sighs and murmurs. Thomas explained the why and wherefore. Peckover located Twitty standing with some elderly ladies. Not elderly to the extent of being frail, but the mayor's wife, for example, Mrs Green. Eleanor Sandwich, the motherly poppycock lady. By resting his elbow on the back of the pew and the top of his head in his palm, Peckover was able to obscure his face to some degree and look about at the choristers without obviously looking to be looking about. Not that anyone paid him attention. They were asking the director scheduling questions. Bob Day had moved from the far-away pew to a position closer to the stage. If he needed more audition information he seemed ready to let it go for the present. Peckover wondered if Day now had enough information not to trouble Robin Goodfellow. The choir chattered among themselves.

Peckover rose and aimed for Twitty. The aisle was fairly jammed, like platforms on the Bakerloo and Piccadilly lines at Oxford Circus. He plucked the seat of Twitty's romper suit, tilted towards the constable's ear, and said, 'Day's the blond one in the safari jacket.'

'I guessed.'

'If 'e asks what you sang at your audition, it was "Rule, Britannia!". I sang "The Road to Mandalay".'

'Road to where?'

'Mandalay. But 'e won't ask because you'll keep clear.'

'Archy's not here.'

'He'll be tearing tickets in two. Couldn't get away.'

Careful of feet, Peckover manoeuvred closer to the stage. By the time Thomas had stepped down from it, Goodfellow had returned to it.

'Tried to phone you,' said Peckover, 'but all your office would say was you were out all day.'

Oscar Thomas said, 'I'm out more than I'm in.'

'London?'

'Why London? In fact, my Ashford office.'

'Motorway busy?'

'I went by train. I appreciate you're with us in an investigative capacity, Peckover—'

'Careful.'

'Exactly. This is too absurd. I saw you speaking to Bob Day. Did you tell him who you are?'

'Not yet.'

'Then I suggest – oh no.'

Alderman Green stood on stage with one arm hoisted for attention please and under the other a briefcase.

'Friends!' Alderman Green called out. 'Fellow choir members, good folk—'

'That's us,' interrupted Robin Goodfellow. His voice was meaty and carrying. 'Good choir folk resuming our rehearsal with the Mozart.' Smiling, he lifted his wrist to his eyes and regarded his wristwatch. 'Mr Mayor – Phil – you have ten seconds on the subject of SCAT, starting – now!'

'Hear hear,' somebody said, applauding.

Peckover was tempted to raise a cheer himself. Good on yer, Goodfellow. Of course, a ten-second deadline might make the mayor maunder on for ten minutes in defiance.

But the mayor looked shaken and a little mottled around the dewlap. Nothing for anyone to get their knickers in a twist about, old boy, ha ha, the mayor said. Merely taking the opportunity to remind those interested that the SCAT march and demonstration would set off from St Vincent's Place at two prompt tomorrow, terminating with a rally and guest speakers, himself included, at the bandstand on West Esplanade, everyone welcome, SCAT lapel buttons now available, volunteer distributors needed, also volunteers for the collection boxes, thank you, friends, for your indulgence. He stepped down from the stage, visibly in a sulk from the peremptory treatment from Robin Goodfellow and the groundswell of support for the whippersnapper from among the choir's oafs, socialists, froggie lovers, sandalled vegetarians, pacifists, and lesbians.

'"Regina coeli!"' roared the chorus in sweet unison. '"Regina coeli! Regina Coeli lae-ta-a-re!"'

At ten o'clock the conductor sang out, 'Goodnight! Beddy-byes! Up timber hill!' Goodfellow was perspiring and wilting. Peckover watched Bob Day heading not for himself, or the exit, but in what might turn out to be the direction of Twitty.

The lad would have to do the best he could. For himself he had a train to catch.

So when Day stepped forward, introduced himself, and suggested coffee, forewarned Twitty said, 'Marvellous, must just catch my friend, be right back,' and as an invitation to Day to step aside he put his hand on a khaki-sleeved arm and applied pressure. Blocked by Day ahead, the front pew to port, piano to starboard, and his retreat cut off by choristers astern, Twitty increased the pressure, smilingly pushed, and squeezed past. He sidled between Dr Willis and a bald

85

fellow reeking of aftershave, tacked past others, and reached the exit, by which time he was probably safe. That he would be back for coffee and discussion with Day was untrue, but it was true that he wanted to catch his friend.

She was walking briskly along the dark path from the church, bag over her shoulder and music in her hand. To each side of the path were the lumpy shadows of gravestones. Twitty wondered if he should ask her, as he would have liked to, will you be my friend?

No, he should not. He had experience of her answers.

'Great rehearsal.' He fell into step beside her. 'What do you think, how we're doing and everything? You're an old pro.'

Possibly not the term he wanted but what was the term? Old hand? Doyenne? Greybeard? She did not reply. Perhaps she wasn't listening.

Twitty said, 'We haven't really met. Not formally introduced. Jason Twitty.'

'I know.'

'You do?'

'You didn't have anything to tell us tonight about how we should pronounce Latin.'

She turned off the path and walked left along Wycliffe Way.

'No, well,' Twitty said. 'But the music, oh, that Psalm, the German chap. Which is your favourite?'

'They're so different.'

Twitty's passion slipped a notch. Of course they were different. Different composers, weren't they? Different bloody centuries. Bloody diplomat's fence-sitting bloody answer. Still, she had spoken. Three sentences and perhaps twenty words if you counted them up.

Striding alongside through the gloom, he said, 'Seriously.' She wasn't going to like this next question but the way had to be prepared. 'This is serious, don't misconstrue.' She was going to misconstrue. 'D'you know, like might you be able to recommend somewhere where a body could lay his body tonight?'

No answer. Probably as well. Her twenty words was his ration and not one had actually dismembered him. He should accept and be grateful.

Sea smells. Latish traffic whizzing occasionally by. Wycliffe Way had trees, hedges, and grandiose Victorian houses. Distantly ahead were lights, perhaps the entertainment hub of Sealeigh. There would be a Kentucky Fried, Chinese take-out, and Archy's Sexplex. The railway station was the opposite direction, behind them. The guv'nor would be about there if he hadn't stopped under a street lamp to pen an ode.

Twitty said, 'Like a decent hostelry.'

'Is this for all night or just twenty minutes?'

'Sorry?'

'Why don't you go home?'

'Home! Exactly! That's it, the problem, I live a little bit out.' Her query could have been taken two ways, one of them not a query but the heave-ho. He couldn't actually smell her, not through the traffic exudations and sea winds and seagull breath and all the coastal stuff, but if he could have done she would have smelled of spices, moonglow, vanilla, and womanhood. 'I'm looking for a bed.'

'I gathered.' Bahama came to a stop.

'Just for tonight.'

'Not permanent.'

'Not at all, no.'

'Just the one-night stand.'

'No! No, no, no!' What he meant was yes. 'I do see that this may seem impudent but if you had a spare couch . . . It could be far away.'

'Like Tahiti?'

'Oh, good, Tahiti!' Twitty, throbbing with laughter, did his best to calm himself. 'A pallet under the stairs or in the cellar so as not to discommode you.'

'I'd like to help but the truth is my place is a mess. Far too untidy. Dust. You'd hate it.'

'No, I like dust. I'll teach you how to dust if you have a duster.'

'There's the beach.'

'Beach.'

'Pebbles, I'm afraid, and dogs do their stuff on it, but it's not that cold tonight, not freezing.'

There she stood in the dark in front of him, not sounding too fierce and insulted, in fact sounding quite placid, perhaps too placid, also

87

implacable and unfathomable like one of the Greek Furies in their milder moments, and possessed of that demonic female power of being everything he right now and pretty well all the time lusted for but which was not, he guessed, going to be on offer. She had resumed walking. He stalked alongside. She halted at a side street, Kimberley Terrace, another of the town's streets not burdened with unnecessary lighting.

'Keep straight ahead,' she said. 'You'll pass bed-and-breakfasts, then on the front you have the Windsor, the Bristol, the Regis, the Ocean Metropole, if you can afford them. The bed-and-breakfasts will have vacancies but I honestly don't know. Sealeigh doesn't have many blacks. Any landlady answering the bell at this time of night and finding a mile-high Sambo in a tracksuit and no suitcase on her doorstep might fall to the ground with a mortal affliction. What do you do, anyway?'

'Do?'

'To live. The hotels on the front will set you back a hundred quid.'

'Spread me a blanket on your floor and I'll tell you all. You'll like me once you know me. I can be a riot, but I'm peaceable, I can sleep alone, I often sleep alone, really. We could practise the April one about the mistress's face and everything. I'll make breakfast.'

'Too generous.'

'Just in case it's high tide and the landladies are timid and the Ocean Metropole costs a bomb, how about a phone number? I promise not to phone after midnight. Not unless I'm really in need.'

She laughed and shook her head.

He said, 'I'll see you to your door. Perhaps a soothing cocoa?'

'G'night.'

Twitty watched her receding figure along unlit, penny-pinching Kimberley Terrace. He called after her, 'You'll be sorry when the coastguard find my body on the beach tomorrow with a piece of paper in my hand with your name on it and a heart and I'm smothered in jellyfish and barnacles.'

Darkness swallowed her. Twitty continued along Wycliffe Way towards the lights and uninviting sea.

Motive Bahama might have. All sorts and species of people

might jump at an opportunity to nick relics and auction them off to a moneybags stymied by what next to spend his money on. Opportunity, as singer and coach driver, she unquestionably had. She'd know the coach's nooks and crannies where stolen goods could be stowed too.

Delectable, capable Bahama? Never.

NINE

Twitty licked fingers anointed by copious cod-and-chips grease from the King Neptune Fish Emporium and dropped the wrappings dutifully in a litter bin. All Sealeigh had gone to bed except the King Neptune and Graham Patel & Sons, Provisions. Thinking with regret of Bahama and her untidy habitation, not that he particularly believed the untidiness, he bought a toothbrush, toothpaste and packet of throw-away razors from one of the sons, a child who rang up the transaction with lightning efficiency and said, 'Cheers.'

He rang the bell of 51 Wycliffe Way. Bed & Breakfast – Vacancy, announced the placard in the window. Round the corner, a mere minute's dash away, he had sighted the Regis Hotel whither he might find himself fleeing with his credit card should the landlady go into shock.

The landlady was robust, hospitable, and offered a choice of rooms. She was Mrs Lemon, she said, and did he have luggage? Stolen, said Twitty. The police were on the trail. The death penalty should be restored for thieves like that, Mrs Lemon said, leading the way through cat and cabbage smells up jazzily carpeted stairs, swinging her bum as she climbed. This room she particularly recommended because it was very nice and you didn't get the noise of traffic. Appurtenances were at the end of the passage. After he had made himself comfortable perhaps he would descend to reception – Twitty supposed she meant the narrow hall with the table and umbrella stand – and sign the visitors' book. Would he care to partake of refreshment in the lounge, included in the tariff? Not really, Twitty thought. He should have known better but having had no dessert he avowed that that would be delightful.

The room was spotless. He was a hundred times better off here than in Bahama's flyblown sty. One message in a shiny frame thanked him for not smoking; another revealed in flowery italic that we pass this way but once, any good that we may therefore do, etc. In the washbasin was a wrapped bar of soap a little thicker than a tea-biscuit. He brushed his teeth vigorously.

Refreshment in what he judged to be Mrs Lemon's private parlour turned out to be a bottle of port and two glasses brought by Mrs Lemon. No one else was partaking. He would have said that he and Mrs Lemon were the only people in the house had he not spied a blade of light beneath one door and heard rushing water from behind another. On the coffee table beside the refreshment lay magazines in a fan arrangement. What magazines it was impossible to tell because Mrs Lemon had turned out the main light. The sole source of radiance was from somewhere concealed low down and possessed of the wattage of a lighted cigarette.

A clicking noise sounded from the closed door where Mrs Lemon fumbled about in deepest shadow. Then she was somewhere close by and insisting that the sofa would be more comfortable.

She sat beside him pouring port and giving her views on interest rates and supermarket prices. She'd had to raise her tariff or she wouldn't have been able to do it, not to the exemplary standards she set herself, she just wouldn't, she would close down rather than lower her exemplary standards. He didn't have to contribute – she seemed satisfied with an occasional murmur of total agreement. 'Chin chin,' she said. Twitty thought this was at least the second, and possibly the third time she had said chin chin. He believed she said it each time she refilled their glasses, or hers anyway. The port was fairly foul. He didn't recall having tasted port before, but you could say this for it, it swilled away both the toothpaste flavour and whatever lingered of the cod and chips. Oddly, the second glass, and successively, tasted less foul than the one before.

Somewhere he had missed a link but the topic had shifted to Roger, Mrs Lemon's first husband, or an early husband, perhaps the original Roger the Lodger. She couldn't begin to tell what a despicable man, what a rotter. Her spare hand, the one not holding her port, was on his knee. What had taken her so long? Help. If he protested would she put him out on the street? Where was Mr Lemon? Was there a Mr Lemon? If there were, would it be better if he showed up or if he didn't show up? Twitty believed Mrs Lemon might have locked the door into the lounge. She had fiddled with it and done something, so if Mr Lemon did show up he wouldn't actually show up, he would just rattle the handle. He might kick the door in. Mrs Lemon was describing how Doug used to take her sea fishing. Twitty did not care where Doug fitted into the scheme of things, not enough to ask, though he did wonder why Doug, having taken Mrs Lemon sea fishing, had not nudged her overboard in mid-Atlantic. Her hand was now on his thigh. A nice glass of port, she explained, did wonders after a tiring day. Twitty uttered a murmur. The night promised to be more tiring than the day. She was allowing her baser instincts to carry her away to a point where he doubted she would take any notice of the doorbell or telephone if they rang. The only escape he could think of was more port for Mrs Lemon, all the port that there was. In the dark he could not see the level of the port in the bottle. He assumed she would have a second bottle, and with luck she would get stuck into it, though how much she could quaff before sinking into a stupor she hadn't said. Currently she was extremely cheerful and had begun to laugh at everything she said. Twitty found her increasingly unintelligible but would have conceded that this might be in part because of his own intake. She groped around for his zip, which his jogging pants did not have. He supposed that was what she was doing. With her other hand she poured port. The level might be low, it couldn't really have been anything else, but the port was not finished because from the sound of the pouring the port was not going into a glass but on to the table, thence presumably to the carpet. He was about to suggest she attend to one matter or the other, and he would propose priority for the port, when she must have heard the sloshing. She slammed down the bottle and swore, a monosyllable more to be expected from a meat porter or an Eddie Murphy film than a landlady with exemplary standards. Laughingly she swabbed and splashed one-handed in the spillage. Twitty could not make out whether she swabbed with her bare hand or with kitchen towels she carried for such an eventuality. The hand that didn't swab she kept on his person. No novice in jogging pants design, Mrs Lemon had now perceived the absence of a zip and the presence of a drawstring and knot. The knot was not a marline-spike hitch or a triple reef with clinch but a simple bow. Moreover she had done with swabbing so could and did go at it with both hands. Should he resist or assist, if only to save the pants from damage? They were new from Ralph Lauren. Already the swabbing hand would have put port smudges on them. Was it included in the tariff, or an extra, or might there be a rebate?

Not that he would be telling anyone of this discreditable episode in the life of Jason Twitty, but his good news was that he awoke next morning alone in the bed in the spotless room with the framed messages. His bad news, he had overslept. He had intended to be at Curiouser and Curiouser at nine o'clock and back in London by noon. His watch said five past nine. Still, time enough to make it to the dining room for orange juice and a muffin, if he could keep them down. His head was chaotic, like a Harrods January sale, but that would pass. On the front of his pants was a port smear. He assumed it was port. He sponged it, creating a darker, wetter patch. He reached the dining room at a canter eight minutes before it would be bolted and barred.

On his way to a table, carrying his choir music in front of the port patch, he nodded to and was nodded back at by, surprise, fellow guests. Not many, a commercial traveller type with the *Daily Mail*, and a couple who looked retired, perhaps on their way to or from the ferry. Double surprise, from the kitchen bearing a teapot came not a serving wench but madam herself.

Mrs Lemon had attended to her hair and applied cosmetics. She wore a butcher's-length apron with SCAT across the bosom. She didn't look haggard, on the other hand she didn't have a lot of bounce in her step. She took little notice of him, neither winking nor screaming. Beyond the civility of bringing fresh tea and removing eggy plates she paid scant regard to other guests too.

She bore down on the guest with the music and inquired, 'The full breakfast?'

'If there were just a slice of toast? It wouldn't have to be brown, you know, bran stuff with lumpy husks and sprouting—'

'The full is included in the tariff.'

'The full, the full,' Twitty enthused. She made the full sound like a command from GHQ. Gesturing as delicately as he could manage at her chest, he said, 'You'll be marching today? From St Vincent's Place to the bandstand?'

'I don't march.'

She might not march but she was a tornado in her kitchen. Inside five minutes Mrs Lemon returned with a plate of fried triangles of bread, two fried eggs, fried bacon, two sausages – fried, everything fried – kidneys, mushrooms, tomato, Heinz baked beans (stewed), and a side plate of toast, butter, and marmalade. And a pot of tea and a bill which Twitty had little doubt Accounts would be able to live with. The bill didn't itemise, it simply pronounced a total that was considerably less than he had paid for his port-stained jogging suit.

Eating like a crusader off to fight somewhere where there would be only herbs and tofu, Twitty thought of Bahama. He loved her.

He speared a segment of banger and smushed baked beans on to it. He supposed he could hardly actually love her. He'd met her only twice and each time she had seen him off with a flea in his ear. What he meant was, how he truly and sincerely felt, he would love it if she would be bowled over by him so they could cuddle up and have a wild time.

In all the dust, wretchedness and misery of her hovel it wasn't as if the police and their sniffer dogs would ever be able to nose out stolen relics anyway.

The retired couple had left. The commercial traveller, who ought to have been out and about drumming up business, was doing the *Daily Mail* crossword. He filled in answers in pen, bespeaking self-confidence, or he might have had no pencil. He might be filling in wrong answers.

Twitty deposited beside his plate exact banknotes plus a fiver for smart service and the chambermaid. He palmed the bill for expenses purposes, checked that his pants pockets held his wallet and toiletries, scooped up his music, and darted, being young, fit, far from crushed by his night of port and romance, and in any case restored by breakfast, out of 51 Wycliffe Way.

Which way to Curiouser and Curiouser?

Curiouser and Curiouser occupied the front ground-floor space of the last terraced house, or the first, on Beach Terrace. You could not see the beach from the shop, though you probably could have done thirty years ago before the developers moved in.

Fleur Whistler came out of the side door, closed it behind her, and said, 'Damn.' Had she locked herself out? She hung from her wrist her sack with the training shoes and leotards and opened her purse. The key was there.

So too the keys to the marital home she had walked away from. Would he change the locks? (No.) Move out? (Possibly.) All Fleur was certain of was that he wouldn't phone or visit while football, cricket, or golf were on the box, which seemed to be most of the time. After class she might drop in at the library for a book on how to separate and divorce. There would be shelves of such in the section dealing with illness, smoking, bereavement, bankruptcy, and buying a house.

Meanwhile, Clemency had welcomed her into the untenanted bed-sitting room behind the shop until such time as she, Fleur the Waif, as she had heard Clemency refer to her, sorted out her life. Some waif. She had put on six pounds in as many weeks. Packing cases were stacked against the walls of her new space, some with bric-à-brac, others empty, and there was no shower, only the claw-foot bath with the rust stain which oughtn't to have been in the flat, in Fleur's view, but in the shop, for sale. The flat was not ideal except in one particular. Her husband was not in it. Two particulars, if you counted Clemency, who lived on the second and third floors. Clemency had pooh-poohed rent but that was unbusinesslike Clemency. Fleur guessed she must have private funds. Clemency not only lacked a flair for selling, at times she positively resisted selling. Fleur had seen her triple the price of a worthless pewter tankard and when the insane customer had brought out his wallet anyway she had snatched the tankard and said it was already sold. The bath with claws and rust might have sold as a period piece if Clemency had been willing to invent a little, claim it came from, say Osborne, on the Isle of Wight, where Queen Victoria had taken a weekly bath in it, also Tennyson, and the Kaiser.

Fleur walked round the corner of the house and into, or almost, a black man fruitlessly twisting the locked handle of the shop door and squashing his nose against the glass, gawking in. He held familiar music. Looked familiar, too.

'It'll be open soon,' Fleur said. 'Hullo, good morning. Our new

Latin pronunciation member, the hard and soft c's and g's. We open at ten.'

'Very civilised. In the forthcoming *Sing a Song of Sealeigh: A History of Sealeigh Choral Society*, I'm the footnote as the Latin pronunciation man. You're Fleur Whistler and you're off to your fitness class.'

'I am?'

'You mean I'm right? Here's how it's done. An altercation at rehearsal, as I recall, with Archy Newby. Overheard chat afterwards, names mentioned. You work here and teach aerobics. Those bulges in your sack could be haggis except it isn't Burns Night. The white shoelace hanging out hints at athletic footwear.'

'Well,' Fleur said, and could find nothing else to say. He was quite a knockout. Flustered, she said, 'Good luck,' and hurried on.

At ten past ten Curiouser and Curiouser was still locked tight. Twitty walked chafing along Beach Terrace and back along the other side, past terraced houses interspersed with poky shopfronts of paralysing uninterest: Spruce Dry Cleaning, Mad Hatter, a women's second-hand hat mart – he couldn't believe it but that is what it appeared to be – an electrical appliances place, an abandoned travel agency, Sunflower Travel, with faded, curling airline posters showing buxom beauties surfing and baring their teeth and cleavage. Oops, beg pardon – on the other side of the glass, between the posters, a face arrived and peered at him.

He crossed the road back to Curiouser and Curiouser. The door opened and Clemency Axelrod stood there saying, 'The Latin. We met. Come in, come in.' She beckoned him inside and closed the door. 'Are you just passing or is there something in particular? Some unusual playing cards have come our way, Egyptian, we think, and rather risqué. I have concealed them so you will have to ask. Here, can you identify this?'

She thrust a knobbly black stick into his hands. The closest it came to any of the stolen relics would have been the madonna but this stick was a yard long.

'Test it for balance,' she said.

Twitty did not understand. Balance it horizontally across two fingers? Vertically on his nose? If he swished it he might demolish curios. Curios besieged them on all sides.

'It's a shillelagh,' revealed Clemency Axelrod. 'Perhaps you'd like to be left to browse. I'm afraid we're low on musical artefacts at present. We had a bugle but it was snapped up. We're open until five o'clock.'

She left him holding the shillelagh and arranged herself at a desk heaped with old books. She started to catalogue or at any rate show interest in them.

Twitty decided to be methodical, starting in the left-hand corner and working his way round. The place wouldn't take him until five o'clock. Ten minutes and he ought to be finished. Cluttered, though, like the contents of a family attic where nothing had been thrown out, only added to. Also smelly. A stale smell of mildew and vermin. Depressing landscapes in flaking gilt frames hung on the yellow walls. Junk lurked invisibly behind larger junk. He saw no sculpted madonna or bejewelled chalice and he was confident he wasn't going to, but he began to circle and scrutinise. As the guv had said, royal charlies they'd look if Clemency Axelrod and or Fleur Whistler were flogging stolen relics here on Beach Terrace, Sealeigh.

The closest to a chalice was a whole rickety tableload of chalices competing for space with ashtrays, cloudy glassware, and sepia picture postcards from Scarborough and Wiesbaden. The chalices were not gold and bejewelled but silver, or at any rate silvery, and once you had them in the right light were inscribed, for example, Cynthia Duckworth, Senior Backstroke, St Aldwyn's School, 1954.

What else? Cracked crockery, mismatched cups and saucers, mugs bearing a coat of arms from Weymouth and Blackpool, an oriental fan, a rare three-legged rocking-horse, a box of cockle shells, a soldier's helmet, a clergyman's gaiters with mud on them, a small flag of an unidentified nation probably long ago swallowed by a larger neighbour, a wine rack, jigsaw puzzles, moulting cushions and a roll of a sort of sackcloth in the soft furnishings section, two croquet mallets but no hoops or balls, obviously irrecoverably defunct radios, record players and TVs, an electric heater with no plug and a lethally frayed flex, a typewriter with its keys bunched against the carriage like a bristly porcupine, and more, more, alas, but he was progressing. The shelves of damp books delayed him. Their spines were furry from having been stored in the dungeons

97

at Glamis Castle. Ethel M. Dell, Victor Hugo, the complete works – surely complete, how could anyone have written more? – of Dornford Yates. He thought of buying *Goldsmith's Poetical Works* for Our 'Enry but it was mottled with fungus and who knew what she would ask for it? Would there be twenty per cent off for choir members? Not many of the items were priced but those that were seemed to Twitty criminally pricey. Four hundred pounds for the wapiti's moth-ravaged head? A tenner for this still unravished bride of quietness, a Grecian urn, with a chip in her lip, a crack like a heart-surgery scar, and on her bottom the surgeons' signatures, Adrian and Belinda Ceramics, Kingston-on-Thames? But, praise be, he had seen almost all of it, circled before and behind cataloguing Clemency, and was but a pace from whence he had set out, the finishing-post, with only one table of wreckage to go.

He had to guard against two temptations. First, buying something because he was here. He was not honour bound, was he, as one of the Sealeigh Choral Society, to be supportive of fellow members in their career goals? Second, he would resist thinking Clemency Axelrod a crook. Her sky-high prices were of no more significance than her glass eye. She could charge what she liked for the wapiti's head. No one was obliged to buy it.

He eyed the garbage on the last table. Here were a clump of dried flowers, a pincushion with demonstration pin, West End theatre programmes (*Careless Rapture*, Ivor Novello), a menu from the *Mauritania* (£75), and sundry pointless boxes. One box was long, flimsy balsa wood that had held dates from Morocco. Another was a musical box. When he lifted the lid, closed it, and shook and thumped the box, watching Clemency to be sure she was not watching, no music sounded forth, naturally. He couldn't hold it against her, she had said she was low on musical curios. He'd have bet the bugle didn't work either. Returning the musical box to the table he saw the thorn.

The thorn minded its business in the space from which he had picked up the box. A quarter-inch of sacred bramble, a brier, a spine of wood blackened and fossilised as it would have been after twenty centuries.

'Ms Axelrod?' he said.

'Coming,' said she, emerging from behind her desk. 'Ah, the

musical box. I'm afraid it doesn't play, the engine is missing, but perhaps you could find one. Shall we say a pound?'

'This.' Twitty pointed a finger at the thorn.

She had to stoop to see. She picked up the thorn and dropped it in the waste-paper basket beside her desk.

'Fleur and I share the cleaning, but you'll appreciate, a place like this, one doesn't care to disturb the antiques more than necessary.' She borrowed the musical box, perused it, pointed, and said, 'It's from here, hardly worth gluing back. I often think of our world of antiques as like that poem, remember, "Things fall apart"?' She handed back the box. 'Shall we say seventy-five p?'

She rummaged in a tea caddy for change. Twitty picked the thorn out of the waste-paper basket and fitted it into the chipped corner of the musical box.

On his way out he bumped into Joe Golightly coming in. All they needed was Fleur to hurry back and they'd have a quartet.

'Our Latin scholar,' Joe Golightly boomed heartily. He carried a matchbox-sized packet, puny stuff compared with Twitty's brown paper bag and its musical box. 'Great little place this.' He rapped Twitty's bag with his beefy plumber's knuckles. Had the purchase been a Sèvres figurine of translucent porcelain, that would have been the end of it. 'What did you find?'

'A musical box.'

'That's the ticket,' boomed Joe Golightly, and he tramped into the shop.

At the station, with fifteen minutes to wait for the train, Twitty telephoned Peckover's home.

'Hullo, Guv? Mrs Peckover? Who's that? Jason Twitty here.'

Somebody had picked up the phone but wasn't saying anything.

'Sam, is it? Mary? That you?'

'I'm Sam.'

'Hello, Sam. Listen, Sam, is your dad in?'

No answer.

'Sam? Your father. Daddy. I'd like a word with him. If he's in. Is he in?'

'Of course, silly.'

'Fantastic. Could you fetch him?' He spoke his clearest English at approximately two words to the minute. 'If it's not too much trouble. Sam?'

Nothing, not even breathing. Sam would be seeing how long he could hold his breath. He might have gone off to play video games. At this rate the next sound would be beeps because his phone card would have run out.

'That you, lad?' said Peckover. 'Enjoying the seaside?'

'I'm catching the next train back. There's nothing at Clemency Axelrod's shop, not on view anyway, not apart from Clemency. I bought a musical box.'

'Ideal. A memento of your days with the Sealeigh choir.'

'It doesn't work.'

'So much the better. Drive you crazy, those things. Mary has one, unbreakable, you can play it under water. 'Ow would you like to hear "The Farmer's in the Dell" from sunrise to sunset?'

'Guv?'

'What?'

'We're getting nowhere. You realise that? We've been on this business, all right, it's less than a week, but it seems like six months and what have we achieved? *Nada. Rien de rien.*'

'We can sing *Regina Coeli*.'

'Speak for yourself. Last rehearsal was as if I'd never heard it before.'

'Me too. It's that load of resurrexit sicut dixits defeats me. I've given up coming in with the right pitch, nobody's going to hear. Trouble is we missed too many rehearsals.'

'I'm not talking about the singing.'

'I know that. Look, don't worry. The tour hasn't started. What we do is what we're doing. Stay undercover, learn the music, meet the choir. Any thoughts on anyone we ought to watch once the tour's under way, that's a bonus.'

'That's exactly it! There's not one member I've met who doesn't convince me they're not guilty.' He watched the digital figures on the telephone dwindle to a few pence worth. 'Henry?'

'Yes?'

'I'd say the mayor's innocent. He's too busy with his SCAT. I'm not going on the march, don't even ask. There's a piece in today's local paper saying all SCAT's talk about rabies coming foaming in through the Tunnel is a metaphor, an excuse for their greedy, frightened Little Englandism. Nobody honestly believes we'll be invaded by rabid dogs and rats and bats, not with all the traps and barriers we've built into the Tunnel. Guv?'

'Still 'ere, lad.'

'I might be becoming paranoid. I have this vision of Curiouser and Curiouser as a thieves' kitchen ruled by Clemency Axelrod. She charges four hundred quid for a wapiti's head. Two of her lieutenants are Fleur Whistler, who's moved in, and Joe Golightly, who looks to me as if he'd like to, he brings her tiny packages—'

Beep beep beep beep.

Twitty hung up. The train was arriving anyway.

He was perspiring and not in the pink. He wouldn't have been surprised if he were coming down with something, a dropsy or the blind staggers, a malady defying the best efforts of the doctors and brought on by breathing the air at Curiouser and Curiouser, Mrs Lemon's breakfast, Mrs Lemon, and port.

TEN

During the next ten days prior to departure for the Continent, nothing happened; nothing at any rate of pith and moment, such as a confession from a relics thief.

Peckover was glad nobody confessed, that no progress into the case was made whatsoever, neither by himself and Constable Twitty nor by Commissaire Mouton and his brigade in Amiens, whom Frank Veal had made mention of, but whom to Peckover remained phantoms. He had begun to look forward to the tour, apart from the singing. He had even started to ponder over what gifts he should find for Miriam, Sam and Mary. Too bad about Andorra but *c'est la vie.*

He phoned Twitty with a development on Sunday, the day after the lad had checked out Curiouser and Curiouser. Not a momentous development but the lad should know. He paced before picking up the telephone, summoning courage, because what he was going to hear would be dispiriting orgy noises, a bacchanal of thumpings, screamings, and heavy rock.

'Jason? That you?' No, not yet. 'Constable Twitty?' There was something, though, not a total silence. ''Enry 'ere. Mate?'

Peckover heard rustling sounds, like sparrows pecking about in a bird-feeder.

'Yuh,' said Twitty. At a guess it was Twitty.

'What's the matter?'

'Bit of a cold.'

'Seen a doctor?'

'Yuh.'

'Liar. What did 'e say?'

'Flu.'

'You're not allowed to have flu. We've got rehearsals. I'm coming over.'

'Nuh,' protested Twitty, a sparrow's protest, throaty among the sunflower seeds.

Might be flu, there was a lot of it around, thought Peckover, and he drifted into a reverie.

'A lot of it, my child, around,
Lost, borrowed, stolen, found,
In fields and on the Underground,
Everywhere the sparrow sound.'
'Sparrows, Mum? The sound of flu?
Methought 'twas more like bubbling glue;
Squelchy retching, hawking, wheezing,
Globs of stringy mucus sneezing,
Spraying here, sprinkling there
Infection through the snot-filled air,
And snorting, swallowing the stuff
As if you couldn't get enough.'
'Speak for yourself, disgusting child!
Endeavour to be meek and mild.'
'But, Mum – ah-CHOOH!'
A cannonade
Of rheum as thick as marmalade
Coateth whomsoe'er it smites –
Bankers, brigands, parfit knights,
Feminists and catamites.

O the pity! O the horror!
Adios to thee, Andorra!

Happened every year, half the population collapsed, the other half immune and suspicious, plotting how they too might inveigle a week off work. In the church, when they weren't singing, the choir was coughing and sneezing.

'Jason?'
'Hnng?'
'We don't have to worry about Bob Day. Day, the Sealeigh copper. He knows about us. Knows who we are.'

Sparrow shufflings.

'I'm calling you this evening, check you're alive,' Peckover said. 'If you're not, I'll be over with ginger soup and drugs. You're doing nobody any favour being brave. You go to sleep now.'

'Yuh.'

When Peckover had answered the phone and heard a voice he wasn't sure he recognised say, 'Henry Peckover?' and he had said 'Yes,' and the voice said, 'Alias Bill Brown? Bob Day speaking,' he had been understandably vexed. His wrath was aimed at the pusillanimous twerp in the bow tie, Oscar Thomas, the only one who could have blown everything, whether deliberately or by accident being neither here nor there. When Day told him that Frank Veal had told him, because Veal had evidently decided that this cloak-and-dagger carry-on between grown policemen was stupid, Peckover was mollified not a whit, though he wondered if Frank Veal might be under strain, such as losing it. Keeping Day in the dark had always been stupid but hadn't it been Frank's idea? If it hadn't, whose had it been? Then when Day had said the relics were Peckover's baby, old squire, and he would stay out of it until and unless he could be of use, Peckover softened to the point of uttering grudging cordialities. He had been won over totally when Day admitted to being a fan. The sonnet in the *Spectator* about the latest gold bullion job at Heathrow with its cunning half-rhymes – Day had quoted bullion, trillion, hellion, and rapscallion – had been a stitch. Peckover had been aware he was the subject of a consummate snow job from Bob Day but never mind, the bloke had done his homework, and why wouldn't he have liked the Heathrow poem? It had offended the Home Office and the entire security police at Heathrow so chances were it might have been quite good. Where was the point in writing anything if it didn't get up the nose of somebody?

'Bye for now, Mr Brown,' Day had said. 'May I call you Bill? See you at rehearsal.'

If Day was the relics bandit, they were up the creek.

Peckover acquired his first spectacles, not cheap. What became of the National Health Service? When he would wear the spectacles in public would happen when it happened. He would don them in private, though, a closet spectacles-wearer, because by golly they did magnify small print, such as everything he read. They were gold-rimmed half-moons chosen by Miriam. He had asked her to choose. In two matters Peckover had no self-confidence: choosing spectacles and Schütz. In his new spectacles he looked like a cobbler in a fairy tale.

Twitty, for three flu-stricken days able neither to see nor stand, emerged for the Wednesday rehearsal unable to sing but offering mouth movements and expressions of rapt musicality. Mr McCurdle trapped him in a pew during the break.

He's in search of sympathy for his doomed Herefords, Twitty guessed, mistakenly.

'The distinction between stressed, tonic vowels and those that are unstressed and atonic is the essential in diphthongisation,' Mr McCurdle said with no preamble other than a hurricane-force sneeze. 'In post-Classical Latin the unstressed vowel became short and usually dropped out altogether. So the diphthongs *œ* – there's your coeli – and *æ* merged with the long and short e respectively.' His hedgerow eyebrows worked up and down in emphasis. 'For example, in Vulgar Latin, and in Italian, *poena*, punishment, becomes *pena* with a long closed e, and in French *peine*. *Caelum*, the heavens, becomes *celo* with a short open e, then the Italian *cielo* and French *ciel*. You'll find no *coelum* or the genitive *coeli* in any self-respecting Ciceronian dictionary. *Coelum* is bad late Latin spelling, like *foenum*, hay, for *faenum*, or *moestus*, sad, for *maestus*. You had it largely right but you could have said more. Jason Twitty, is it?'

'Yes.'

'Teacher?'

'Representative.'

'Representing what?'

'A variety. Imponderables. What about the hard and soft g?'

'Hard or soft g for *regina* and c for *coeli* is a matter of sonorisation of intervocalic surds, in other words, palatalisation, shifting the point of articulation to the palatal zone. In Classical Latin c and g were hard velar consonants but Classical Latin isn't what Mozart set his music to. I hazard that is what you had in mind.'

I did? marvelled Twitty. 'Pretty much,' he agreed.

At the Friday rehearsal and again at the Saturday dress rehearsal Oscar Thomas reminded the choir of the importance of dress. No scuffed shoes, please, and white shirts and blouses, not cream, ivory, eggshell, pearl, or lint.

They practised arriving on the tiered stage, when they stood and when they sat, and opening their music in one discreet, simultaneous flick, not like a mob consulting their programmes at a football match.

Singing, however, at the dress rehearsal, with instrumental accompaniment beyond the piano, threw Peckover into confusion. He had believed he had been making headway, but the orchestra, some eight of them, went its own way, leaving him lost. They were professionals, presumably they could read music, and Goodfellow never scolded them as he scolded the choir, but what they played bore little relation to what the choir sang, or so it seemed to Peckover. They were unnecessarily loud, the trumpet and trombone in particular, blasting away like à champion Yorkshire brass band, and everything lasted twice as long. With an introductory chord or two and some rippling effects from Keyboard Kate, the choir had in the past sung and that had been that. Now there were orchestral overtures, entr'actes, folderols, and lengthy stretches where the chorus simply stood, trying not to yawn and scratch itself, while the instrumentalists interminably sawed and blew. This was no doubt how the composer had intended it to be but it took getting used to and there wasn't a lot of time. Tomorrow people would be paying to listen.

Five of the orchestra had played on the last tour so had to be watched. Their instrument cases were not the worst place for stashing a madonna.

Sunday's two performances passed off to a packed church and what to Peckover sounded like suitably frenzied acclaim. The choir looked dashing in its performance costumes and sang its best because here was the audience and there was no going back. Dinner-jacketed on the back row between Witherspoon and the barrow-boy with the pencil moustache, a building contractor named Crisp, Peckover concentrated as he had never concentrated. He held his music up, his head high, and watched Goodfellow's eyes and baton every instant when he was not labouring to follow the music. He was desperate for a pint of beer.

His opinion was that he acquitted himself decently. Indeed, he regretted having dissuaded Miriam from coming to the concert with the bairns (the audience had several bairns, squeaking and being shushed) to see for herself what he could do under pressure. She had allowed herself to be dissuaded more readily than he approved of. He failed to hear Twitty, somewhere to his right among the tenors, so that was fine. The lad wasn't singing out in the silent bits.

After the second performance the choir and friends of the choir had a party in the church hall where they partook of cakes with Day-Glo icing and bowls of Presbyterian fruit cup. Not a drop of beer closer than the Jolly Sailor on King Street.

The single most distressing feature of Peckover's experience with the Sealeigh Choral Society was neither the fruit cup nor the nail-biting probability that sooner or later he would commit a major singing gaffe. The torment lay in his inability to be rid of the music he had so conscientiously laboured to master. This ailment in which a tune rackets relentlessly about in the skull, never shutting up, had not yet struck, quite, though he had had inklings of it. At three o'clock next morning it visited him in its full awfulness when he awoke with 'And so do his sisters, and his cousins, and his aunts' bouncing in his head. G&S, Mo, April in his mistress's face, the lobets and herring even, would next day and in coming days, with no warning, strike up in his head and go on and on, over and over, continuous as an old seventy-eight record with a nick in it. Was there a cure? His affliction could not be unknown to medical science and probably had a name, an acronym like CMMS (Chorister's Melody Malady Syndrome). In a milder form it afflicted everyone over-exposed to advertising jingles or popular music of the catchier sort.

Chief Superintendent Veal added to the Sealeigh file copies of Peckover's and Twitty's by now fairly copious reports on the choir and passed it on for translating and forwarding to Interpol. The translating shouldn't be too taxing, not to Sergeant Czyz, the Factory's resident polyglot. It was not as if it had to be translated into Tagalog or Lapp.

Peckover said, 'So tell me what you know about Ghent, apart from 'ow they brought the good news to it from Aix.'

'Who did what?'

'The poem, lad, the poem.'

'One of yours?'

'Browning, pity's sake!'

'Browning's the one eloped with the woman who languished on a couch, right?'

Peckover supposed that could be said about Browning but probably oughtn't to be the first thing said. He, Twitty, and a couple of dozen early arrivals stood with their baggage by two ancient silvery Leyland coaches outside Sealeigh Presbyterian Church, waiting for someone to open up the baggage lockers. The Scotland Yard pair had given up avoiding being seen together. Natural enough for the new boys to gravitate to each other.

No sign of Bob Day so far. Oscar Thomas had vanished into the church with the union coach driver.

Peckover felt fairly sure that all anyone knew about Ghent (other than those who had visited it, but who had?) was Browning's 'I sprang to the stirrup and Jorrocks and he, They galloped, you galloped, we galloped, all three.' He suspected he hadn't got it a hundred per cent right. He didn't recall what the good news had been, either, and why Ghent to Aix, why not Aix to Ghent, or, come to that, St Tropez to Vienna. Now he thought of it he wasn't surprised Twitty had never heard of the poem. Probably he hadn't heard of Wordsworth's 'Daffodils'. Harrow's trendy Eng. Lit. teacher would have concentrated exclusively on the loss-laden gripings of Philip Larkin. Actually it wasn't loss, because you couldn't lose it if you'd never had it. 'Give me your arm, old toad; Help me down Cemetery Road.' Gawd, I asks yer.

Peckover guessed that Twitty had assembled his touring costume with careful thought for his role as Englishman abroad. It was a mixture of stockbroker belt, grouse moor, and salmon fishing on the Spey. Daft tweed fishing hat minus the hooks and flies; tweed jacket with leather shoulder patches for shouldering your gun while waiting for the ghillies to beat the pheasant out of the heather; regimental tie of the Queen's First Dragoons, cavalry twill trousers, and brogues.

He himself wore his parka with the hood because Miriam had insisted the boat would be breezy; jacket, flannels, psychedelic tie as sole tribute to cockney vulgarity, and comfy suede shoes. Perfect travelling weather, the sky dishwater grey and not a hint as to what it might do, whether turn sunny and blue, or slosh down rain, or remain black.

Joe Golightly's baggage included a carrier bag of pork pies, Cornish pasties and Scotch eggs bought at the last minute for freshness. He was holding the bag open for Clemency Axelrod to see in with her good eye, his big face troubled as if he might not be bringing enough to see him through the foreign cooking to come. Clemency, similarly concerned, touched his arm in sympathy. Peckover wondered if the package Twitty had seen Joe Golightly bring into Curiouser and Curiouser might have been an engagement ring.

Bereaved for his slaughtered Herefords, Mr McCurdle stood apart, sneezing and guarding his suitcase, an outsize piece of tartan canvas that would unfold and hang up like a wardrobe. The chorus, either sensitive to his misfortune or intimidated by his strong character (what kind of man built Brighton's Royal Pavilion out of thirty thousand matchsticks?), left him to himself. Peckover decided that given the opportunity, and the ride to the ferry being only twenty minutes, he might sit next to Mr McCurdle, if not to swap jokes at least to demonstrate to the choir that he was not contagious.

On second thoughts, what if he was? He had a cold, he might have the mad cow bug too.

He certainly wouldn't be sitting with Archy Newby, in conversation with a couple of the younger females, neither of them Fleur Whistler.

Not actually conversing but standing together as if for security against the foreignness to come, were Ms Whistler in blue, and Eleanor Sandwich in a hat of a glittering, metallic material with attachments of gauze or net and a clump of artificial roses.

Alderman Green shunted about making his mayoral presence known, jovial in spite of or because of his wife having been ordered by Dr Willis to skip this trip because, as the mayor explained, she was 'a bit under the weather', as if that explained anything. Gladys Green, present to see her husband off, had given up trying to keep up with him and stood abandoned. Alderman Green circulated with a word and a quip for everyone as though hosting a sherry party at the town hall.

Dr Willis, in a commanding knitted suit from Yves St Laurent or one of those, and surprisingly flashy earrings, chatted briefly with Gladys before turning her attention to her suitcase, adopting quite a sexy curtsey posture to unlock it and retrieve seasickness pills or playing cards for bridge. If any of the choir fell ill on the Continent, here on tap was a proper English doctor, not a Monsieur le Médecin whose first and last remedy would be suppositories.

First in need of treatments was going to be turtlenecked Witherspoon if what he was up to was a habit, not an aberration. He stood swallowing Coca Cola from a can in one fist and taking bites from a sixteen-ounce Toblerone bar in the other.

Superintendent Day arrived by taxi. Its driver could not have known he was a policeman because an altercation took place, Day on the kerb with money in his hand and showing his watch to the driver, then leaning through the window to point at the meter. He handed over money whereupon the taxi accelerated off with a squeal of tyres and spatter of gravel.

Robin Goodfellow arrived in a Volvo driven by his wife, if the haughty vision off the cover of *Vogue* was his wife. Might be his sister. Unlikely to be his mistress, decanting him among what was getting on for the full complement of choir and instrumentalists.

Peckover counted seven, possibly eight, instrumentalists. Though they had accompanied at the dress rehearsal and performances, he had been far too involved with his singing and Goodfellow's baton to give them a look. Mainly he identified them by counting the misshapen black boxes which held their instruments, some more cumbersome than others, such as the cellist's, and matching the boxes to those persons who stood close and kept an eye on them.

He knew by sight the instrumentalist without an instrument, Keyboard Kate, who was hardly going to haul a piano across the Continent. Having jettisoned her shawl she looked less like a countrywoman on her way to market. For the performances she had worn a long gown. Now she had on a raincoat. Everybody had an opinion on what the weather would do.

No ringers. Veal's word, ringers, in the Feathers, three weeks ago, which equally to Peckover might have been three days or three years, such was the discombobulation brought about by this world of choral singing and Schütz. The absence of ringers, Witherspoon had told him, meant their leader, Robin, was satisfied with the choir as it was. Peckover had never once received the impression that Robin Goodfellow was satisfied. More likely Oscar Thomas had told him there was no money for ringers.

Thomas had emerged with maps and the driver from the church. He stood bow-tied by the door into the first of the two coaches, holding a clipboard on which he checked off the names of choristers as they entered. Peckover was able to name one in every five or six. Clemency. Eleanor. Unknown. Peter. Unknown. Archy. Phil Green. Fleur. Batches of unknowns.

He thought he and Twitty might be better off in the second coach – Bahama's. The driver of the first coach was bossy. When one of the instrumentalists put her violin case in the empty luggage compartment, the driver whipped it out, shooed the woman away, and announced to the populace, 'It would be happreciated if horganisation of this 'ere locker was left to the driver, all right?' He was Augustus Briggs, known among the choir as Gus the Bus. He treated the choir in a lordly fashion, as if they were children who would meet with disaster but for his care and guidance. He wore an enveloping jersey knitted from thick brown wool by his mother over a considerable period of time. She must have had it in her head that her son was a giant because the sagging, billowing garment would have fitted King Kong.

Peckover swung his suitcase containing concert wear, leisure wear, music, and handcuffs, into the luggage locker of the second coach. Bob Day stood by the door with a clipboard. 'Bill Brown,' Peckover told him, and climbed aboard.

Where was Mr McCurdle whom he wanted to demonstrate to the choir by sitting beside him, perhaps laying a hand on his head, was personally free from mad cow disease?'

Who in this lot was nicking holy relics?

Who honestly cared?

Honestly, when he thought about it, he did. Not because of possibilities of acrimony within the European Community or even because thieving was squalid. But holy relics. A madonna. Not to be solemn about it but some people still lived and died by what they believed to be holy.

Constable Twitty in his landed gentry costume climbed aboard. Beamingly to the driver he held up a high five, arm aloft, fingers spread. Bahama O'Toole wore a quilted jacket and had sunglasses ready just in case. She put out her tongue.

Twitty adored the tongue but accepted that it was not nor probably ever would be for him. He achieved a carefree smile. He failed to see what she didn't see in him. Usually they were smitten. What had he done to switch off Bahama? He dropped his high-five arm, took a step along the aisle, and felt his tweed sleeve plucked. Leaning back in her driver's seat, holding his sleeve, Bahama said, 'Sorry.'

'Sorry?'

'It's . . . I don't know. You come on a bit strong. Perhaps later.'

'Later?' He had to stop talking like an echo chamber.

'This evening.'

'Ghent?'

O Ghent! Fair inamorata of cities, bower of dalliance, flower of Flanders, perfumed garden of the EEC!

'We'll see,' said Bahama, releasing his sleeve and swinging back into a coach driver's position, alert over the steering wheel, ready to go.

Treading air, reprieved, practically solicited – had she not said This evening and We'll see? – Twitty swung along the aisle in search of a seat with no neighbour, where he could fantasise.

In Twitty's head a flight of archangels sang, 'We'll see because we'll see because we'll see because we'll see!' And on and so on. Some lyrics there were that seared the soul and fizzed the loins.

ELEVEN

Sergeant Pépin, Criminal Brigade, Service Régional de Police Judiciaire, Amiens, stood beside his Yamaha motorcycle on the dock at Ostend and watched the arrival from Britain of the Channel Ferry and Hovercraft Services vessel *Princess Diana*.

He wore a black leather jacket and leggings over a designer blue denim suit. From the motorcycle's handlebar dangled his helmet and goggles. Considering the wild goose chase to Andorra and the rail strike, the commissaire had had little choice but to allow him a vehicle from the transport pool. When he wore the helmet and goggles he looked like one of the angels of death in Cocteau's *Orphée*, not that he had ever heard of the film.

According to the Scotland Yard file in the saddle bag, one of the choir, the mayor, was a shareholder in this ferry company, and an influence. Therefore the choir used the *Princess Diana* on the long crossing to Ostend, squandering its budget while lining the pockets of the shareholders. The choir might have done better with one of the rival ferries plying the shorter, cheaper routes to Calais, Boulogne, and Dunkirk. Small wonder that England had been known in history as the sick man of Europe. If it had not been England it should have been. Certainly it had not been France.

True, from Ostend to Ghent was barely a half hour's drive. From Boulogne it would have taken half a day. If, that was to say – a big if – a certain driver of one of the choir's coaches did not reverse into the ocean, or hit the Customs shed, or take the coast road to Knokke, or miss Ghent and carry on to Brussels and Germany. A woman driver! *Une poufiasse!*

Une poufiasse noire, nom de Dieu!

Sergeant Pépin regarded with disdain the pathetic British cars driving off the ferry. A Rover, a Vauxhall, an overpriced Jaguar,

113

Ford Fiestas and Escorts, lorries setting off on the international highway to the Middle East, a stupid two-seater MG with its roof down, a vintage Rolls-Royce asking for trouble. Park that Rolls unattended in one or two places in Amiens he might mention and somebody would have its brass lamps and horn off it in a couple of shakes and serve it right. Now came a passable Mercedes. Now an honest Volvo. Straggling down a gangway on to Belgian soil, or to be exact, concrete, trooped those without cars: British back-packers, unruly school parties, hooligans with suitcases, and paupers.

Tiens, a Citroën! This was more like it. Sergeant Pépin almost came to attention.

Next a Peugeot Estate! *C'est magnifique, ça!* The sergeant's eyes brimmed. In his head he heard massed bands and the people of France singing the *Marseillaise*.

Not that his country was perfect, not with flabby, pinko sots like Commissaire Mouton in positions of authority. *Pouf, ce chiffon mou!* The commissaire was soft, self-indulgent, mentally unstable, and probably a Communist.

To restore public trust to the Police Judiciare, and honour to France, Sergeant Pépin had not the least doubt that it was up to himself to bring to justice the Sealeigh relics thief. Little help the undercover pair from Scotland Yard would be. Off their own patch they would be useless.

He had no intention of allowing the coaches out of his sight, not at any rate until Ghent. The Ghent police were proving co-operative and why not? They didn't have a dissipated Communist chief feeding them false information about Andorra. Inspector Spaak was less fleshy than the commissaire but he was not, being Flemish, a skeleton. At their recent meeting Inspector Spaak had treated chocolate, pastries, buttery sauces, beef, French fried potatoes, and Kriek beer, as his inalienable birthright. With fifty of his finest he would stake out the museums and St Bavon's cathedral, where the choir was to sing, and which possessed four bronze candlesticks. The candlesticks had been ordered for his tomb by the lascivious English tyrant Henry VIII and sold to Ghent by the odious puritan, Cromwell.

The cathedral had also a painting, *Adoration of the Lamb*, by a Van Dyck or Eyck. The painting was in sections too huge to be robbed but needed to be watched because two panels had in fact been stolen, in 1934, and only one ever recovered. So Inspector Spaak had chompingly said in the café in the shadow of the cathedral, dribbling masticated pastries and chocolate down his chin.

Eyeing the exit of vehicles off the *Princess Diana*, the sergeant chewed his lips, salty and dry from the wind off the Channel. What if Inspector Spaak turned out to be less competent than he seemed to be and the Eyck or Dyck was stolen? Sergeant Pépin wondered if he would kill himself.

Here they came, one following the other down the ramp, two scratched silvery coaches. In the slot above the windshield where Ghent or some such destination ought to have been displayed was the word SING. The coaches halted at customs. Sergeant Pépin unslung his helmet and goggles from the handlebar. This might take an hour or it might take a couple of minutes.

It took a couple of minutes. From the leading coach stepped a Britisher with abysmal dress sense, as who of them had not, wearing a bow tie and bringing papers to a customs officer. A second customs officer heaved open one of the doors to the luggage compartment and peered in. A third and fourth climbed aboard the second coach. They climbed out again, weak, Sergeant Pépin surmised, from the sight of distressing British dress and smells of teabags, cabbage water, and cricket bats.

The sergeant sat astride his Yamaha and roared the engine. Goggled and helmeted he followed the coaches from the dock. *De Dieu*, but he had better keep well back from the woman driver! *Femme au volant, mort au tournant!*

In Flanders fields the poppies blow, between the crosses, row on row. Who said that? Someone in World War One, must have been. Through the window Peckover watched the hurtling landscape. Bahama O'Toole drove fast as a train. Did Belgium have a speed limit?

No poppies. Either it was too early or too late. Flat, though. Like Norfolk.

'What time do the churches and museums close?' he said.

'In Ghent?'

'No, the Isle of Skye.'

'Hold on. Five o'clock, I think.'

Twitty occupied the aisle seat because of his long legs. He turned the page in his guide book. They should not have been sitting together, they should have been chatting with unmet members of the choir, but here they were. Henry's twenty minutes to Folkestone with Mr McCurdle had evidently been enough. Mr McCurdle had instructed him in the development of the south coast as a resort area from the time of the Prince Regent.

The guide book being for all Europe, its pages on Belgium were not copious. Still, it had more on Ghent than on Gap. Bra it had never heard of.

'Six o'clock, the cathedral, April to September.'

'Why don't you tell your girlfriend there's no rush. We don't want the cathedral open and people slamming off into it the moment we arrive.'

'Why not? Unleash the choir, let the filcher filch, get it over with. Everywhere's under surveillance.'

'Any idea 'ow much surveillance it's going to take for a treasure-house like Ghent – Athens of the North?'

'It's not the Athens of the North, it's the Florence, it says here, and it's not all relics. It has a mammoth flower festival but not this year. Who said she's my girlfriend?'

'You'd like 'er to be. I've got eyes. No shenanigans, lad. I want you single-minded and scintillating. What else about Ghent?'

'Population close on half a million. It's an industrial port with canals and ships.' Twitty held out the guide book. 'Help yourself.'

'I don't read on buses. Too bouncy.'

Ghent 36 kilometres, announced a road sign. Divide by eight, multiply by five. Too taxing, fractions. Thirty-two kilometres would be twenty miles. At Bahama O'Toole's rate, another five minutes and they'd be there. At least they were on the right road.

'Marvellous hotel here, Guv. The Saint Jorishof, twelve twenty-eight, oldest hotel in Northern Europe.'

'Think yourself lucky we're not going there. Gale-force draughts and creaking floors. It'll be full of Common Market grandees on expense accounts. I hate quaint.'

'Napoleon stayed there.'

'Pish. Advertising stunt. I'll bet 'e didn't stay long, all those sloping floors. If our Novotel has wall-to-wall shag and lots of plastic and luxury, that's the place for us. That all?'

'Azaleas and begonias were developed in Ghent,' Twitty said.

'Well, well. Ghent – Gaunt. John of Gaunt was born in Ghent.'

'Time-honour'd Lancaster. "This royal throne of kings, full of sound and fury, so are they all, all honourable men." What about relics?'

'There's a chunk on where we sing, the cathedral of St Bavon, mostly about the Van Eyck. And the four candlesticks made for Henry the Eighth.'

'His Flanders mare.'

'His what?'

'Anne of Cleves, one of his wives. Can't be far from 'ere, Cleves. He'd never seen her before she arrived for the wedding, he'd only seen her portrait. Called her his Flanders mare.'

'Where do you get all this?'

'You're not the only one went to school. Anything else?'

'Other places – Brussels, Bruges, Antwerp.' Twitty flipped the page. 'Favourite sports, cycling, soccer, pigeon-racing. Cock-fighting but it's illegal. High obesity, stomach problems, gout. They don't like authority and don't pay their taxes. How do they get away with it? Three official languages. You don't suppose English might be one?'

'It will be as far as I'm concerned.'

'The Flemish in the north are Teutonic, orderly, clean, and have big families. The south is scenic and has French-speaking Walloons who have small families and are anti-Church and more urbane.'

'And dirty?'

'Doesn't say. Doesn't matter, we're not going to the south.'

'Who knows where we might be going?' Peckover said darkly, and fell to brooding on Clemency Axelrod's glass eye. Were glass eyes hollow? Presumably they were not solid like marbles. He suspected they might not be glass either, but of some advanced shatter-proof plastic, and maybe not a globe but a disc, a cosmetic saucer. Just as well Clemency Axelrod was an alto. A glass eye made of glass and worn by a soprano might shatter if she held on long enough to her high C. That would be something to see.

Twitty, lifting himself a little way out of his seat, observed over

117

the heads of choristers the back of the head of shampooed thick hair that was Bahama. Perhaps later, she had said, and we'll see.

O best Bahama!

Rumours, as events turned out. Twitty had not anticipated Bahama waltzing off with Witherspoon and others to see St Bavon's cathedral before its doors closed.

He was stuck with Henry, Bob Day, Dr Willis, Eleanor Sandwich, Clemency Axelrod, Joe Golightly, and an additional half dozen from the choir footing together through the streets of Ghent in a makeshift clump. Guideless sightseers, they soon tired of the medieval buildings with shops and airline offices inside, especially when for the third time they passed the same baroque window displaying chocolates. For fear of seeming philistine, nobody was prepared to admit having had enough, except, of course, Peckover. Outside another chocolate shop he announced, 'How quickly one sees all there is to see of any city and would be content to move on.' He sounded like a fop in a Restoration comedy. Dr Willis declared that the decay of curiosity was the death of the soul. 'Only expressing an opinion,' muttered Peckover.

A splinter group returned to the hotel restaurant. The remaining magnificent seven dined abundantly and for far too long, in the view of Twitty and some others, though not Peckover. The Relais Pax was big and noisy. A child waiter pushed two tables together, dealt out cutlery and napkins, and brought, unasked, gross panniers of bread, litre wine bottles containing water, and other wine bottles containing wine. Then he set down a Rabelaisian platter of cold cuts, beetroot, radishes, chicory, artichoke hearts, a jug of possibly mayonnaise, and ample butter. The butter looked as if it had been sliced from a corner of the EEC's butter mountain. There didn't seem to be any menu. Twitty guessed that the Relais Pax would not have been the first choice of Eleanor Sandwich and Dr Willis but nobody had asked them. On the television over the bar, athletes in coloured jerseys were kicking for the most part a football but occasionally each other.

Peckover and Joe Golightly asked for beer and were brought a fizzy brew named Trappiste which made them gasp. Unidentified fish in much juice arrived. Eleanor Sandwich pronounced it delicious.

She was enjoying the wine too. '"Let them have dominion over the fish of the sea" – Genesis,' Eleanor said. Joe Golightly reached into his shopping bag and produced ketchup and Worcestershire sauce, setting them beside his plate. Dr Willis said, 'You'll be charged corkage.' 'I'll pay,' said Joe Golightly, and summoned more beer.

Peckover moved on to red wine. Clemency Axelrod sipped water. Superintendent Day said little and drank sparingly but poured for others and passed bread, anticipating desires like a butler. The child waiter, speaking for the first time, offered a choice of biftek, lapin, or foie de veau, and departed with a muddle of changed orders which he was not possibly going to remember. Superintendent Day said, 'Don't they have child labour laws?' He had started sparingly but moved by indignation he now swilled down half a glass of plonk. Peckover ventured that the waiter might be older than he looked. 'True, he could be nine,' said Day, and swilled again, emptying his glass. Twitty, deprived of Bahama, would have preferred sitting at the bar watching the football, though he didn't know who the teams were and couldn't understand a word the demented commentator was shouting.

The waiter's big sister, aged ten, brought a tureen of smoking pommes frites. 'Skinny little devils, aren't they?' Joe Golightly said. Eleanor Sandwich giggled and said, 'The chips or the staff?' The waiter brought platters of meat and his sister returned with back-up chips. Peckover said impeccably, *'Ma'm'selle, encore du rouge, s'il vous plaît.'* The rouge wasn't quite finished but it soon would be, not least because of the thirst of an alto at the table's far end, Audrey Belcher, a pert young thing about whom Peckover knew nothing except her name and that she had taken over one of the bottles of red and clearly wouldn't be giving it up without a struggle. She was undergoing reasonably discreet pawing from her neighbour, Sydney Crisp, the pencil-moustached barrow-boy and building contractor. Married with several children, Sydney was at home a pillar of the community.

Peckover's neighbour, Eleanor, said, 'Mr Brown, I really shouldn't, but would you pass just a soupçon of that scrumptious bread?' The name Brown failed to register with Peckover and he passed nothing. He was telling Dr Willis, 'Avoid all books, poems, music, paintings, plays, and films with the word dream or dreams in the title. They are invariably duds.' Twitty reached out a tweed-sleeved arm and brought a bread basket to Eleanor Sandwich. Dr Willis, surprisingly slurred, said, 'You have heard of *The Interpretation of Dreams* by that dud, Freud?' '*Dream of Gerontius*,' Clemency Axelrod called out. Titles with the word dream became a parlour game. Bob Day offered, 'I dream of Jeannie with the light brown hair'. Joe Golightly said, 'What's this muck?' and scraped Bordelaise sauce off his steak. He cut into the steak and said, 'Raw. No point sending it back. They just don't know. Let's try the rabbit.'

Dishes of green beans enlivened by whole cloves of garlic arrived. 'You should be in bed,' Day told the child waiter. When the child stared, blank, Day stiffened the sinews, summoned up the blood, and said, '*Vous devrez être dans votre lit*. Wait – *tu, ton lit. Mon petit.*' Was Day, Twitty asked himself, a pederast? He accepted that it might all have been worse. Archy Newby was not present, or Oscar Thomas.

Sydney Crisp at the end of the table was eating one-handedly and growing visibly fonder of Audrey Belcher. His other hand was out of sight. Audrey, beginning to look a little pale, took a curative gulp of the house red. Golightly boomed, 'This beer is potable once you get the hang of it. Where's the waiter?' Clemency Axelrod touched his arm and said, 'Oh, Joe!' Twitty believed that he himself, Clemency, and possibly groping Syd, were the only ones not drinking themselves towards oblivion. Dr Willis said, 'Who plays bridge?' When the reply was silence she said, 'Does anyone know the words to, you know, Burns, "My love is like a red, red rose"?' Superintendent Day's light tenor broke into 'Roses of Picardy'. The table joined in except for Twitty and Audrey, who did not know it, and Sydney who was not listening. Eleanor Sandwich started a chorus of 'Abide with Me', and next, before anyone could stop her, 'Lead, Kindly Light', both of which Twitty knew from school and sang along with. Why not? The choristers produced a stirring sound. Clemency Axelrod instigated 'Hang down your head, Tom Dooley' and kept it going through several verses until it dawned on the party that she knew only two verses and was repeating herself. Joe Golightly put an end to Tom Dooley with a sonorous

'Shenandoah' so uninhibited that the table allowed him a solo turn and hummed richly, cotton pickers on the old plantation. Eleanor Sandwich, carried away, threw in a 'Yes, Lordy!' and an 'Oh, sweet Jesus!' Her minister at Sealeigh Presbyterian Church would not have approved but he wasn't here. The bartender lowered the volume on the television. Bar customers and families at tables turned to watch and listen. Audrey, wan and swaying, started a round, 'Life is but a melancholy flower'. In sequence and with fervour, Joe, Clemency, Bob, et al, joined in. Even Robin Goodfellow's perfectionist demands might have been met. 'Life is butter, life is butter, melon cauliflower, melon cauliflower,' warbled the chamber chorus to the tune of 'Frère Jacques', and might have been warbling it still had not Twitty, to his astonishment, heard himself embark on a tedious old song his dad at one epoch had sung without cease. '"Hey Jude, don't let me down,"' crooned Constable Twitty. Support overwhelmed him, not excluding his flushed guv'nor's baritone, and not only from the Sealeigh table. 'Laaa la la la-la-la laaa,' sang the table, the Belgian blokes and their birds at the bar, and families who hitherto had been concentrating on their chips. Twitty knew the song went on for quite a while, it always had when his dad got started on it, but he had not known it went on quite as long as this. The barman switched the TV off and sang, 'Laaa la la la-la-la laaa.' The child waiter, not singing, arrived with ice cream and a few pastries: éclairs, almond puffs, cheese turnovers, straws, custard shells, chocolate shells, chocolate tartlets, caramel cornets, profiteroles, napoléons, madeleines, and flaky fruited confections no one at the Sealeigh table could have put a name to.

The television returned to life. A bristly grandmother presented a bill. Up to now she had been in the kitchen plucking hens and tending the stockpot. Would the infant staff see any of the tip? Bob Day examined the bill and said, 'Seems reasonable.' The choir tossed into the kitty Belgian francs, English sterling, and credit cards.

In the hotel lift Twitty said, 'I'm going up another floor, Guv.'

'You're going nowhere tonight. It's midnight. She's asleep and you're off to bed – your own.'

'That an order?'

121

'It's common sense. Heavy day tomorrow. One concert and our relics robber on the loose among the treasures of Ghent.'

Twitty pouted. The guv was right of course. Wasn't the end of the world. Still nine days of the tour to go.

He was mistaken in that. Neither he nor Peckover had an inkling just how heavy tomorrow would turn out to be.

TWELVE

The first drama of the next day, concert day, was that the concert was cancelled.

The Bishop of Ghent evidently had not understood that Gilbert and Sullivan were an English team whose operas offered moral values on a par with those of cabaret under the Weimar Republic. Also revealed to him was that much of the programme's English folk music was wholly unsuitable for the House of God, particularly a work entitled 'Blow the Candles Out'. Accordingly and with regret came the message from the Bishop's secretary: His Grace had no choice but to deny permission for the concert to be held in the cathedral of St Bavon.

On the prompting of Sergeant Pépin, Inspector Spaak had spoken of the programme's depraved elements to his wife's cousin, Monseigneur Claus, who had referred them to the Bishop's Palace. Pépin and Spaak, conspirators, judged that the less time the choir spent in the cathedral the safer its treasures would be. Choir members could not be excluded altogether. A group had visited yesterday evening and had been kept under surveillance. Any of the choir entering today would also be watched, and more easily in their tourist twos and threes than if there were a concert and the entire choir were milling about. Dumping the concert would not frustrate a determined thief but it could do no harm. Ghent had no need of this Sealeigh concert. Though Pépin knew none of the music on the programme he was ready to believe it was pornographic, certainly the English songs.

By urgent appointment, Oscar Thomas, Robin Goodfellow, two committee members (sopranos), and Alderman Green, who insisted on being present in his capacity as mayor of Sealeigh, were granted an audience with the Bishop. Thomas, spokesperson, presented His

Grace with sheet music and stressed the central position in the concert of the sacred Psalm 150 and *Regina Coeli*. Goodfellow explained that folk music was frequently misinterpreted. Chancing his arm, he sang with feeling part of 'April Is In My Mistress' Face'. Mrs Jobson, committee member and soprano, sang too. They sounded like the Angel Gabriel and St Cecilia. Recent scholarship, Goodfellow said, held that the mistress was a metaphor for the Apostolic Church Triumphant and that April, month of daffodils and rebirth, represented the risen Christ. Alderman Green informed His Grace that he could guarantee him the freedom of Sealeigh and tickets for himself and one other aboard the *Princess Diana*.

Rarely, mused the Bishop, have I encountered such rogues! He had to cough and lift his fingers to his lips to hide his smile. He mooted in flawless English that 'Blow the Candles Out' be withdrawn; unless, naturally, Mr Goodfellow were able to persuade him that these candles accompanied a sacrament following which the priest asked the altar boy to blow the candles out. The deputation left the Palace too drained to exult, but the concert was on again.

The concert was for nine that evening. At three in the afternoon, chorus and orchestra assembled in the cathedral for the ironing out of rough spots and to rehearse seating and walking on and off a tiered platform set up in the nave in front of the chancel.

It was as well the rehearsal did take place, because an entire row of ten chairs was found to be missing from the platform. A beadsman, possibly a verger or deacon, someone anyway in a long gown, a soutane or a chasuble – Peckover was inexpert in church nomenclature – led a group of the able-bodied, Peckover included, into a vestry or sacristy, anyway a place with spare chairs. Peckover observed that whereas the cleric in the gown was pretty certainly authentic, several others hanging about in gowns were not. They were cops in copes. The same went for a tourist couple too touristy to be real, he in a lurid holiday shirt which bulged at the hip, she with a bulky shoulder bag, and both showing more interest in the chorus than in the architectural mix of Gothic, Romanesque, and baroque, the pulpit of carved wood, and the voussoirs, volutes, and squinches. The believer in a headscarf, kneeling at her devotions in an empty pew with her hands over her eyes, but her eyes open and blinking through parted fingers, was the most obvious copper of all.

The police presence reassured Peckover. If nothing else it suggested that no nicking had happened, not so far, nothing anyway that would have left as visible a gap as making off with the *Adoration of the Lamb*, which was twelve feet wide and eight feet high. If Ghent were duplicating this level of surveillance in other churches and museums, the thief would have a hard time of it.

A television crew was setting up cameras and sound equipment. Not every day did a choir from England praise the Lord in Ghent. Electric cable lay in coils. Lengths of it snaked across the worn flagstones. A chorister tripping over a cable and bumping his head on the floor would be unlikely to wake up until after the concert was over, if then.

Robin Goodfellow led the choir and orchestra through a rough passage or two of the Schütz, though in Peckover's opinion, and everyone else's including Goodfellow's, if they weren't spot on now they never would be. Surprised sightseers and a few of the faithful in the pews looked on, together with the too-touristy tourists and fake curates and divines. The woman at prayer continued kneeling and blinking.

'Save your voices,' Goodfellow advised the choir. 'No talking, no drinking, no chips. We have a late collation at the hotel after the concert. We reassemble here at eight fifteen. Full regalia. Knock 'em dead. Oscar?'

'Nothing, I think,' Oscar Thomas said. 'For those of you whose concert wear may be rumpled, the hotel has an ironing room. Peter, you have something?'

Peter Witherspoon announced, 'It's just that one or two of you have asked me about the Van Eyck, indisputably one of the masterpieces of Renaissance art. It is a polyptych painted by the brothers Hubert and Jan van Eyck as an altarpiece over five and a half centuries ago, in fourteen thirty-two – the year after Joan of Arc was burned at the stake – and remains almost intact and unutterably glorious in spite of war, fire, dismantling, and incompetent cleaning. I will gladly try to say a word or two about it.' He pointed. 'Anyone interested, it's through there and to the left in the Vijd chapel. We have permission to view it as a group, though I got the impression that a coin in the box, say a pound apiece, wouldn't be amiss. Thank you.'

'When?'

'Now,' said Witherspoon.

'Let me remind you the cathedral closes at six and will reopen at eight for our concert,' Oscar Thomas said. 'Don't be carried away by the Lamb and find yourselves locked in.'

Alderman Green said, 'Friends, chorus members, citizens of Sealeigh—'

'Not now, Phil!' somebody said. Someone else groaned. Others started shuffling down from the platform.

'I would just like to say,' said the unsinkable mayor, 'that I spoke on the phone this morning with my dear wife, Mrs Green, who as you know is unable to be with us due to being under the weather, but I am happy to inform you is feeling better and soon will be right as rain again. She asks me to convey her warmest wishes to the Sealeigh Choral Society. Anyone who'd like to send her a card, she'd be tickled pink. Thank you, one and all.'

No one could remember having heard the mayor deliver so brief a speech before.

Dr Willis remained impassive. It was not for her to set the record straight, but the mayor's dear wife would never again be right as rain. She would do well if she lasted through the summer.

St Bavon's cathedral smelled of stone and incense. Sopranos, altos, tenors, and basses of the chorus dissolved from the platform. Friends coalesced in clumps of twos and threes. Some headed along the nave for the west door and daylight, some for the Vijd chapel to hear Peter Witherspoon's thoughts on the *Adoration of the Lamb*. Others stood aimlessly awaiting guidance. Ahead stretched four free hours.

The Ghent police surveillance unit in its surplices and tourist shirts mingled and watched.

Twitty, mingling, watched Archy Newby in conversation with Fleur Whistler beneath an enormous effigy of the crucified Christ. About the crucifix were dingy stained-glass windows which would dazzle when the sun shone, or might if someone washed them. What had Fleur to say to the plump weasel? Hadn't they had their happening and it was over? She should have had more sense, walked away. He found Henry. Peckover was looking thoughtful, perhaps composing, while fondling the stone toes of a prophet.

'What's the plot, Guv?'

'Be quiet. You're supposed to be saving your voice.'

Twitty whispered, 'We ought to see the Van Eyck, agreed? We can't be in Ghent and not.'

'Can't hear you.'

'The painting.'

'Bahama's there?'

'You've got Bahama on the brain.'

'*Moi?* That's rich. Come to that, we should see 'Enery the Eighth's candlesticks.'

'I've seen them.'

'Where?'

'Miles away. That way. Beyond that sort of tomb.'

'Show me.'

Peckover followed Twitty along an aisle. They passed Audrey Belcher and Sydney Crisp studying a guide book. They looked tired. 'Hullo,' Twitty said to them. They didn't hear. Peckover sang softly, 'I'm 'Enery the Eighth, I yam, 'Enery the Eighth I yam, I yam.'

Twitty led past a railed-off area behind which were ladders, buckets, and sacks of cement, but no workmen. In this corner of the cathedral was nobody, working or otherwise. A blue and pink statue of a madonna and child, crumbling statues of apostles, brass plaques with Latin inscriptions, side chapels with altars, closed doors to steps, crypts, rood lofts. Above soared panchromatic windows.

'I got married to the widder next do-o-oah, she's been married seven times befo-o-oah,' droned Peckover.

Twitty halted in front of four caged candlesticks. They did not look especially secure. They stood in a row on a narrow wall-shelf, two slack chains keeping them from toppling out. Perhaps they were bolted down. Perhaps they were considered safe by being in this part of the cathedral where nobody ventured. Except that here at last was someone, a gowned curate with brown boots, sitting on a kitchen chair holding a missal and looking at the intruders from the choir. Peckover guessed that brown boots did not have to mean he was not a curate, but he didn't know. Instead of Ms Macrae's lesson in art and antiques, he and the lad should have been given the rudiments

127

of church vestments. Not that it mattered. Curate or armed guard of the surveillance squad, he wasn't a Sealeigh chorister, he wasn't filching the candlesticks.

'*Dag*,' the man said.

Peckover said, '*Dag*,' and added, '*Mijhneer*,' though *Mijnheer* might not have been correct for a curate.

Twitty, somewhat in awe of men of the cloth, bowed and said, '*Mijhneer*,' then '*Dag*.' He had never spoken Flemish before.

They retreated from the cleric and the candlesticks. Peckover sang, quiet yet breezy, 'Every one was an 'Enery, she wouldn't 'ave a Willie or a Sam—'

'Guv, d'you mind?'

'What?'

'That song.'

'You know it?'

'I do now.'

'There's one more line.' Peckover sang, 'I'm 'er eighth old man named 'Enery, 'Enery the Eighth I yam!'

Not only in the vicinity of the candlesticks but everywhere, unless Witherspoon had an audience, the cathedral was now sparsely populated. A few sightseers; in the pews a handful of the faithful; some clergy, genuine or fake, one carrying a tower of prayer books; television cameras, but the crew had gone off on a break. Peckover wondered if, mid afternoon, perhaps the Ghents, Ghentians, dropped everything for a stein of Trappiste and a pastry. He felt uneasy. He headed with Twitty in the direction of the Vijd chapel.

He said, 'You're the relics thief, lad. You'd like another relic. When do you choose?'

'You mean in here?'

'Wherever. You prefer a blank time like now or a busy time like Sunday morning mass or just before or after, say, a concert, loads of people swarming about?'

They negotiated a font without water, an unattended table with pamphlets appealing for aid for the Third World, and another statue of the Virgin, less than life size.

Twitty said, 'If I could break in, three in the morning. Commando assault gear, flashlight, and a mate outside who'd do owl hoots if the fuzz hove near.'

'You can't break in. You're an amateur, remember? You don't know locks and crowbars. You couldn't get in through an open window.'

'It's only you keeps harping on about an amateur.'

'Never mind that. You don't have your commando gear with you, the battery of your flashlight's dead, your mate's down with Napoleon's revenge, and at three in the morning you're in bed because you like your eight hours.'

'What you're asking is would I choose busy or calm?'

'Take your time. Call me soft in the head but I thought it was a simple question.'

'I'd go for calm, like now. Never could stand the rush hour. Guv?'

'What?'

'Don't look but we're being watched. Over your right shoulder. By a sort of lectern thing.'

Peckover looked up. Awed, he turned slowly through three hundred and sixty degrees. Twitty hoped he would not overdo it and fall in a swoon crying, 'The fan vaulting! Frozen music!'

'The geezer with the brown boots,' Peckover said. 'What about it? He's stretching his legs.'

'He's suspicious and he's following us.'

'If he is he ought to be sacked. He should stay at his post. Keep going. I spy choir.'

Here now were people, fifteen or so packed inside a narrow chapel and another dozen outside peering in. A bronze frame enclosed a painting which occupied the entire length of one wall. Its wing panels on iron hinges could be opened or closed and today were open. As Peckover and Twitty arrived, three Sealeigh choristers, familiar but nameless, were leaving.

Twitty's height gave him an advantage. Peckover, a paltry six feet two, had to stand on his toes to see more than the upper reaches of the painting over the heads in front of him. One or two true shorties could see only the shoulder blades of the person in front. Peckover had observed the phenomenon in his salad days, assigned to crowd control at rock concerts and soccer matches.

Somewhere in the crush in the chapel Witherspoon could be heard but not seen.

'The marble altar, those of you who are able to see it, is somewhat lower than the brick altar which it replaced in nineteen fifty-one.'

Peckover wondered if Witherspoon had said all he had to say about the painting. He could have been lecturing for twenty minutes.

'The original altar-table was a predella with a central tabernacle for the Eucharist. A sculptured baldachin crowned the altar. Archaeological evidence for the tabernacle and baldachin were hidden until forty years ago behind the baroque aedicule which we see framing the altarpiece.'

That was all right, then. Peckover glanced at Twitty. The lad was not looking at the *Adoration of the Lamb* but at some point in the crammed audience. Peckover followed the direction of the gaze. Bahama O'Toole. Adoration of the Coach Driver.

The audience was not exclusively Sealeigh chorus members. As with all guided tours, a few interlopers had been attracted. They hearkened on the fringe, ready to flee if a cap were passed round.

'What's the word you said?' said somebody. 'Polyptych?'

Dr Willis had clearly recovered from her musical dinner of the evening before. She enunciated polyptych with a note of scepticism, as if hearing for the first time of a newly identified species of pimple.

'Beyond tryptych,' Witherspoon explained. 'An altarpiece arranged in at least four hinged, folding panels. Here we have twelve. *Mystery of the Incarnation* when the wing panels are closed, as I've pointed out, and the *Adoration of the Lamb* when they're open, based on Revelation, chapters three and twenty-one, I believe. Do observe the towers representing the New Jerusalem where the blessed rest in the sight of God. An advantage of panels, to my mind a dubious one, is that the whole may the more easily be dismantled and stored. This was removed to Pau in the war for safekeeping.'

'Which war?' asked someone too young to know any better.

'Nineteen thirty-nine forty-five. Then to Germany. The Americans liberated it.'

Peckover felt a tap on his shoulder.

Bob Day said in his ear, 'You'd better come. Forget relics. We've got a murder.'

THIRTEEN

Some minutes later, by the time Peter Witherspoon said, 'Any more questions?', four Ghent police officers stood at the west door of St Bavon's cathedral allowing no one in or out. Two more policemen led by cathedral staff checked that every other exit and entrance was locked. Though the murder was fresh as spring lamb, blood still seeping across the flagstones, such precautions were probably already too late. If the murderer had wanted to leave the cathedral he could and by now would have done so, or so Peckover observed to Twitty. If he had wanted to mingle, to become one of the shocked and innocent, he could have done that too.

'Or she,' Twitty said mechanically.

On the flagstones with the back of her head stove in lay Eleanor Sandwich.

No blunt instrument. No handbag as far as could be seen. Only choir music of the richest red. Closest to her head, 'April Is In My Mistress' Face' had come off worst, its title page curled from the weight and wet of blood.

She lay by King Henry's candlesticks, near the railed-off area where reposed buckets and ladders, and not far from where Audrey and Sydney, enfeebled lovers, had stood with a guide book. That had been twenty minutes ago. Peckover looked at his watch. Unable to get a decent view of the Van Eyck, giving up on it, Eleanor Sandwich could have been on her way to or from the cathedral's second choicest item, Henry VIII's candlesticks.

The shelf which had held the candlesticks had suffered a violent assault. It hung askew from a single bracket. One candlestick lay on it, caught by the chain. Two others were on the ground among masonry chippings and dust. The fourth was missing.

131

The chair where the brown-shod cleric had sat was empty. As it would be. Nobody sat at a time like this.

A different cleric peeled off his own gown as if it were infected. Clearly wanting to cast it far from him but knowing he didn't do this in a cathedral, he folded it, saying, '*Monsieur Peckover? Je m'appelle Pépin, Sergeant de Brigade Criminelle, Amiens. Je sers de jonction entre la police anglaise et la police française. À votre service.*'

Peckover did not believe the *à votre service* bit. One of Frank Veal's memos had mentioned Sergeant Pépin. The fellow was evidently heavily political. He had watery blue eyes and no eyebrows to speak of. He wore, now that he had divested himself of the Papist garb that had seemed to bother him so much, a tailored blue denim suit.

'Not Peckover,' Peckover said. 'Bill Brown, for the time being.' Did it matter any more? 'This is Jason Twitty.'

Pépin ignored Twitty. He introduced a tourist in a loose, lurid shirt. 'Inspector Spaak.'

''Ullo.'

'*Mijnheer.*'

'*Monsieur.*'

'*Dag.*'

Outside the cathedral wailed police sirens, or ambulances, or both. Not the rising, falling whine of London's police, or the whirring wha-wha-wha of Los Angeles, but a punchy pam-pom-pam-pom, not that police departments didn't change their tune from time to time for change's sake. By the minute the number of cops at the murder scene was increasing.

No press yet. At the guarded west door they cajoled, threatened, and presented cheque books. Most furious and frustrated was the television crew who had set up equipment for the concert. Having stepped outside for air and coffee they now found themselves barred from re-entering and deprived of the scoop of the year. The cops were obelisks, deaf to threats, blind to cash, and unstirred by the erotic winking of a seasoned woman reporter who had covered war in Chad and dined with King Baudouin. They were unyielding as the cathedral's gargoyles and less fun. They were big, armed, without imagination, and effective.

Technicians with bags were allowed in. Detectives with ribbon cordoned off a wide area around Eleanor Sandwich. Bob Day answered questions from Inspector Spaak. Her name was Eleanor Sandwich, one of the Sealeigh Choral Society, he had known her for eight years. Her body had been found by two more members of the choir, Sydney Crisp and Audrey Belcher, or so Day gathered. No longer holding hands, Sydney and Audrey answered questions from Sergeant Pépin. From where Peckover stood there looked to be language problems. He noticed an officer in brown boots, still wearing his gown, immersed in the contents of his notebook.

You left your post by the candlesticks, Peckover reflected. You came tracking after me and Twitty. You're in trouble.

He might have been in bigger trouble if he'd stayed put. Might have had his skull bashed in too. Assuming, that was, that the murderer and the relics thief were one and the same, and serious enough to kill if caught in the act.

'Might have been worse, Guv.'

'What might?'

'All this.'

'God's sake, what could be worse? Look at 'er.'

'What I'm saying, the police, we're here already.' Not looking at Eleanor, he drew Peckover aside. 'No trampling of evidence. It's clean, sort of, the scene.' His prattling voice sounded a tone or two higher than usual. 'And Dr Willis, she's a doctor.'

'What're you on about?'

'Too late, though, the police. Futile. You know, I know nothing about her, Eleanor. We were talking before the rehearsal, only for a moment, about chocolate. She said she was a chocaholic and didn't want even to try Belgian chocolate. She'd tried them all, Lindt, Fanny something, Canadian I think she said, and you couldn't beat Cadbury's milk. She was very funny and scathing about Europe's bureaucrats wanting to rename British chocolate vegolate because it was low in cocoa and high in vegetable oils. Guv?'

'Shut up.'

'I will. Got to save our voices.'

'Forget that.'

'All right if I go and sit down?'

'No time to feel queasy, lad. Yes, go. What you do while you're sitting, you write down Witherspoon's name and under it everyone in the chapel with him, far as you noticed. Those whose names you don't know, write what they looked like before you forget and we'll find out who they are. Elimination exercise. If they were adoring the Lamb they weren't near the candlesticks. I'll be with you soon.'

The exercise was routine but necessary. On the other side of the nave, there being no further questions, Peter Witherspoon and his audience surged out of the Vijd chapel and into the arms of the police.

The police herded the group still further from the candlesticks area and Eleanor, and into an ante-room which smelled of disinfectant. Battered storage cupboards lined the walls. In a corner lay four bowls of cat food.

One of the altos fainted at the news. Names were taken, questions asked.

So many police. Sometimes when they were needed, there they were.

'Tonight's concert will of course be cancelled,' Oscar Thomas said.

'Yes,' agreed Robin Goodfellow, and, after reflection, ruffling his fingers through his red mane, 'Unless we're being hasty.'

'My dear fellow.'

'And the rest of the tour?'

'Naturally it's off. How can we continue?'

'Eleanor's musicianship was second to none, but one fewer among the altos isn't going to make a difference.'

'You know that's not what I mean.'

Superintendent Bob Day looked at Inspector Spaak and said, 'The decision may not be entirely up to us.'

Inspector Spaak said, 'I 'ave no, ah, *répugnance* – objection? – to the concert of tonight. Is probable we learn nothing, but possible we sense, ah, intangibles.'

Sergeant Pépin said, '*Qu'est-ce que vous dîtes?*'

Day asked Peckover, 'Where stands Scotland Yard on this? To sing or not sing?'

Peckover said, 'Inspector Spaak has a point. I'd say go ahead.'

Especially now he was more confident of his lobets and herrens.

That latter thought was in poor taste and not to be shared. He suspected that it might have amused Eleanor. He knew no more about her than Twitty. She was a Presbyterian who laughed easily and was not averse to tattle. She it had been who had fed him the rumour that Archy Newby and Fleur Whistler had once had something going. Such rumours were almost invariably true, she had said.

Goodfellow clearly wanted the concert. He had worked harder than anyone. He had brought the choir to a standard which could only enhance his reputation.

Not that Oscar Thomas hadn't worked. Singing and paperwork, both.

Peckover could not recall either Day or Thomas having been in the audience in the Vijd chapel. Goodfellow, either. But he hadn't looked. They might have been there. Then again they might have been roving around.

Ghent's medical examiner arrived, a woman with scarred cheeks, as if she had been born at a trading post in the Belgian Congo and had survived smallpox. Peckover marvelled at her gorgeous green eyes. Any normal bloke would have fallen in love with her and sod the scars.

St Bavon crawled with coppers. The mayor of Ghent arrived.

The mayor of Sealeigh did not. He stood with the media outside the west door, clamouring for admission.

Twitty had not enjoyed his single look at Eleanor Sandwich. Queasy in a pew he said, 'That's the end of our cover, Guv.'

'What is?'

'Who's going to answer questions from a couple of sing-along warblers in the choir?'

'Some who might not be happy with questions from coppers is who. But you 'ave a point. As two of their own we can 'ardly pin 'em to the wall and put the knee in. But we can mix and listen. There's the whole Ghent police can be menacing and put questions, but they're not going to be able to put questions in bed, like you might with Bahama O'Toole.'

'That's pretty rough.'

135

'Rough is where we are, mate. One of us choristers happens to be on her face with her brains oozing out.'

'You've such a way with a phrase. Bahama was in the chapel with the painting and Witherspoon. She's acquitted.'

'She'll know who else was in the chapel and can also be acquitted. Blimey, it's just pillow chat. You don't 'ave to pull out her finger nails. If you don't want to share 'er pillow, that's up to you. All I'm saying, there's something to be said for staying undercover, and something for unmasking ourselves.'

'Whatever you say. I don't feel great.'

'We'll keep as the choir for the moment. Frankly, damned if we do, damned if we don't.' Peckover sounded distracted. He leaned forward as if about to pray, elbows on the shelf where lay prayer books. He leaned back. 'It's ugly, disgusting.'

'Eleanor?'

'Us. Me. Three weeks we've been with this Sealeigh lot. Three weeks today if you've kept track. Three weeks and we 'aven't a clue. We've learned nothing except how to sing sodding Schütz. We've done everything wrong starting with imagining we're watching for someone who nicks relics. There's more to this than relics, lad. Don't ask me what. We've arrived nowhere and look what 'appens.'

'Be reasonable, Guv. How could we have foreseen this?'

'I don't know how,' Peckover snarled. 'It just happens to be our job.'

The consensus of the four senior policemen from three European Community nations gathered by the cordoned-off candlesticks area was that Eleanor Sandwich had lucklessly surprised the relics thief.

He in turn had surprised her by bludgeoning her to death with a blunt instrument, more than likely the missing candlestick.

Otherwise the murder of Eleanor Sandwich made no sense; neither at this stage of the investigation nor, fairly certainly, at stages to come.

Trouble was, this theory made little sense either. To put it another way, it was stupendously flawed. Why had the relics thief left without the candlesticks, three of them anyway, when they were there for the taking?

Because, observed Superintendent Day, the thief was suddenly a murderer. He had murdered Eleanor Sandwich. Caught with the candlesticks, he'd need to talk his way out of accusations more dire than theft.

Without going as far as to say that Eleanor Sandwich was beloved by all, Day believed she had no enemies. If she had he was in the dark about them, and he was confident he knew her as well as anyone in the choir. She was a gossip. She had a quirky humour which could be surprisingly disrespectful. She was God-fearing and given to quoting the Bible. As far as he could see, none of these attributes seemed sufficient for anyone to kill her. She was dead because she had been in the wrong place at the wrong time.

Inspector Spaak translated into basic English for Sergeant Pépin, and the trickier passages of Pépin's French for Day and Peckover. Day took notes. Peckover, thirsting for a pot of tea, frowned and plucked his earlobe.

Reconstruction. Eleanor Sandwich, after the rehearsal, may or may not have started out by attending Witherspoon's talk on the Van Eyck. If she had attended initially – there would be witnesses – she had wandered off because, stumpy of stature, she could not see the painting. Or she was bored but had read about Henry VIII's candlesticks. For whatever reason, she had found herself approaching the candlesticks. They were not under surveillance, their guard having tracked off after two suspicious characters, one of them black, who had briefly visited the candlesticks, demonstrated that they could not pronounce *Dag* and *Mijnheer*, then left. When Eleanor Sandwich arrived, in place of the guard was the Sealeigh relics thief, attacking the shelf with the candlesticks. He switched his attack to her because she had discovered him and they knew each other.

Consensus meaning general agreement, not necessarily unanimity, a dissenting opinion was allowed, Peckover being the odd man out. He was unhappy with this reconstruction. Not all of it, but something he was unable to put his finger on. Perhaps simply that he had never envisaged the relics thief as a murderer. But most murderers did not see themselves as murderers until suddenly that was what they were. He fiddled with his earlobe and kept silent.

Bob Day said, 'Whoever he is he'll have blood on him.'

The lovers, Sydney Crisp and Audrey Belcher, if lovers they were, had found Eleanor. Of the two, in spite of her headache, Audrey was the more coherent.

They had listened to some of Peter Witherspoon's talk and were wandering round the cathedral with a visitor's guide book. They obviously would sooner someone else had found Eleanor. They were sickened, as who would not have been. Eleanor had still been moving, they had told Superintendent Day. She had even talked, tried to, saying something about murder and being mad and banning Jack.

'Jack?' questioned Sergeant Pépin. '*Qui c'est Jack?*'

A forthright alto in her life, in the moments before death Eleanor had been face down and capable of only whispers. In any event, Sydney and Audrey had not dawdled over her. The first person they had run into had been a deacon who failed with their English but understood their gestures. Next they had come upon Bob Day and a quartet of choir members admiring the pulpit.

Neither had blood on them. Day insisted there would be blood on the murderer. There was blood everywhere else.

Peckover thought it possible that the blood on the murderer might have been light enough for him to have mopped it away to an extent where only eagle eyes in search of blood would spot it. He might be in the cathedral now, exuding innocence, pondering how best and soonest to dispose without trace of the clothes he stood in.

Sergeant Pépin, having eyed Day's collar, cuffs, sleeves, pants, and shoes, gave Peckover's the same scrutiny.

He said, '*Où est Twitty?*'

'Meditating.' Peckover jerked his thumb in the direction of the nave. '*Allez voir là-bas.*'

He watched Pépin's departure with pleasure. Not that it was going to happen but the lad was in no mood to be messed with and he was bigger than Sergeant Pépin. Probably fitter too. They came no fitter than young Jason, jock of Lavender Hill. If there were to be bloodied clothes, they might yet be the sergeant's denim, house of God or not.

Sooner than anyone had a right to expect, a Ghent police officer recovered the death instrument.

138

Acting on her own initiative, until such time as her sergeant would hiss at her in his reverential cathedral voice to stop being a horse's arse, Gardienne de la Paix Claire Baudoin, twenty-two, stalked along what looked to her to be the most direct route between the corpse and the west door, searching. Discovering nothing, she retraced the route, looking to left and right on ledges, behind statuary, and along pews. Then to the west door again. Stolidly back. And again, mulishly, to the west door. By now she was making detours, as if recommended by *Michelin*. Her parents would not have believed it. They had always thought her flighty, capable of looking for nothing except boys. Now she climbed into a railed-off chapel acrid with dust and there, treading carefully, sought among sacks of cement, bricks, and buckets. She saw on a mound of sand, half buried, a reliquary bronze candlestick stuck with bloody clumps of probably white hair. Scattered like a paper chase across the builders' rubble were drenched red tissues. Claire stood sentry at the rail awaiting the first person to pass within summoning range. Come fire, plague, even her sergeant's hiss, she would never desert her discovery.

'*M'sieu*,' she called to a rangy Brit in a turtleneck sweater named, she learned later, Witherspoon. The name made no sense to Claire, and was less pronounceable than were *Mijnheer* and *Dag* to Peckover and Twitty.

Gardien de la Paix Claude Merveille found an empty, bloodstained handbag, asking to be found, in a tulip bed twenty metres from the west door. He handed it to his sergeant and stood there, smiling, awaiting promotion. The sergeant told him to piss off and find the handbag's contents.

'I didn't understand half what Pépin said but I got the impression I'm not his type,' Twitty said. 'The bad news is he didn't understand what I said.'

'What did you say?'

'I told him to stick a Duke of York up his bottle and glass or I just might take a hit and miss on his daisy roots.'

'Where did you learn that sort of talk?'

'You.'

'Rubbish.'

139

'You calling me a holy friar?'

'I don't do rhyming slang. Haven't 'eard bottle and glass since I was wearing short round-the-'ouses. Stick it up your Khyber's what you should have said. Khyber Pass, arse, all right? Remember next time you see 'im.'

'I will. I think he was hoping to see Eleanor's blood on my hands. He said his chief was on his way from Amiens.'

'Already?'

'The word he said was chef. I thought a cook was on his way and it didn't surprise me because you know the French. Then he said commissaire.'

'Commissaire Mouton. I 'ope he's more amiable than his sergeant. So where's your list of acquittals?'

They sat in discomfort in a cushionless pew. Twitty's long legs were stretched sideways. Peckover sat slumped, knees pressed against the pew in front, feet dangling. He noticed that the prayerful woman on her knees, watching through parted fingers, had gone.

Twitty said, 'Witherspoon's the only certain acquittal. There's no knowing who else until someone asks questions and we can corroborate who was in the chapel the entire time. People were coming and going.'

'Bahama was there.'

'Bahama, Witherspoon, Dr Willis. Those not in the chapel, not when we were there, include Oscar Thomas, Robin Goodfellow, the mayor, Clemency Axelrod, Fleur Whistler, Archy, Mr McCurdle, Bob Day, Audrey Belcher, Sydney Crisp, and forty or fifty others who, not being in the chapel, might have been trying to lift candlesticks. Take your pick. On the other hand, they may have been in the chapel. I didn't take notes.'

'Witherspoon eliminated. A small advance.' After three weeks our only advance, brooded Peckover. 'Eliminated from the murder of Eleanor Sandwich. He might still have lifted the madonna.'

'Might have. One other thing.'

'Astonish me.'

'I'm talking. I should be saving my voice. You too, all of us, or it's going to be croak concert. We're going ahead with the concert, right?'

'So I gather.'

140

Homage to Eleanor. Peckover was in favour of that. But he detected rumblings as to the rest of the tour. Oscar Thomas was canvassing opinion and swaying it where it was undecided. Seemliness was the question. With Eleanor murdered, could the tour in all decency go on? Peckover's belief was that Thomas argued seemliness but thought costs. Fair enough. Andorra was off. Ghent was now a disaster whether the concert went well or poorly. Why not be shot of the rest of the tour, poky Gap and Bra?

A day which had opened with the Bishop bent on cancelling tonight's concert might well end, Peckover guessed – correctly as things transpired – with the cancellation of the rest of the tour.

FOURTEEN

'Alleluia! Alleluia!' tumultuously sang the massed voices of Sealeigh
Choral Society, less Eleanor Sandwich.

Homage and farewell, Eleanor! Peckover watched like a cat
Goodfellow and his baton for entries, cut-offs, and clues to whether
more or less accelerando or ritardando were required. The cathedral
organ throbbed under the flailings of Keyboard Kate, the strings
mewled, the sopranos – the skyscrapers of music! – surpassed
themselves, the brass bleated their cavalry charge. Forward, the
Light Brigade!

'*"Lobet Ihn mit Pauken und Reigen!"*'

Dinner-jacketed Peckover warbled forth from the tiered platform's
back row, wedged between Peter Witherspoon (acquitted) and
Sydney Crisp (pretty certainly acquitted), neither of them the
strongest among the basses, both in fact leaners. He, Bill Brown,
no longer leaned but took responsibility. He held high his head and
his music in its shaking black folder. Why did his hand shake? He
was surely too young for so sudden an onset of Parkinson's and he
had not tippled abnormally. He wrote it down to nervousness. No
time to worry about it now. By gripping his dithering right wrist
with his left hand he brought the music under control.

Flame-headed Robin, pro and charmer, delicately mopped his
brow with a cerise handkerchief and turned to the audience to
introduce each work in English, French, and could it be Flemish?
Whatever it was, the audience beamed in appreciation.

Was the bishop in the audience, checking that 'Blow the Candles
Out' was not being sung?

G&S time. Mrs Boothby sang her plaintive 'Poor Little Buttercup'.
Peckover, overtaken by reflections on the news media, worked hard
at not grimacing. How was he going to avoid the BBC, ITV, *Mail,*

Sun, Telegraph, etc? They would be on their way. He would need his niftiest evasive action.

'When constabulary duty's to be done,' boomed out Joe Golightly, 'A policeman's lot is not a happy one.'

Any moment now the lickety-split jaw-wrencher.

Go!

'And we are his sisters and his cousins and his aunts!'

Peckover's mind was not wholly on it. It was on Audrey and Sydney. It had better stay on sisters and cousins and aunts if he were not publicly and grievously to err.

'His sisters and his cousins, whom he reckons up by dozens, and his aunts!'

The audience loved it. How could they? How could they understand a word of it?

Not that Gilbert's rhyming didn't make better sense than Eleanor's dying 'murder, mad, and banning Jack'. Peckover believed he would have to have a friendly session with Audrey and Sydney. Murder, mad and banning Jack was not good enough.

The audience wended out of St Bavon's and into the floodlit night. The instrumentalists packed away their instruments and the television crew their equipment. Elated, exhausted, the chorus remarked among themselves on those passages that had gone well and those that had gone ill ('But do you think anyone noticed?'). Many congregated round Robin Goodfellow, asking his opinion or eavesdropping on it. Others straggled out of the west door and back through the streets to the hotel and supper. Not a few recalled only now that one of their number was in the mortuary, her body to be flown back to England at such time as the Ghent police permitted.

Outside the illuminated west front Sergeant Pépin nudged Commissaire Mouton and pointed.

The commissaire said, 'I know, I know. Obviously. With the black.'

Commissaire Mouton stepped forward, introduced himself, and shook the hands of Peckover and Twitty.

Peckover said that since he and Constable Twitty were undercover, might it not be better if they talked somewhere discreet, perhaps a pub or its equivalent?

143

They started walking. Commissaire Mouton said he was on his way to police headquarters. He would have liked Messieurs Peckovair and Tweety to be there too but as they were incognito he understood. Could they meet early tomorrow? Peckover agreed it would need to be early because the tour might be cancelled, and they might be returning to England tomorrow. Sergeant Pépin butted in with a salute, fingers quivering against an albino eyebrow, and confirmation on the authority of Monsieur le Directeur, Thomas, that the tour was cancelled. The Sealeigh rosbifs and nègres would return to Angleterre demain, Pépin said. All names and particulars had been noted for further questioning and extradition as necessary.

Pépin's French was so gabbled as to be barely comprehensible, deliberately in Peckover's opinion. Peckover spoke to Mouton in valiant school French, boosted in recent years by Bordeaux vineyard holidays with Miriam. Mouton spoke to Peckover in stricken English boosted not at all by his sole visit to Angleterre, a day trip with Madame Mouton, at her insistence, to Dover and its Marks and Spencer. That had been years ago. Madame Mouton had bought shoes and dresses and indescribable sausages. She had badgered him ever since to forgo the summer holiday on the Atlantic coast and head instead for England, Scotland, Ireland, even Northern Ireland. Even Wales. But for the Welsh rugby team the commissaire did not think he would have heard of Wales. He certainly had no intention of going there in the summer when there would be no rugby.

'Constable Twitty and I are under no obligation to leave tomorrow,' said Peckover.

'You have it perhaps the wrong way round,' said Commissaire Mouton. 'I and Sergeant Pépin are not obliged to stay in Ghent. If our murderer is, excuse me, one of your Sealeigh choir, and the choir returns home tomorrow, our place may have to be in Sealeigh. At your invitation, naturally.'

Peckover liked Commissaire Mouton. He could not believe Mouton was eager to go to England. But the bloke was serious and ready.

Twitty's eyes had locked with Sergeant Pépin's. After a few moments endeavouring to stare the sergeant down he gave up. He did not consider it a defeat. To back down against this sort of weird official, to refuse even to be provoked, was a victory.

Abandoning his coffee, Twitty pushed his chair back and said, 'There goes Bahama. If it's all right with you, Guv, I thought perhaps a gentle interrogation.'

'Gently interrogate 'er in that lounge place. You can take things further if needs be, lad.'

'I can't imagine what you mean.'

'I'll be 'aving a word with the adulterers if ever they stop pawing each other.'

'You don't need me?'

'I'm Bill Brown, especially concerned about Eleanor's dying words because 'er second cousin in Sheffield turns out to be a friend of my wife. Something like that. Bill Brown plus J. Twitty would only complicate it.'

The hotel restaurant had pink napery and a profusion of daffodils and tulips. Peckover had kicked off with the trout, fish for his health, after which he would be able to enjoy his meal. He had ordered the pigeonneau, which would presumably be a small pigeon, or some sort of pigeon, maybe squab. He had hoped there would be enough small pigeon or squab, but he couldn't be in Ghent and eat routine filet mignon he could find anywhere, or the chicken even if it was forestière. Miriam would have despaired. There was not a lot of pigeonneau, not enough for a Texan, or for Joe Golightly, but it had a nicely reeking sauce (chicken liver and cider? puréed rabbit hearts?) and lay on slices of fried bread spread with foie gras. Plus braised endives, peas, and chips. He had urged Twitty to try the frogs' legs fritters because it wouldn't be every day he'd find them on Lavender Hill. With the frogs' legs fritters he should have the Brussels sprouts au gratin, this being Belgium and Brussels a mere hop and skip down the road. Twitty, who didn't mind much what he ate, had thanked Henry for his suggestions and ordered the steak, medium not bleeding, *s'il vous plaît.* '*Pas bleu,*' Peckover had told the waiter helpfully, '*même pas saignant, peut-être brûlé un peu.*' The steak had arrived raw all the same. These victuals the policemen had washed down with something red from the Rhône, half a glass satisfying Twitty, Peckover taking care of the rest. Twitty had then tackled the ice cream and hot gaufres Parisienne, a kind of waffle like the ones at Polly's Pantry on the Lambeth Road.

He said, 'You never know, Guv. Bahama's been with the choir three years. I might learn something.'

'You never know.'

Twitty loped in pursuit of Bahama. Until such time as Audrey and Sydney got up off their bums and left too, Peckover decided he might as well test the brandy.

Armed with the choir roster and room numbers, Peckover stalked the fourth floor. He had given Sydney and Audrey eight minutes' start, long enough for them to bid goodnight to the moon (they had skipped the moon) but not long enough to become so busy with each other that they would ignore a knock on the door, or fail to hear it. He could be wrong of course. Their hearing might be heightened. They might spring to answer a knock on the door. Love was an enigma.

If they had not gone their separate ways they could be in Sydney's room. Most of the choir shared, like Audrey sharing with a soprano named Eve Swindler, which would render assignations tricky. ('Eve, would you mind awfully if you spent tonight in the park?') Fat cats like Sydney evidently wanted not to be on his own but to be free to choose whom he would not be alone with.

Peckover put his ear to the door of room 406, heard nothing, and knocked.

He knocked again.

Someone within said, 'Who is it?'

'Bill Brown.'

Dodgy, this. Mouth against the door, he had to be loud and clear enough for Sydney to hear but not for doors to right and left to open and heads to pop out.

'Won't take a moment,' Peckover mouthed against the door, which smelled of fresh paint. Inhaling glycols, acrylic resin, titanium dioxide, arsenic, and cyanide, on top of the plonk and brandy, could make a bloke light-headed.

'Wait.'

Exactly what I'm doing, mate. He looked both ways along the corridor. No doors flying open so far.

The time he was waiting he could have had another brandy. Why didn't Sydney just tell him to buzz off? If he had been Sydney he'd have told Bill Brown to buzz off.

He hoped it *was* Sydney. What if there had been last-minute room switchings? A clerical error on the roster? No way of knowing if it was Sydney from the few muffled words from the other side of the door. He hoped it wasn't the mayor. He had no reason to speak to the mayor. Waking him up would have to be an honest mistake. He would be contrite and probably fetch up joining SCAT.

Waiting anxiously, Peckover rehearsed the spiel for his interest in Eleanor. Eleanor's niece in Aberdeen, though he hadn't met her himself, was acquainted, the niece, with this pal of his . . .

The door opened. Here was Sydney, overdressed if anything in blazer and tie, the tie a trifle crooked but none the less a tie. He might even have brushed his moustache, what there was of it. He had his trousers on. Beyond his ear, also dressed, Audrey sat reading in an armchair. You'd have thought they had so many visitors she didn't notice any more.

'You're a copper, aren't you?' Sydney said.

FIFTEEN

Peckover walked in saying, 'Evening, Audrey,' and looked for somewhere to sit and be friendly.

There was not a lot of choice: the armchair in which Audrey pretended to read and an upright chair at a table. On the table were Booth's gin, Vermouth, and two glasses with contents, so he thought he wouldn't sit there. He sat on the edge of the bed.

Sydney closed the door, sat on the chair at the table, and said, 'I'm right, aren't I?'

'Do I look like a copper?' asked Peckover, shocked.

'You and your mate, the blackie, and the Frenchie, Pépin, and someone behind him during the concert, you were all being chummy outside the cathedral.'

Betrayed, mused Peckover, by his own ilk, by the very company of coppers. He was surprised to hear Audrey ask for his identification. A lass not to be underestimated. Studying his warrant card, she read aloud, 'Henry Peckover, Detective Chief Inspector, Scotland Yard. Goodness!' Peckover waited for them to cry out, 'Not Peckover the Poet!' Neither did. Audrey passed the card to Sydney, who held it genteelly between thumb and forefinger, little finger extended, as if he were taking tea with the vicar. He returned it to its owner.

Peckover said, 'Murder, mad, and banning Jack. Eleanor's last words. We have to be able to do better than that.'

Sydney said, 'What it sounded like.'

'That's right,' said Audrey. 'I mean, approximately.'

'Ah, approximately,' said Peckover. 'See?'

Sydney shrugged. Audrey shook her head.

She said, 'She was so faint.'

'She was dead – dying. I've never seen a dead person, anyone like that, not before.'

148

'I know you'd sooner not be reminded,' Peckover said. 'But you were there, you heard her. It may be important, it may not be, but try to remember exactly. Consonants, sibilants. You both have a terrific ear. Smashing singers. Shut your eyes, open your ears.'

They did not shut their eyes. They gazed at each other, evidently trying to remember. Peckover wondered if he were mistaken or had they turned a little sickly? When they spoke it was to each other. Peckover might not have been there.

'After "murder" there was something,' Audrey said. 'Like a shushing. She was whispering, and like, I don't know, shushing, and sort of gargling. There was somethig after "mad" too. Madder, might it have been? Maddening? And after "Jack", there might have been something, but you couldn't tell.'

'After Jack there was just aah. She was dying. Jack was the last I heard.'

'Jack and aah.'

Peckover brought out his notebook and pencil. 'You're doing well.' He didn't know if they were doing well or not. He was probably wasting his time, and theirs, when they might have been consoling one another. But they were trying.

He said, 'After "murder" came this shushing sound—'

'More a chuh or chah,' Sydney said. 'Look, I'd not swear she said "murder".'

'Chuh, yes,' said Audrey. 'But not a real word. Not church. Or chop. And she kind of hissed. Oh, all that blood!'

Peckover allowed them time.

'Banning might have been banner,' Sydney said.

'Bandage?' queried Audrey, looking hard at Sydney for corroboration. 'No, not really, no.'

Peckover said, 'You're doing so well.'

He waited for more but that seemed to be it. He jotted down words and phonetics.

'Murder,' Peckover said. 'Eleanor's first word, the first you heard, you're reasonably happy with that? Or not?'

The pair looked at each other, then at Peckover, and nodded. Audrey said, 'Not much, is it? Who's Jack?'

'We'll 'ave to find out, love,' said Peckover. 'Either of you know a Jack in the choir?' According to Oscar Thomas the choir hadn't had a Jack for ten years. 'Joe Golightly, is he ever called Jack? Like a pet name?'

'You think Joe—?'

'Absolutely not,' said Peckover. 'Is he ever called Jack?'

Sydney and Audrey lifted their eyebrows at each other and shook their heads.

'You've been very 'elpful, both of you.'

Peckover wished he could believe it. He stowed away his notebook. They were not going to offer him gin, for which relief much thanks. He would probably have accepted.

'We'll keep in touch,' he said vaguely on his way out.

The hotel slept, or at any rate was silent. Peckover and Twitty's room on the third floor was empty. Names and room numbers in hand, Peckover rode the lift to the ground floor. He looked in the bar, which was closed, and where he wouldn't have expected to find Twitty anyway. In the lounge were only Bob Day and Mr McCurdle in deep chairs, taking coffee and a nightcap together. He retreated before they saw him and summoned him to join them.

No one else anywhere apart from a receptionist reading a book behind the front desk.

Peckover unfolded his roster of names and room numbers. Bahama O'Toole, 248. He ran his eye down the list. No one else was in room 248. Likely as not a single room was a perk for the coach drivers. Bahama and Gus the Bus could hardly be expected to share, and they'd need all their beauty sleep to be fresh for battle with these Continental motorists.

Sorry, lad, but here I come. No, it won't wait till tomorrow.

Peckover rode to the second floor. An arrow pointed left to 200–221, another arrow right to 222–250. A door opened in the corridor to the left and Archy Newby came out. Before Peckover could go right and seem not to have seen him, having no wish for chit-chat, Archy saw him. So Peckover lifted a hand in greeting, received barely a nod in return, and walked off in the direction of Bahama's room 248.

At the end of the corridor was a T-junction, 248 to the left. He looked back. The corridor was empty. Peckover scurried along the corridor, past the lift, and stopped at the door Archy had come from. The plaque said 205. He walked back towards Bahama's room, fishing from his pocket the names and numbers.

Archy Newby, room 50.

So 205? The roster was alphabetical. You had to hunt for room numbers. 'Lobet Ihn mit humpfen and bumpfen,' Peckover sang softly, hunting, and halted at the T-junction.

Fleur Whistler, 205.

Foolish girl was Peckover's opinion on that. *It's rumoured they had an affair, but of course it's over*, Eleanor Sandwich had said. He shouldn't assume, she and Archy didn't have to have resumed the affair. His earlship could have breezed hornily in and Fleur could have breezed him out again with her aerobics girl's arm and feet.

Not my business, the love lives of the Sealeigh Choral Society, Peckover resolved.

A door behind, or a couple of doors behind, quite close anyway, opened. Peckover looked round.

Clemency Axelrod emerged from room 210 and exclaimed, 'Oh!'

'Evening,' Peckover said.

Flustered, Clemency said, 'Yes, good evening.' She had a cardigan draped over one arm. 'Thank you.' She clearly would have liked to run. 'Such a nice hotel.'

If she'd had her wits, better to have said, such a confusing hotel, such a muddle, would you believe I ventured quite mistakenly into the wrong room?

'So sorry,' apologised Clemency. Clutching at the sliding cardigan she scuttled for the lift.

Peckover stepped round the end of the corridor and brought out the names and numbers. Axelrod, Clemency: 340. She was on the wrong floor of the nice hotel for a start.

Room 210: Golightly, Joe.

Joe Golightly was sharing with Mr McCurdle who was down in the lounge.

Bahama's room was now all the way back along the main corridor. Peckover pocketed the roster and set off. After he had passed the lift a door a few steps ahead opened. Out came Dr Willis.

No avoiding her. Might even be her own room. So why was she

151

leaving it, this no-nonsense figure in a knitted blue suit? For a stroll under the stars?

At least she was composed. More accurately, after a momentary freezing she recovered her composure. Obviously she had been on a professional visit, administering to a case of the Belgian gripes.

'We were discussing the negative double and the unusual no-trump,' she said. 'They originated in New York. You don't play, do you?'

Play what? Peckover had no intention of playing anything. He shook his head.

'I thought probably not,' said Dr Willis, walking past him in the direction of the lift. 'Goodnight.'

She hurried, the lift having arrived. Out from it and striding away along the corridor went Alderman Green. On a secret SCAT mission, no doubt.

Peckover perused his roster. Willis, Helen: 306. She wasn't even on the right floor. He looked at the door from which she had come: 227. This Ghent hotel was one steaming swamp of lust. At one o'clock in the morning, after the murder of one of their own, and a concert, an entire endless day of drama and trauma, and too much food and drink, Dr Willis wanted him to believe she had been discussiong the unusual no-trump?

Avec qui had she been discussing? Out came the crumpled roster. Room 227: Robin Goodfellow.

Peckover was shocked. The bloke was married. He was a candidate for knighthood. He probably had children, perhaps a dog, a decent house in Ealing or Greenwich, and an agent lining up an American tour. If a sirdom were ever to come his way he'd need to shape up.

Peckover walked fast in search of 248: O'Toole, Bahama. The next sex maniac to emerge out of somebody else's room he would ignore utterly. He right-turned at the T-junction.

Wrong turn. As far as he could determine, the room numbers had no logical progression. He reversed into the alternative arm of the T-junction. Here it was: 248. He knocked.

They sounded as if they had the television on. He waited, giving them a chance, but he would not wait for ever.

The television's muffled burblings continued. Some Belgian

chocolate commercial. Either they were rearranging themselves, or agreeing to brazen it out by not answering, or they hadn't heard. Of course Twitty might not be there. Peckover raised his knuckles. Now, before Ms O'Toole came to the door, was his chance to disengage, withdraw, much as he and his mates when in short trousers had rung doorbells and run away. Bahama might after all be watching the box alone. He knocked hard.

''Ullo? Bill Brown 'ere.'

The television fell silent. The whole hotel was silent, as if embalmed. Peckover knocked again, whereupon the door opened.

'Hello, Guv. I mean Bill Brown. Mr Brown.' Twitty wore a sequined bolero, once presumably the property of a toreador, and baggy red and white checked pants such as Coco the Clown might have coveted. 'Anything up? We were singing.'

'Come in,' called Bahama O'Toole.

Peckover advanced a step. The room was a single, identical to Sydney Crisp's, except that in this armchair sat Bahama, giving him a wave, and on the table, instead of gin, were books. Bahama, bare footed, wore jeans and a jersey. The television was off. Peckover wondered if it had ever been on.

He said, 'Singing, eh? Golden oldies, I suppose.'

'You heard, Guv? Bahama knows them all!'

'Like the Beatles?'

'C'mon, that's the dark ages. You know, Bob Marley, Jimmy Cliff. Notting Hill Carnival stuff.' Twitty, snapping his fingers, crooned, 'You can get it if you really want.'

'Very catchy. Makes a change from Schütz. Bahama, sorry to break things up. Private matter. We'll see you tomorrow.'

Peckover locked the door of their room, took off his jacket, and said, 'Murder, mad, banning Jack. Remember?'

'I do.'

'Sit down.'

He tore a page from his notebook and handed it to Twitty. Twitty read, *Murder. Chah (chuh). Ssss. Mad-er. Ban-er (Ban-ing). Jack-aah.*

'Very revealing,' Twitty said. 'It's worse gibberish than before.'

'Sing it.'

153

'You're joking.'

'You can sing. You're in the choir. You sing oldies like Notting Hill Carnival stuff. You don't 'ave to sing it out loud, I don't mind not hearing. Chew it, swill it, try it different ways, listen to it. If it's still gibberish, I'm going to bed. I'm going anyway.'

'You've been talking to those two who found her.'

'For what it may be worth.'

Peckover went into the bathroom, scrubbed his teeth, showered, shampooed, and returned combing his hair. He wore a kimono, a birthday present from Sam and Mary that Twitty would have had something to say about had he been awake.

'Mate!' Peckover barked.

'Sir!' Twitty came to attention in the armchair. 'Love your peignoir. It'd go a treat with your poofter shoes.'

'Less of your impudence. Let's hear your translation.'

'The chah or chuh could be church. Strictly, St Bavon's is a cathedral and if anyone knew the difference Eleanor probably would. She thinks she's in heaven, or on her way, and sees the banners of the armies of Christ. Onward, Christian Soldiers. I don't quite believe that's what she was trying to say but I'm not being flippant. The ban, banner, or banning, stumps me.'

'Go on.'

'If the sibilant prefixes the mad or madder we could almost have smash, smatter, smeared, but I don't see where it gets us. Sorry, Guv. Doesn't amount to much. At least we've made progress with Jack.'

'How?'

'It isn't Jack, it's Jack-aah, so we can forget Jack. No Jack. Jackal perhaps, Jackass, jack-in-the-box, jack up the price, and jack it in.'

Peckover contributed, 'Jacuzzi, Jacobean, Jack Frost, Jack the Ripper. None of that lot means anything to me. Jack might not be the start of a word. Might be the middle or the end.'

'I've tried it. I've sung it every way. Ban-ah-jack-aah. Isn't there an actor, Victor Bannerjee, he was in *Passage to India*? It isn't the same, though, doesn't fit, and he isn't in the choir. On the other hand,' Twitty frowned down at the pencilled gibberish from Peckover's notebook, 'mad-er could be madonna. Chah with the sibilant could be chalice.'

154

'Where's the thorn?'

'Good question,' Twitty said, searching the words for a thorn.

'Give it up, it isn't there.'

'Guv, you're ahead of me. You spotted the chalice and madonna. Why didn't you simply say?'

'Because I'm not ecstatic about them. Or I wasn't. Now you've come up with them I'm a bit more confident, and much, much less ecstatic.'

'What's that supposed to mean?'

(Also, what are you doing to your hair? Twitty wanted to ask. Our 'Enry, seated in the flowery kimono on his bed, had placed the flat of each hand on either side of his parting and was crimping, pressing the wet hair into two hillocks, a ravine between.)

'Think,' Peckover said.

'Henry, here's the truth. I'm tired.'

'Whose fault's that? Sitting up 'alf the night singing reggae with that bird, if that's what you were doing.'

'She didn't nick the relics and she didn't murder Eleanor.'

'Says who? Convince me.'

'You can be a right bastard. For a start, she hasn't time. She's doing a degree course, she's driving a coach, she's singing with the Sealeigh—'

'I'm convinced. Don't be so solemn.' Dissatisfied with his crimping, Peckover went to the mirror over the dressing table and combed out his hair over his forehead. 'What I'm not ecstatic about is why in her dying moments Eleanor Sandwich would talk about a chalice and a madonna. Maybe a thorn too if Sydney and Audrey had listened harder. Where did Eleanor hear about the relics? Someone tell 'er? How would she know about them?'

'She stole them.'

Peckover plucked stray hairs from the comb. The constable in his bolero and clown's pants sat slumped in his chair.

'Don't give it a thought, lad, not now,' Peckover said. 'Let's finish with these last words. Any of 'em we 'aven't dealt with?'

'No.'

'What about the first word we've got?'

'Murder? It's the only word makes sense.'

'Exactly. Odd that one word makes sense when none of the

155

rest do. What about Sydney and Audrey hearing what they took to be the word murder because that's what they were looking at? Most sacrilegious murder breaking open the Lord's anointed temple.'

'You're brimming with quotes these days, Guv.'

'I 'ope so. One apt quote's worth a power of mindless prattle.'

'Murder,' Twitty said. 'Girder, sheepherder – got it! Absurder!'

'You're too precise. This is someone choking in blood and overheard by a couple who don't want to hear. Murder, muddle, udder, burden, surgeon. Does Dr Willis do surgery? Dirndl? What's a dirndl and is it Flemish or Swiss?' Peckover peered in the mirror for signs of ageing: bags beneath the eyes, crow's feet. 'Bumble, burble, McCurdle. McCurdle's got a fierce cold. Pockets probably stuffed with Kleenex.'

'Bahama telephoned her parents this evening from one of the card phones. She said McCurdle was on one of the phones for ages and when she walked past later he was still at it, only in French. He wouldn't call from a public phone if he was up to no good.'

'He might if he didn't want the call to show up on 'is room bill. Murder, McCurdle, it's stretching it. Murdoch is closer. Do we know if Rupert Murdoch's in Ghent? What else did Bahama regale you with?'

'The mayor's paranoid about the Tunnel. He was upset when Eleanor walked out of SCAT a while ago.'

'She did? He was?'

'She's not convinced Clemency Axelrod has a glass eye. Clemency may only pretend she has a glass eye to win sympathy, and she's tougher than she looks. Did you come up with anything?'

'Half the choir's having assignations with the other 'alf. Tryst Hotel, this place. It's a seething love nest. Clemency and Joe Golightly. Archy Newby and Fleur Whistler. Sir Goodfellow and Dr Willis. And that's only on one floor. Jason Twitty and Bahama O'Toole. Singing, eh? That's rich. Pull the other. And 'urry up and turn off the light.'

Peckover unrobed, slid into bed, and pulled the sheet over his head.

* * *

At 4 a.m. Constable Twitty woke up, sat up, and in the same four-quarter time and on the same G natural as his tenor part in *Regina Coeli* he sang stereophonically, 'Bank of Djakarta!'

'Wha'?

Twitty opened his eyes to pitchy dark. 'Sorry.' He was panting.

'Was that me?'

'Wasn't bleedin' me. Nightmare. It's over. Go to sleep.'

'Your fault. You keep saying sing it. Ban-ah-jack-aah, Bank of Djakarta.'

'Where's that?'

'God knows. Other side of the world.' Twitty flung out and waggled his arm, an impatient gesture in the dark pointing possibly to the east. 'There might be one in the City. They've got scores of banks nobody's heard of. I'm not saying I'd want to put my money in them, if I had any. Credit this and Commercial that. Yemen, Oman, Gabon, Lebanon.'

'Phone the Factory. Special for Frank Veal.'

'Me?'

'Now. Tell 'em if there's a Bank of Djakarta what we're looking for is a deposit box with a madonna and chalice and thorn in the name of someone in the Sealeigh choir. Tell 'em to kick off with the name Eleanor Sandwich. We should be so lucky. And don't wake me again.'

SIXTEEN

Round the table in the conference room at Ghent police headquarters sat Peckover and Twitty (Scotland Yard), Bob Day (Sealeigh Constabulary), Commissaire Mouton and Sergeant Pépin (Amiens), and Inspector Spaak (Ghent) with a half dozen of his senior colleagues.

Some debated more hotly than others. One alone contributed nothing, his expression alert to the issues under discussion, every sinew of his body taut with readiness. This was Constable Twitty. Never before had he been confined in a room with so much top brass. In his stockbroker's weekend fishing tweeds he sat with open notebook, ballpoint poised, and at his elbow a tumbler of flat, sanitary Evian water.

Also available from a side table was coffee, beer, and red wine.

No tea. No women. One of the Ghent commanders, a blue-eyed Fleming whose tailored pin-stripes were no excuse for his table manners, had brought in his breakfast, a fat, hot, onion-filled pastry that steamed, reeked, and on to the table shed flaky crumbs which he swept with his forearm to the carpet. One of his compatriots eyed him with disgust, another with envy, but both furtively, clear evidence to Peckover that the pastry-eater outranked them both.

Though introduced with much handshaking, Peckover had failed to sort out who was who among the local lot. He believed it possible that he might never sort them out but it would hardly matter because he would probably never see them again after today. *Lady of Kent*, sister ferry to the *Princess Diana* – 'A gem of a ship', as Alderman Green, shareholder, had been going round describing the plastic tub – was to sail from Ostend at 6 p.m. Peckover saw no reason why he and Twitty should not be aboard with the rest of the Sealeigh choir.

He might see them in court one day, these Hercule Poirots. (Not a whit of disrespect intended – they seemed competent, by and large, but the world's best-known Belgian kept intruding on his thoughts.) A trial, however, was some distance in the future. As Mrs Beeton might have said, first catch your criminal.

Two of the Poirots smoked white cigarettes and a third a yellow cigarette. Gauloises fumes, or Gitanes, pungent as a slowly burning cat, subdued to some extent the onion smell from the pastry. The smoke performed shifting minuets in the oblongs of morning sunlight which fell through the windows. Twitty, that tender plant, his throat and lungs unsullied as a maiden's thoughts, had begun to cough.

Peckover shot Twitty a warning look. This was the Continent, these were Continental cigarettes, so what was the problem? What did the lad expect? He didn't want the Poirots to interpret Twitty's coughing as a reproof, which is what it was. If he were allowed to get away with coughing every time someone ignited a Gauloise, next he'd be clapping his hands over his nose and fainting at the wafts of garlic-breath from anyone within whispering distance.

Twitty, silent apart from his coughing, believed the brass would have listened had he dared speak. That the majority were foreign brass – never mind they were on their own patch, they were still foreigners – was all the more intimidating. Several were bilingual, perhaps trilingual, though the one most ready to speak English, continually interrupting to explain the course of the discussion to the English policemen, was easier to understand when he spoke French.

Sergeant Pépin contributed almost as little as Twitty, following a garrulous start. Early in the proceedings he had advanced a recommendation that the coach driver, Bahama O'Toole, being of a certain ethnic minority, therefore unreliable, should be closely interrogated. Sooner or later she would reveal herself in her true colours.

This was not, Sergeant Pépin had said, a matter of racial prejudice, though he had been accused of that, and he would be prepared to defend scientifically proven data on the inferiority of certain ethnic types due to brain size and other factors. Simply, the woman O'Toole being of an alien culture, her values were not those of the West. Any practitioner of voodoo would be only too eager to thieve Christian relics for use in perverted rites. The same person committing a murder would without question consider a cathedral the perfect place and a holy candlestick the ideal weapon. Similarly, the crimes plainly deriving from a twisted depravity, the likelihood of the Lord Archy Newby as the black woman's accomplice should be looked at. The Lord Newby had been caught red-handed stealing Christian relics at school. Everybody knew that the British artistocracy was depraved. The reason behind the toppling of Margaret Thatcher, sole Britisher of honour and integrity of the twentieth century, was less well known because of the secretiveness of the British establishment, the Defence of the Realm Act, draconian libel laws which encouraged juries to obliterate at a stroke any individual or public print, and the public prints themselves, concerned only with football, royalty, photographs of women's breasts, and court dramas of sexual whippings, another of the manifold *vices anglaises*. As for the intellectual press, it did not count, being either the lackey of the banks or written by and for left-wing schoolteachers. Madame Thatcher had been forced from office when her plan for wiping the British aristocracy off the face of the earth was betrayed to a powerful conspiracy of ethnic immigrants and Marxists. It was common knowledge.

Commissaire Mouton had suggested to the sergeant that it was common nonsense. What was common knowledge to anyone who had done his homework, such as studied the fact sheets supplied to all present, was that Mademoiselle O'Toole had attended the Witherspoon lecture from start to finish and was therefore eliminated from the murder inquiry. True, Archy Newby had no such alibi, claiming to have returned to his hotel after the rehearsal to read a history he evidently found engrossing. The commissaire read aloud from page four of the fact sheets: '*Courtesans, Concubines, Lesbians: Life at the Court of Marie Antoinette*, by Sylvette Vestale, Privately Printed, Paris, 1947.' As he, the commissaire, understood matters, it was not Archy Newby who needed particular attention. What about this Joe Golightly, who, he gathered, had the strength to crush a skull with a candlestick? Let not their efforts be sidetracked by brain size, voodoo, Madame Thatcher, and sexual whippings.

Twitty smiled sweetly across the conference table at Sergeant Pépin. The sergeant glowered. Thereafter, still glowering, he said nothing.

Inspector Spaak gave his opinion that brute strength was not an essential for crushing a skull with a brass candlestick that weighed over four kilos. Women members of the choir should not be automatically excluded from the inquiry.

Neither, interpolated a Ghent colleague with an open-neck shirt and gold chain, should anyone who happened not to be a member of the choir be excluded. Not one scrap of evidence pointed to the murderer being a member of the choir.

A policeman with a languid air and a white carnation in his buttonhole said that if women were not to be excluded, quite rightly, neither should the choir's more public and prominent members, for example – wearily he sought through his fact sheets – Robin Goodfellow. Oscar Thomas. Alderman Philip Green.

A policeman in uniform wanted to know exactly what was known about the other coach driver, not the woman, the one who was not one of the choir. Augustus Briggs. He had driven the coach on the previous tour, had he not? When the relics went missing?

Inspector Spaak remarked that while they were not excluding people they should also not exclude Angus McCurdle simply because there was sympathy for him on account of his Herefords. Too bad that he was missing, if missing were not too loaded a word.

Peckover, Twitty, and Day thought that it was. Still, McCurdle had left Ghent, telling Oscar Thomas that he had much on his mind and needed time to himself. 'The world is too much with us,' Oscar Thomas had said he had said. McCurdle had promised to rejoin the choir at Ostend for the six o'clock ferry. Inquiries at the railway station had revealed that a gauntish man with spiky eyebrows and a tartan suitcase who spoke good French had bought a ticket to Calais.

Superintendent Day pointed out that the problem with focusing on McCurdle because he had left Ghent was that eighteen or nineteen other members of the choir, at the last count, had also left Ghent or were proposing to do so. These others, moreover, unlike McCurdle, had no intention of returning to England on the evening ferry.

Having arrived this far, Ghent, which was not far at all, these free spirits intended to journey on. They had cancelled the milk and newspaper and left the key next door with Mrs Jones who would see that Pusskins got her sardines. Now, by bus, train, or rented car

161

they would head off independently on pot-luck holidays to wherever funds would allow. Eleanor, they agreed, would have wanted them to. She would have done the same.

Inspector Spaak did not care for this scattering of the choir but he had no power to prevent it. Probably it didn't matter. He had statements from everyone. None of the choir were going to vanish for ever. In England further questioning would be up to the English police. All the same, he would be at Ostend for the departure of the ferry, and to meet this McCurdle, if he showed up. If in the course of the day the least crumb of evidence against Monsieur McCurdle, or the coach driver, or mayor, or no matter who, came to light, he would bring him back to Ghent.

A policeman in springtime shirtsleeves came into the room. He carried a piece of paper and wore a surprising red tulip. Ghent, city of flowers! Baffled by the array of upper-echelon officers, at sea over whom to salute, he lowered the hand he had begun to lift and saluted no one. He whispered in the ear of Inspector Spaak.

The inspector said, 'Monsieur Peckover? Chief Superintendent Veal is on the telephone.'

''Old the fort, lad,' Peckover murmured, and followed the tuliped policeman from the room.

The conference resumed in French, or in double Dutch for all Twitty understood. One of the policemen looked at his watch, stubbed out his cigarette, gabbled something to Inspector Spaak, gathered up his papers, and left.

Twitty was grateful to his guv for not having aired in this lofty company his, handsome Jason's, musical epiphany. First opportunity, he would buy Henry a beer. If the Bank of Djakarta was housing relics in its vaults, they would hear about it in good time. If the Bank of Djakarta had no relics, less said the better.

What Bank of Djakarta? Was there a Bank of Djakarta?

Regina coeli! Twitty heard in his head.

Djakarta? He didn't know where the place was, either, except vaguely out there in the Orient, far away. He would look it up, though.

Peckover returned. Twitty could not tell from his expressionlessness whether he brought good, bad, or no news. He wanted to know and he didn't want to know. Was this what it was like in the dock awaiting the jury's Guilty or Not Guilty? Our 'Enry took his seat. A hush had fallen. That had been the Yard on the phone. They hadn't called with the football scores. Peckover drummed meditative fingertips on the table.

It's good news, Twitty guessed. If it weren't he'd have got it over with. He's milking this all he can.

What a ham! *Quel jambon!*

Peckover addressed Commissaire Mouton. 'We have recovered your black madonna from Amiens cathedral, Monsieur le Commissaire. *Elle est tout à fait secure, um, sûr. Hors de danger.*'

'*Zut!*' said Commissaire Mouton, and punched Sergeant Pépin on the shoulder.

Peckover could not resist grinning, whether because the madonna was safe or because of his French was impossible to say. He retrieved his impassive look and swivelled his eyes to include everyone at the table.

'We 'ave also recovered one chalice, property of the church of St Mary of the Angels, in Padua, and one thorn from the Bruder Klausenkirche in Basel.'

'*Extra!*' cried a Ghent copper, cigarette quivering wetly on his lower lip.

Inspector Spaak was applauding. His handclaps commenced heartily then petered out, cowed by a glare from the pastry-eater.

'*Félicitations, M'sieu',*' said the pastry-eater.

'Our CID took possession of the relics at nine-thirteen this morning from safe deposit box number two-o-nine at a foreign bank in the City of London,' Peckover said. 'Without going into details, I'll add only that credit for their recovery goes in large measure, I might almost say exclusively, to investigative work by my colleague 'ere, Detective Constable Twitty.'

'*Chouette!*'

'*Formidable!*'

Peckover said, 'Deposit box two-o-nine was rented in the name of Eleanor Sandwich. The CID is verifying the authenticity of her cheque to the bank, which is the Credit Bank of Djakarta. The description given by the assistant securities manager of the woman who rented the box two weeks ago, Friday, March twenty-third, fits Eleanor Sandwich. Am I going too fast?'

'*Non, non!*'

'If Eleanor Sandwich deposited the relics in the bank's custody, we may fairly and reasonably assume that she it was who stole them on the choir's last tour, or at the very least was an accomplice to their theft. Our theory that Eleanor Sandwich surprised the relics' thief by the candlesticks in St Bavon's cathedral, and was thereupon murdered to silence her, is therefore flawed and must be reconsidered. To put it another way, that theory now looks like a load of cobblers.'

Like I always said, Peckover wanted to add, but didn't, it's bleedin' amateurs, innit. An amateur thief who should have stayed at home with her knitting, murdered by an amateur, a bungler who disposed of the murder weapon twenty yards from the scene and threw her empty handbag into the tulips to try to make it look like theft. Amateurs made no sense. There was no knowing where to start. The whys and wherefores had no answers.

That was to say, he didn't have the answers. From their mumblings and blowing cigarette smoke neither did anyone else at the table. Of course, amateurs made sense to themselves. No such beast as a literally senseless murder ever existed.

He raised his hand six inches and said, 'Assume Eleanor Sandwich is our relics thief. If we knew who murdered 'er we'd 'ave a fair chance of finding out why. Since we don't know who, perhaps we should tackle the question why? Why should anyone kill Eleanor Sandwich? Personally, I've no idea.'

Bob Day said, 'One thought for what it's worth. Neither Eleanor nor her assailant strike me as being professionals.'

Peckover said, 'Good thinking, Bob.'

'The unprofessional Madame Sandwich escaped the law for quite a time,' objected a Ghent commander. 'She would be escaping it still had she not, with her last words, as I understand it, spoken of this bank.'

'She was lucky,' observed a colleague.

'An unfortunate choice of word.'

'You know what I mean.'

'Your ambiguity does not make it easy.'

164

'Perhaps you would like to refer the matter to the Académie Française?'

'*Messieurs, la calme, je vous en prie,*' urged Inspector Spaak. 'Supposing, as a hypothesis, Madame and her assailant were accomplices who had, say, a falling out, a difference of opinion?'

'Some difference,' said the policeman in uniform.

'Supposing,' said the languid one with the gold chain, 'the assailant was not an accomplice but wished to be. Even over the victim's dead body, somebody determined to take over the relics business for himself.'

'Supposing a mugger off the street looking for an easy handbag.'

Nobody was impressed. Nobody had made a move to open the windows either, though the room was as fuggy as a bar in a Maigret story. Twitty edged his notebook to Peckover. He had written, *Chunnel? Eleanor poss. threatened by looney SCAT fanatics?*

Peckover slid the notebook back and murmured, 'Go on, then, tell us about it.'

'No.'

'Yes.'

'Not I, Guv.'

'Do it.'

'I'd be embarrassed. There's nothing in it.'

'You've 'eard the level of contributions we've had so far.' He hiked up his hand and announced, 'Constable Twitty has an offbeat thought which may merit attention. Constable?'

A coughing attack shook Twitty's frame. Unnerved by so much seniority, bent on flight, cough lozenges for his throat, he pushed his chair back. Peckover stood and pushed chair and constable back to the table. The chair legs screeched on the parquet. He slapped Twitty's back, sat, and offered the glass of Evian. 'All right, lad? 'Ow about the Heimlich manoeuvre?' Normally Peckover had little patience for the anti-tobacco stormtroopers who hung the greeting 'Thank You for Not Smoking' in the hallway of their home and fanned the air, retched, and reeled about at the first whiff of tobacco smoke. This time he was on Twitty's side. 'Bit dense in 'ere,' he said. 'Can we 'ave the windows open?'

The pastry-eater, probably commandant-in-chief of the combined

165

Ghent and Flanders Sécurité and Judiciaire, brought Twitty a tumbler of red wine, said, '*Courage, mon petit,*' and exhaled Gauloise fumes.

Twitty sipped and choked. The coughing subsided.

'Thank you. Sorry. It's just that, see, it probably doesn't add up—'

'Speak up,' said the one in uniform.

'Sorry. The deceased once said—'

'Who?'

'Eleanor Sandwich told me I shouldn't dream of joining SCAT because—'

'What SCAT is, please?'

'It's in your fact sheet,' Peckover growled.

'Sealeigh Campaign Against the Tunnel,' Twitty said. 'Because some of its extremists positively terrified her. I think those were her words. Actually I may have them.' He flipped through his notebook's early pages. Dr Willis and bridge stuff. *Bahama O'Toole & castration possibilities – ouch!* Political spat, Fleur Whistler v. Archy Newby. Political speech, Ald. Green. Financial speech, Osc. Thomas. *Leader G'Fellow's weird Latin. Yrs. truly opens mouth, inserts foot.* 'Sorry. It wasn't even what she said so much as how, sort of with a shudder as if she were genuinely anxious.' Audrey Belcher. Dr Willis. 'Here, Eleanor, quote, she was "positively terrified". She said the police should take very seriously the threats of the SCAT lunatic fringe to bomb the Tunnel, and the most dangerous were some who didn't belong to SCAT so couldn't be easily identified. She didn't name names. Perhaps she didn't know names, though I have a feeling she did. That's all.'

Twitty shut the notebook and stared down at his hands.

'*Voilà!*' Peckover said.

Commissaire Mouton said, 'The Mayor Green is to do with this SCAT?'

'Chairman,' said Bob Day.

'Bomb the Tunnel?' queried the commissaire. 'Is possible that M'sieu' Twitty 'as put the cats among the pigeons.' He shrugged, a small yet infinitely Gallic hoisting of the shoulders. 'Then again, as 'imself figure, per'aps not.'

Sergeant Pépin caught Twitty's eye and leered.

Desultory discussion ensued. Superintendent Day agreed that providing a SCAT membership list should be no problem. Alderman Green almost certainly would have one with him.

Twitty whispered, 'Told you, Guv. They think I'm a nutter. It's a non-starter.'

'Shut up. Drink your wine.' To the assembled police Peckover declared, 'Eleanor Sandwich is dead, murdered. From the sound of it she may have believed she was in danger. 'Er opinion of the SCAT extremists was that they were dangerous and terrifying. Some there are, as we in Britain know, who threaten bombings. This may be a red 'erring that has us barking up the wrong tree.' Something askew there. Only the lad would spot it. 'And it may not. You'd think that with the accumulated experience, professionalism, and brainpower at this table we'd be able to come up with something.'

But they didn't. Six hours later, Peckover, Twitty, and Superintendent Day joined the rest of the returning Sealeigh choir on the coaches bound for Ostend and Blighty.

SEVENTEEN

Oostende, proclaimed a harbour sign twenty metres long. The first car in line drove up the ramp and into the belly of the *Lady of Kent*.

Sergeant Pépin identified the car as a hopeless Ford, probably not even made in the United States. He sat astride his Yamaha wearing his black leather jacket, goggles pushed on to the top of his head, and happy to be here. Happy to be anywhere after the suffocating conference with the commissaire, all the high muck-a-mucks, and the Scotland Yard banana boy. Not that there was any action here either. He had watched the Customs fools paying hardly any attention to the Sealeigh coaches. They had looked in only half a dozen of the rosbifs' bags, confiscating nothing.

The rosbif coaches were far back in lane three. They would not be there long because the queues were boarding at a steady lick. In a fine white Simca behind the rosbifs were the police: Inspector Spaak, a driver, and a couple of cohorts, not about to embark but in attendance. The wind was brisk, and tufts of white frolicked on the sea. But they were no more than tufts, inadequate for a roller-coaster crossing for the rosbifs. *Tant pis*, thought Sergeant Pépin.

He observed a hurrying figure on foot, hefting luggage and listing as he strode between lanes of vehicles He passed Spaak's Simca, and paused, looking up into the windows of the Sealeigh coaches as if deciding which was the more desirable. McCurdle? The big folding suitcase was plaid. Why didn't he just get into the first coach, or either coach? Both had room. The Scotland Yard flics were in the second coach. Whichever he got on he would only be getting off again in five minutes after the coaches were on board. He was swinging open the door to the luggage locker of the leading coach. Now he was pushing his tartan case inside. There didn't seem to be a great deal of space but he was lifting and pushing. He removed a black box from the locker. A music case? He removed two more, rearranged baggage, and returned the music cases. Now what was he playing at? Opening his case? He needed his bowler and umbrella? Inspector Spaak was stepping from the Simca.

Sergeant Pépin would not have been surprised if McCurdle had murdered the Sandwich woman in collusion with the depraved aristocrat, Lordship Newby. The black woman driving the second coach had an alibi for the time of the murder but she might well be involved.

McCurdle and Spaak were talking. Spaak had brought out his notebook but was writing nothing in it. McCurdle reached up and hauled down the door of the luggage compartment. They were shaking hands, the Belgian flic and the rosbif. Sergeant Pépin wondered if Spaak was in collusion with McCurdle, the Lord Newby, and the black woman. He had never trusted Belgians. Everything said about them was true. When the coach honked its horn, McCurdle climbed aboard. Following a Bentley, the silvery Sealeigh coach drove forward, stopped while Gus the Bus handed through the window an embarkation ticket, then proceeded up the ramp.

Sergeant Pépin watched the two Sealeigh coaches disappear into the *Lady of Kent*. Scowling, he made a fist with his right hand, crooked his elbow, and with his other hand slapped the bent arm.

'*Salauds!*' he said. '*Assassins!*'

Mr McCurdle's tribulations were not yet over. Minding his business in the cafeteria with a pot of tea, *Le Monde*, and a view through the window of choppy ocean, he found himself borne down on by the choir's two newcomers.

They clutched their duty-free goodies: Peckover a bottle of Scotch and two bottles of claret, Twitty a bottle of brandy which he expected would last him four or five years, unless he threw a party, in which case forty minutes. Peckover had sundered Twitty's illusions that they had saved mightily on London supermarket prices. This lot had seemed pricier than the same stuff in Waitrose. Somewhere along the line were those who had to make a profit and as likely as not one would be Alderman Green, shareholder, Channel Ferry & Hovercraft Services, Ltd.

Peckover had also selected Shalimar for Miriam, and for Sam and Mary comics for their developing minds, chocolate bars for their teeth, a kite each for flying on Primrose Hill (he knew who would be flying the kites if ever he got them up in the air), and mugs bearing a blurred picture of a boat and the inscription *Lady of Kent*, which, if dropped and broken first time they were used, would be no loss.

They sat beside McCurdle, who said, 'Chief Inspector Peckover, I presume.'

'Word seems to be out.'

'But you are still J. Twitty.'

Twitty nodded.

Peckover said, 'Pure routine, sir. Would you mind telling us where you were today?'

'I don't mind. Calais. This is in connection with Eleanor? A Belgian officer – Spaak? – just asked the same question.'

'Why Calais?'

'Excuse me, but first Spaak, now you. Am I to infer – this sounds melodramatic – that I'm under suspicion?'

'No more than the rest of the choir, the adult population of Ghent, and yesterday's visitors to the cathedral. It's a matter of trying to keep tabs.'

'You say visitors to the cathedral? He may have been a random thief or madman?'

'Calais, now. Unless one had friends there, or a specific purpose, like a Saturday outing from Dover, one might think Calais an odd place for a day out.'

'Why d'you say that?'

'You've already seen Calais. Everyone has. One other thing I'd say is you're asking more questions than I am. If you stick to answers this shouldn't take a moment.'

'What was the question?'

'Why Calais?'

'You know I've lost my herd of Herefords?'

'I know.'

'Now Eleanor. We weren't intimate but we always gave each other the time of day. She was in the choir when I joined twelve years ago. There was respect. Perhaps even fondness.' He took a swallow of tea, made a face, and pushed the cup and saucer aside. 'At Ghent station I didn't know where I was going and didn't care, just as long as I didn't kick my heels in Ghent all day. Calais was up there on the departure board. Antwerp would have served. Bruges. The Calais train happened to be due.'

'That's the only reason?'

'The act of travel may in itself be sufficient. Nothing is as solitary. Travel clears and deadens the mind.'

'What did you do in Calais?'

'The cathedral. The Rodin monument to the six burghers, though I never cared for Rodin. Walked. As you surmised, I have seen Calais. Everyone who crosses the Channel by sea has seen Calais, Boulogne, Dieppe, probably Dunkirk. Same difference, wouldn't you say? We suppose they're the same because in fact we have never seen them. Off the ferry we come and slam away as fast as possible. No one lingers in the Channel ports. The truth is, Calais is not without interest.'

'You almost convince me.'

'About Calais or my going there?'

Peckover made a meaningless gesture.

'It's a little delicate,' McCurdle said.

Twitty said, 'If it's a woman we're broad-minded.'

McCurdle winced. Peckover refrained with difficulty from hacking Twitty's shin under the table.

'It's tax,' McCurdle said. 'Unfortunately, I have no knowledge of how closely our police work with the Inland Revenue.'

'Personally,' said Peckover, 'at the longest distance possible and with trepidation. On any official basis you don't 'ave to worry about us. We're not the fraud squad and I'm not interested.'

McCurdle mulled this over. 'Calais has a college of veterinary science. They might not have the last word on bovine spongiform encephalopathy but their approach is different from ours across the Channel. I might have paid the college a visit for professional reasons.'

'Though you didn't.'

'Who's to know? Calais is a business expense.'

'If the first train had been to Antwerp or Bruges, do they 'ave veterinary colleges?'

171

'Everywhere has something that might be a business expense.'

'You ate in Calais?'

'At Le Channel. A far superior restaurant than its name would suggest. Too superior for me. I had the duck pâté, salmon, no dessert.'

'Decent wine?'

'A glass of Muscadet. Water. I'm not a great drinker. I believe I have the receipt.'

He dipped into an inside pocket but Peckover gestured, dismissing the receipt.

'You took your suitcase with you?' Peckover said.

'Yes.'

'Wasn't that a little cumbersome?'

'I don't understand.'

'You could have left it at the hotel, picked it up when you got back from Calais.'

'I was not going back to the hotel. I was going to Ostend.'

'Ostend to Ghent, a taxi to the hotel, it's only another, what, forty minutes?'

'You should have told me all this this morning. Obviously you would have arranged my day better than I did.'

'Why back to Ostend? Calais to Dover and Folkestone has frequent ferries. Wouldn't that have been simpler?'

'I'd paid my fare for this ferry. I'm not paying twice.'

'So you lug your case from Ghent to Calais then back to Ostend. Oscar Thomas or anyone would have put it on the coach for you.'

'I do not impose.'

'A fiver to the hall porter. He'd not 'ave felt imposed on.'

'Correct me, Inspector—'

'Chief Inspector. It's not important.'

'I was merely about to ask if I'm right in my impression that this has turned into quite an interrogation?'

'It's just that it seems a pity that on your day off, so to speak, you lumber yourself with a great suitcase. The tartan one, isn't it?'

'It'll not be the only tartan suitcase in the world.'

'I don't follow.'

'I don't follow your obsession with what is only a suitcase.'

'Well, it's not a monster, it's 'ardly a cabin trunk, so I can see

172

you can cope with it from Ghent to Calais and Calais to Ostend. Depends what's inside. Truth is' – Sir? Mr McCurdle? Angus? – 'I'm with you all the way on suitcases. We're both obsessed, seems to me. I don't let mine out of my sight either. Leave your suitcase unattended these days and what 'appens? Either some bugger swipes it or the bomb squad hauls it off and takes it apart. Have you seen the notices at Charles de Gaulle in Paris? "Any Unattended Suitcase will be Removed and Blown Up." Bet they do it, too. The French love explosions. Ever been in France on Bastille Day? Come to think of it, they're not the only ones. We've got Guy Fawkes Night.'

'July the Fourth,' Twitty said. 'That's the Americans. Their Independence Day.'

'I'm grateful for the information,' McCurdle said.

'So there you are in Calais,' said Peckover, hurrying on. 'They'd remember you at the restaurant if nowhere else. Eccentric Brit arrives for lunch carrying capacious tartan suitcase.'

'The port happens to have travellers. It must happen all the time. Since you're so excited about my suitcase, I did not carry it in Calais.'

'I was 'oping not. What did you do with it?'

'Checked it in at the railway station.'

'They 'ave lockers there or a real 'uman you give it to?'

'Probably both.'

'Where did yours fetch up?'

'In the left luggage with staff.'

'May I see the baggage claim?'

'You hand it over when you collect your bag.'

'They don't let you keep something they tear off along the dotted line?'

'No.'

'No receipt? Nothing?'

'I told you.'

'Someone like you, a business expenses zealot? I mean, the pennies add up. I'd 'ave thought you'd have asked for a receipt.'

'If there was a receipt, I wasn't aware. I probably dropped it in a bin.'

'Quite right. Not worth cluttering up your wallet. If you come across it, let us know.' Peckover gathered up his duty-free booty.

'On the off-chance we need to talk to you again, you'll be at your Sealeigh address? Rivermere Farm, is it?'

'You're a pest, Inspector.'

He's demoted me again, this time with malice aforethought, Peckover thought. Couldn't really blame him. The bloke had amazing eyebrows. Did he not know any decent barber would trim them for him or did he really like them as they were?

'It goes with the job,' Peckover said. 'Rivermere Farm?'

'I'll be there.'

'C'mon, lad. I always like to see the White Cliffs. "There'll be bluebirds over",' sang Peckover, '"the White Cliffs of Dover".'

'We're going to Folkestone,' Twitty said.

'You can see 'em in the distance though, can't you? Bluebirds, that's something else, unless the tourist office spray-paints the seagulls.'

Grey un-spray-painted seagulls screeched overhead. Clemency Axelrod and Joe Golightly stood at the rail, pressed together and throwing gobbets of bread to them. They didn't need to have been pressed together, there being nobody else at their section of rail. Twitty wondered if the gift-wrapped packet that Joe Golightly had brought into Curiouser and Curiouser might have been an engagement ring, as the guv had suggested.

'You were pretty hard on McCurdle, Guv.'

'Never mind McCurdle. Unless we scarper quick we're going to be received by the mayor.' Peckover glanced again over Twitty's shoulder. 'Too late. He's yours, lad. You can be hard or gentle, your choice.'

Alderman Green wore a jovial red anorak and a peaked cap with a bobble on top such as golfers wore in the twenties. He reached out a hand for shaking.

'Mr Brown, hello. I'm Phil Green. After all this time and we've not had a chat. *Mea culpa* – is that correct? Mr Twitty, the Latinist, you should know. Hello. The new boys and most welcome. Not, I'm afraid, what I'd call one of our happier tours.'

'No,' said Twitty. Somebody had to say something. The guv nodded politely but said nothing. He had passed the mayor down the line. Twitty said, 'Shocking.'

174

'Excuse me one moment,' Alderman Green said. 'I must have a word with Oscar. Where's the fellow been hiding?'

He strode across the deck to where Oscar Thomas, Robin Goodfellow, and four or five of the choir sat talking on a life raft.

Twitty said, 'Mayor, top SCAT cat, Mr Vote-for-Me, and he doesn't know who we are? We're just the new boys? If he doesn't know by now, he's the only one.'

'He's self-absorbed,' said Peckover.

'He is. He's like a celebrity, or imagines he is. You wouldn't think he'd think he needed to introduce himself, not after all this time.'

'He likes introducing himself.'

'I say he's fishy and so's his SCAT.'

'Hm.'

First on, first off, or so it was with the vehicles aboard the *Lady of Kent*, more or less.

An excited, unshaved seaman in shirtsleeves, efficiency itself, pranced and pointed, beckoning cars forward, halting others with outstretched palm. Woe to cars that did not accelerate away the instant he pointed, and double-woe to those that budged before being commanded to do so! He rolled his eyes, gesticulated, clapped both hands to his forehead, and caused the errant driver to feel like a grub. He may not have been a seaman, he may have been a landlubber traffic attendant in the employ of the Folkestone Harbour Authority. Whatever he was, he imposed discipline and certitude where otherwise there would have been a turmoil of clogging, horn-blowing, dented bodywork, and bloodied noses. (The more thoughtful of those awaiting his signal reflected that this was a car deck of largely British motorists, patient and sensible, and were grateful. The internecine chaos had they been French, or, worse, Italian, did not bear thinking about.) Superb at his job, the attendant bounced and beckoned as if he had been given a time limit which, if not met, would result in the boat reversing at thirty knots back to France with the cars that had not made it ashore still aboard.

Nose-to-tail, the Sealeigh coaches awaited their turn. When it came, the fevered attendant gave a hop and a skip, beckoned Gus the Bus forth, then with a skip and a scamper slammed the flat of his hand into the air in front of Bahama's coach. He summoned cars from the right and cars from the left. By the time coach number two steered down the ramp, coach number one was eight or nine vehicles ahead and about to be looked over by Customs.

The majority of cars, lorries, and coaches jaunted unmolested through Customs. A random few were singled out no matter their windshields wore a green Nothing to Declare sticker. Idle and bored these dockside Customs officers in natty black might be, but dense they were not. Over the years they had developed an eye for the family sheltering behind a Nothing to Declare sticker which all too risibly was a barefaced lie and needed to be dealt with.

Officer Belinda Heptonstall, as it happened, saw nothing unusually suspicious about the coach which said SING. Simply, she had done nothing for twenty minutes except watch traffic roll by. Time for an inspection. She asked Gus the Bus to open the luggage locker.

'What are those?' she said, peering in.

'Music cases, aren't they?' Gus the Bus said. 'Violins and stuff. Sealeigh choir, innit. We 'ad a murder, didn't we. Our Mrs Sandwich slaughtered in the church. Was it on telly?'

'Bring them out.'

'All of them?'

'Yes.'

'Well, I dunno, bit hexceptional. Shouldn't I fetch their owners?'

'By all means, if you want to be here all night. Funny smell, isn't there?'

'What smell?'

Gus lifted out the music cases.

Officer Heptonstall said, 'Open this one, this, and that.'

Gus sprung a catch and opened a lid. Together they observed a trumpet. Officer Heptonstall took it out, examined it, peered inside, gave it a shake, looked in the case, and put the trumpet back crookedly.

'Now you mention it, there is a pong,' Gus said. He opened the next case. A violin. ''Orrible Camembert, that'll be what. We've been in Belgium.'

Officer Heptonstall looked down at the violin and said, 'You can close it up.'

'That it?'

She was already walking away. Besieged by music cases, Gus the

Bus emitted a blubbery raspberry, though softly. 'Women,' he said.

Now separated by three cars from the natty gaggle of Customs officers, Bahama O'Toole inched her coach forward. Stop, start, stop, start. Someone in a hutch looking at passports did not speed matters, though he barely looked. Did the brave new Europe intend to remove barriers or didn't it? Bahama wanted to know. Halfway along the coach Peckover craned for a better view of the first coach, Gus, and the litter of music cases.

''Ere, lad.' Peckover jabbed an elbow in Twitty's ribs. 'Count those boxes. Quick – that's the first one he's putting back.'

'One, then,' counted unquestioning Twitty. 'Two, three, four, five, six, seven. Seven. Next question?'

''Ow many did we take on board?'

'Where?'

'When we left Sealeigh.'

'Seven. Don't ask me. I didn't count.'

'You were too busy slavering over Bahama. There were six. We've won one.'

'Somebody bought an extra flute in Ghent. What's so special? There might be more on this coach. We might have won half a dozen.'

'All the instrumentalists are on Gus's coach, right?'

'No idea. I don't think I see any in here.'

'Bob Day will know. Up front. Ask 'im.'

Ahead, Gus put his coach into gear.

Bahama grimaced, swung her coach's steering wheel, and pulled out of line. Had she not done so the Customs woman standing in front and pointing would have been flattened into the concrete. She switched off the engine.

Officer Heptonstall having looked at one SING coach thought she might as well look at the other. The Sealeigh coaches were news, she could regale her mum with it, and her job did not give her many privileges. A clutch of Folkestone Harbour police were keeping unprivileged reporters and cameramen back from both coaches. A deal of back-and-forth arguing seemed to be taking place.

Peckover watched Gus drive from the dock. 'Damn,' he said.

Officer Heptonstall's examination of the green-stickered second coach was more cursory than the first. She climbed the step and put

177

a foot inside to check that its passengers were not armed terrorists, then asked the driver to open the baggage compartment.

Bahama did so. Officer Heptonstall looked in at layers of luggage. With coaches it was hard to know where to start.

Not really hard. You just got on with it.

Peckover watched through his window. He couldn't hear what the Customs officer was saying. He wanted to put a firework up her skirt, tell her to snap to it, chop-chop.

Officer Heptonstall inquired, 'No bonbonnes?'

'No what?' said Bahama.

'Bonbonnes.'

'You mean like chocolates?'

'Like carboys?'

'Cowboys?'

'Carboys.'

'I'm sorry?'

'Carboys!' Officer Heptonstall spoke more loudly than she had intended.

'Oh, carboys.' What was the woman talking about? 'You mean like stowaways?'

Oh boy, some people. Officer Heptonstall straightened her tie, though it was straight enough. Mum would love hearing about this one.

'Demijohns,' she said. 'You've heard of demijohns. Demi—'
She observed utter blankness on the driver's face. 'Never mind. Off you go.'

Peckover awaited Bahama by her driver's seat. She wore scuffed spongy-soled sneakers with dangling tongues.

He said, 'Fantastic driving, you've done brilliantly. I mean, those Belgians and all. So don't spoil it, I'm not suggesting a coach chase. It's too late anyway. Incidentally, the lad, Constable Twitty, he's all right. Honourable. No, I'd not exactly say honourable. But he might have some leave coming up. I'll put in a word for him. What I'm saying is, if we catch up with the other coach I'll buy you a box of strawberries.'

'The traffic shouldn't be too bad at this hour. We'll see what happens.'

Bahama pressed down on the accelerator with her sneakered foot.

178

EIGHTEEN

Deep dusk on the Kent coast, coldish, the sky straining to drizzle but not quite managing to. Sooner or later a downpour would provide real weather, something to discuss. The coach would reach Sealeigh in another twenty minutes and in the dark, if it reached there. Bahama was treating herself to some hairy overtaking. Had Peckover been a traffic cop he would have flagged her down, lectured her, and handed her a ticket. He wouldn't have bothered lectured just anyone, let the macho and the drunk go to hell in a handcart, but Bahama was smart enough to benefit from judicious words from the sage.

Every now and then Peckover hoisted himself from his seat to look ahead and see if Bahama had caught up with Gus's coach, but she hadn't.

'"*Lobet Ihn mit Saiten und Pfeifen,*"' he sang absently.

'"*Lobet Ihn mit Psaltern und Harfen,*"' joined in Twitty.

'Stop it,' Peckover said. 'You'll have the whole coach singing. What else do we know about McCurdle?'

'My feeling is we should focus on the mayor.'

'Not Archy?'

'Curious, that. I haven't given Archy a thought for two weeks.'

'So tell me about McCurdle.'

'He gave me a free tutorial in diphthongisation.'

'Perhaps he was giving himself a free close-up of one of the choir's new boys. Sussing you out.'

'He asked if I were a teacher.'

'And you said?'

'Representative.'

'Representing what?'

'He didn't want to know. Representative is a conversation-stopper.'

179

Peckover's coccyx had begun to ache. The seats were too close together. Seats were always too close together.

He said, 'I'd still like to know why he went to Calais. He had too many explanations. One good one would have done, like the veterinary college as a tax dodge.'

'You thought that was good?'

'Confess to a small sin without being asked, like finagling your expenses, and the assumption is you've nothing else to hide. People suppose you must be dead honest.' Peckover hoisted himself up. Nothing in front. No SING tail-lights. Where was this, then? Dark. Ribbon development. The sea somewhere to the left. They couldn't be far from Sealeigh. He sat down. 'I'd like to see inside his suitcase, and I'd like to know who brought that extra music case on board and what's inside that.'

'Not relics, anyway. That was Eleanor's game. Drugs?'

'Explosives?'

A fat raindrop detonated on the window.

'Coach ahead!' Bahama called out, like a sailor with a spyglass.

Peckover stood and strained to see. More raindrops burst and dribbled.

'Where are we?'

'Milford,' said Audrey Belcher across the aisle. 'First stop for the suburbanites. Sealeigh's another mile.'

'Milford,' Bahama called out, braking. 'Anyone for Milford?'

Yes. Mrs Boothby. Mr Charlesworth. Audrey. Sydney kissed Audrey's hand in parting. Ahead, Gus the Bus's coach was pulling away.

Peckover swore. He put his face to the window and cupped his hands against his eyes. Outside was a glare of shopfronts and the beginning rain. Several of the choir stood talking beside a taxi. The only one he knew by name was Archy Newby. Two instrumentalists, each with a suitcase and one music case. Half Gus's passengers might have disembarked and evaporated into the night.

Most of whoever remained had gone their ways by the time Bahama caught up with Gus's coach at the next and final stop: Sealeigh Presbyterian Church. A few had waited to say goodbye to friends in the second coach but nobody Peckover was interested in. He bearded Gus by the luggage compartment.

'Did you happen to notice Angus McCurdle leaving?'

'Who's 'e, then?' Gus the Bus said.

'Late forties, lean, dour, dark overcoat, eyebrows, big tartan suitcase. Did he also take a music case?'

'One of the band, is 'e?'

'Has all the luggage been claimed?'

'It 'as.'

'Mind if I look in the luggage locker?'

'Just told yer, mate. It's empty.'

'I'd like to see.'

Twitty said, 'Did you notice if the mayor took away a music case?'

''Is Worshipful the Mayor, Mister Halderman Green, not being the band, would not of taken haway a music case, would 'e? Who are you lot, anyway?'

'Police,' Peckover said, taking out his notebook. 'Let's see your driving licence, then.'

The luggage compartment was empty, the Sealeigh concert tour was ended, the singers were gone, and the police learned from Gus the Bus nothing other than somebody must have been bringing in Camembert that smelled like a sewer, though he'd once 'eard somebody say, must of been a Froggie, that Camembert smelled like the feet of God.

Peckover telephoned Miriam from Sealeigh police station, telling her he was back on Albion's blessed soil, rain was deluging, he would not be home tonight, and how were Sam and Mary? Miriam said it might be as well he'd not be back tonight because the archaeologists' leftovers were Greek, not usually his favourite – Peloponnesian haddock and braised okra – though it was so good she might freeze it. Sam and Mary had consented to be pianists and she had made an appointment with a piano tuner.

He telephoned Veal to say he was no longer Bill Brown, he was out of the closet, and he'd not say no to staying on the case. Twitty too. Superintendent Day had alerted Kent's bomb squad. Whatever Sealeigh's top hotel, that's where he and Twitty would be, so don't even think of arguing. They had sung Schütz and lived to tell about it. Over and out.

Day telephoned the Chief Constable of Kent, who agreed that the police watch on the mouth of the Channel Tunnel be doubled. Quadrupled, old boy. Couldn't be too careful. But discreetly. No leaks, no media, no panic.

Twitty, made lonely by all the telephoning around him, but unable to choose between six or seven girlfriends, called his parents and told them about abroad and Belgian chips.

He failed to find in the directory, O'Toole, Bahama. Her pad, that dusty Elysium, was on Kimberley Terrace, off Wycliffe Way. Fat chance he'd have tonight of carrying her off to paradise.

Over mugs of ɔrange tea, Peckover and Day speculated on the extra music case, if Peckover had counted correctly. Twitty had counted with him.

Explosives did not smell of Camembert. Except to a dog, they smelled of nothing. A score of Sealeigh's choristers might have brought home ripe Camembert, leaving Gus the Bus no alternative but to call in the fumigators and open wide the luggage locker to breezy ozone vapours.

But something was going on. There existed SCAT rabble who talked of blowing up the Tunnel. Not many but it wouldn't need many. Crazies, the political equivalent of soccer hooligans. They would have to get their explosives from somewhere, and it had been got before now from the Continent. By the IRA for one.

Without going so far as to say it out loud, the policemen drinking their orange tea were aware they had fouled up. The choir had evaporated and with them one supernumerary music case. The additional music case might contain a guiltless viola or bassoon of Continental manufacture. Then again it might not. Whatever, they would never be issued warrants to search for the case in the home of every member of the choir on what amounted to no evidence at all.

Alderman Green would have to be questioned about SCAT's lunatic fringe, their names, the degree of their passion and involvement, but not tonight. First thing tomorrow. Day assumed he was the obvious choice for a preliminary chat with the mayor, alas, but the prospect somewhat unnerved him. Judging from a word in his copper's ear from Dr Willis, Gladys Green was not under the weather but extremely poorly, and she didn't want her husband to know.

Still trickier, indeed hardly to be thought about, was the mayor the upstanding pillar of the community that he appeared to be? Because SCAT's chairman spoke out against violence didn't mean he might not privately be promoting it. Day needed a little time to gear himself up before tackling the mayor. Like a night's sleep.

He said, 'Phil Green wasn't at Witherspoon's lecture in the Vijd chapel. He says he toured the cathedral, on his own, then went outside for air and couldn't get back in because the police sealed it off. Phil's rarely on his own. He needs an audience. Now, Eleanor was an early member of SCAT but got out because she couldn't take its extremists.'

'She told me she was terrified,' Twitty said. 'She said I must think twice before joining SCAT.'

Day said, 'Could Phil Green have killed Eleanor because she left SCAT?'

'No,' Peckover said.

'You sound very positive. How d'you know?'

'I don't. You're saying he kills 'er out of pique? He's affronted. Codswallop. With respect.'

Twitty said, 'If she quit SCAT with sensitive information, like plans for bombing the Tunnel, he might have wanted to shut her up. What if she'd been putting some kind of squeeze on him? Not that I see Eleanor as a blackmailer.'

'Why not?' Peckover said. 'She nicked relics.'

This they mulled over in silence, three sages too full of wisdom to speak.

Day said, 'Suddenly about six months ago McCurdle was chatting up Eleanor every rehearsal, which was peculiar because he's unsociable, he doesn't talk much to anyone—'

'He talked to me,' said Twitty.

'The exception. Then just as suddenly he wasn't talking to Eleanor. Almost as if he'd been proposing and she'd turned him down. Proposing something, enlisting her. It's probably not significant. I don't know.'

'I know it's the sort of background info you don't have when you're parachuted into the choir at five minutes' notice,' Peckover said. 'Is McCurdle in SCAT?'

'No. But he's always loathed the Tunnel because the new rail link was going to lop off a corner of his land. He didn't want compensation, he wanted his land. Anyone barmy enough to build Brighton Pavilion out of matchsticks might be barmy enough to try and blow a hole in the Tunnel.'

Peckover finished his tea. On the table, between bookends, were law books, gazetteers, a dictionary, a Bible.

He said, 'McCurdle has a tartan suitcase easily big enough to hold a music case.'

'I saw him put it in the luggage locker at Ostend,' said Twitty. 'He practically climbed into the locker with it. He could have removed a music case from it, put it with the others. If customs look inside, nobody's to know it's his.'

'So 'ands up who's for Rivermere Farm,' Peckover said, raising his hand.

'It's seven miles,' said Day. 'Might as well be sure he's there. We'll send a car.'

He picked up the telephone.

Sergeant Dick Pennyfather and Constable Rose Bailey drove through bucketing rain along the waterlogged driveway to Rivermere Farm. They had visited only last month, in better weather, when mad cow disease had been rumoured. Tonight they found a ghost farm. A single dim security light burned in the downstairs. Sergeant Pennyfather kept the lights of the patrol car on and the wipers swishing.

'Our horrible luck,' he said. 'One of us is going to get soaked. Try the doors, Rosie. I'll look after the car.'

'Is that an order?'

'Would I order you? Kiss, please.'

They kissed and fondled. Each was married, not to the other, but they were good friends, and without friendliness shifts could become tedious . . .

They both got wet. No one answered their ringing and knocking. The doors and windows were locked. In outbuildings were two tractors, a Land Rover, a fairly ancient Jaguar, farm machinery, rope and twine, ladders, and scores of baskets for the apple harvest. The beams of their flashlights swung into corners and up to haylofts.

'We see a music box, we stand back, right?' Rosie said.

'You can stand back. I'll be running like the clappers.'

They unlatched the door of a shed, trained their flashlights inside, and recoiled from an outburst of grunts and squeals. Armies of gargantuan pigs lumbered to their feet. Three, anyway. The sergeant and constable slammed and latched the door. Two cow byres stood empty, scrubbed, reeking of disinfectant.

'Radio the station, Rosie. Nobody's at home.'

Two hours later, a dozen police let themselves into Rivermere Farm with a search warrant, six inches of wire, and a piece of plastic. Peckover stood impressed in front of the unfinished Brighton Pavilion. He was less impressed with himself. 'I'll be there,' McCurdle had said in the *Lady of Kent*'s cafeteria. Our 'Enry, innocent, thick as two planks, had believed him.

Superintendent Day divided the team in two: one for the farmhouse, the rest for the outbuildings, not neglecting kitchen gardens, chicken runs (Rivermere Farm had no poultry but Superintendent Day was not to know), and the entire farm, including orchards. A freckled constable who objected that the farm had a zillion acres of orchards was assigned to the orchards and told to get on with it. Being wet already, Sergeant Pennyfather and Rosie were also assigned to the outdoors.

The search confirmed what they thought they had said quite a while earlier. McCurldle was somewhere else. So was his music case, if he had a music case.

The public having been kept ignorant of the possibility of explosives smuggling through Customs at Folkestone, it was, not surprisingly, a police constable who identified the music box, or at any rate a music box.

The hour was three in the morning and the box stood unattended on the pavement outside the Dog and Pot, beside a deserted bus shelter (at this hour everywhere was deserted) in Bournemouth, a hundred and forty miles from Sealeigh. While not looking new, the box did look to the constable like a music box that would accommodate a French horn, an instrument he was familiar with, being a concert-goer. Briefed, forewarned, he radioed his desk sergeant. They arrived in force: police, forensics, four bomb specialists from the police, three more from the army. The constable backed away as a gloved explosives handler tenderly opened the case. Inside was a French horn and a gummed label bearing the name of its owner, Patrick J. Mulvaney, a musician with the Bournemouth Symphony Orchestra. Mr Mulvaney, it would transpire, had a quick one or three too many taken in the Dog and Pot following an evening concert.

Sensibly, deservedly, luxuriously asleep in Sealeigh's Ocean Metropole, Peckover and Twitty knew nothing of this incident, nor of two false alarms, until the next day, when they would be present at the opening of an altogether more revealing music container.

At dank dawn, prior to its discovery, Chirpy Charlie began his whistling postal delivery. Loaded satchel of letters, cheques, and junk over his shoulder, he set out on his mail delivery up and down eight gentrified streets of terraced houses in north Sealeigh.

Seven years on the trot Chirpy Charlie had won Sealeigh's Postman of the Year Award. He knew all the town's inhabitants, had a chirpy word for everyone, patted the dogs, and put the string which bound his bundles of mail into litter boxes. Infinitely friendly, yet knowing his place, Chirpy Charlie's piercingly tuneful whistling of tunes on everybody's least-favourite-tune list ('Pop Goes the Weasel', 'How Much is that Doggie in the Window?') prevented anyone from sleeping after seven-thirty but warned that he was on his way. This allowed the residents to stay out of sight until he had passed.

Charlie ceased whistling, stared, but still could not place the small orange dog attacking the rear off-side wheel of the Wilsons' Volvo. He recognised every dog in the neighbourhood. This was an intruder, slavering, snarling, and savaging the tyre.

He looked up and down the street for someone to discuss the matter with but there was no one about.

'Garn!' Chirpy Charlie shouted at the brute, not too loudly lest he be thought to be bringing common rowdiness to the street. The dog took no notice.

He took from his satchel the Granny Smith intended for Veronica Satterthwaite, today being her sixth birthday, and flung it. To his astonishment, and the animal's, he scored a hit on a hind leg. The beast streaked away down the street.

186

Chirpy Charlie was shocked at what he had done. What if the apple had missed and dented the Volvo? Omitting the apple, he related the incident to Mrs Peters when she signed for a registered package. Mrs Peters told Jennifer Benson when they delivered up their offspring to North Sealeigh Primary, and Jennifer told her friend, Roberta Day.

Roberta passed the story on to her spouse, a police superintendent, at eight-thirty when his alarm clock awoke him from a three-hour sleep. Five minutes later the desk sergeant telephoned Superintendent Day with word of evidently a particularly foul-smelling music case discovered at Stonebridge.

By then, at the speed it had been going, the small orange dog could have been in the next county.

'Camembert, you said,' were Peckover's first words of the new day, spoken on the telephone in his room at the Ocean Metropole to Gus the Bus. 'Were you being polite?'

'Yus I wus. There wus ladies present, wus there not?'

Peckover could not recall. He said, 'What you in fact smelled was dog – er – ' Gus the Bus was sensitive to this mild four-letter word? Unbelievable – 'dirt?'

'Hexcrement of dog, yus. I'd go along with that. What's this all about, then?'

Peckover, Twitty, and two dozen police stood by the grassy verge of a country crossroads at Stonebridge, awaiting action from the explosives specialists. Here on the verge a vigilant patrol car had spotted a black music box. There in the grass it lay, closed and dewy. If it had been thrown from a car, a little more force would have sent it into the ditch where it might have remained undiscovered until the Second Coming. Not that there was much traffic but two uniformed police stood in the road to speed dawdlers on their way.

Semper Fidelis, Chief Constable of Kent, shook Peckover's hand and said, 'Good to have you on board.' He shook Twitty's hand. He was Brigadier (retd.) Alec Semple-Field, a trim figure, no fool, and present, not back at HQ waiting for the bar to open. No one called him Semper Fidelis to his face but he would not have taken too strenuous offence if they had. Always Faithful. There were far worse nicknames. 'Cutting it a bit fine, Day,' he said as Bob Day came from his car.

A captain and a warrant officer from the Royal Engineers bomb disposal unit opened the music box.

Empty. Apart from hexcrement. Dog? Cat? Human?

The bomb team closed the box, placed it in a plastic bag, and handed it to the forensics officer, a woman aged thirty or so in a raincoat. Peckover wondered if she would perform the analysis herself or pass it to an assistant. Not a job he'd fancy at all.

NINETEEN

The animal in the music case had been a dog.

The dog may have been a fox (dog family *Canidae*), most probably a common red fox (*Vulpes vulpes*), though this guess from the laboratory at Maidstone was based merely on the colour of hairs taken from the inner walls of the case. Hair colour was not conclusive. Such canines as Labradors and golden retrievers – slobbering, soft-hearted creatures which did not gnaw car tyres, in Peckover's opinion – had in many instances coats of similar colour.

A pit bull terrier the dog was not, but that had been plain from Chirpy Charlie's description. Always assuming the animal from the music case was the one on which he had scored a hit with his Granny Smith.

Pit bulls, Labradors, and golden retrievers would in any event have had to have been contortionists to have fitted into the music case. Two dozen air holes had been drilled in the lid and sides. The animal had been intended to survive.

Whatever the breed, the dog had become frenzied inside the case. The interior had been clawed, chewed, and thoroughly savaged. Mucus and saliva tested positive to a neurotropic virus, probably rabies.

The rabies virus, continued the preliminary report, caused acute encephalomyelitis leading to death usually ten to twelve days following the onset of mad-dog syndrome. The syndrome might be furious or paralytic.

In humans and other warm-blooded animals, untreated rabies was fatal.

Also present in the dog in question was morphine hydrochlorine, a pain-killer which worked by depressing the cerebral cortex. It was widely used to produce narcosis in dogs.

'Alert the media,' Semper Fidelis ordered.

* * *

Superintendent Day telephoned Alderman Green at home to ask if it would be convenient if he dropped by. He seldom asked, he simply arrived, but the mayor was the mayor, and that called for delicacy. Not a scrap of evidence could be mounted against him, so far, but if a rabid animal had been smuggled into the country, SCAT was where to start asking questions. A major SCAT coup would be to be able to blame the Tunnel for rabies finally entering the country. Everyone's worst fears come true. The smuggling had been bungled because the rabid animal had demonstrably not entered through the Tunnel, but someone had tried.

Gladys Green answered the phone. Philip was not in. She was not sure where he was. Perhaps the Town Hall. She expected he would be home for lunch.

'Are you going to arrest him?' she said.

Day did not know what to say. Or how to say it. Be outraged? Uncomprehending? Laugh it off.

'Good heavens, nothing like that. Routine. Bye for now, Gladys.'

Did she know something about her husband that no one else knew?

He telephoned the Town Hall. The mayor's secretary had not seen him and did not know whether she expected to. The mayor was to have been with the choir on the Continent. He had no engagements.

'For close on a century – eighteen ninety-seven to be precise – we have had no rabies in Britain because of the most stringent quarantine laws. The last case of rabies contracted by a human in Britain was in nineteen eleven. In the thirteen cases diagnosed here since nineteen forty-six the rabies was contracted abroad. Rabies is a nerve disease endemic in the western hemisphere, and at times epidemic, in various rodents, skunks, dogs, foxes, and vampire bats. Worldwide the only areas free of the virus are Australia and Antarctica, areas of Scandinavia, except for Denmark's border region with Germany, and certain quarantined islands such as New Zealand, Hawaii, Ireland, and, until now, Britain. From what you give me to understand, Britain may now have been invaded. All it takes is one rabid animal.'

Speaker: Dr Janet Waterman, PhD, Deputy Director, Animals

Division, Dunwoody and Bauer Research Laboratories, Ashford, Kent.

Venue: Superintendent R. Day's office, Sealeigh police station.

Audience: A fluid score or so of urgently arriving and departing police, health officers, and Members of Parliament for Kent and Sussex constituencies, rabies being not merely a matter of life and death but of votes.

Outside Day's office the Member for East Kent told a reporter for the *Sealeigh Examiner*, 'This is something for you to sink your teeth into. Don't quote me.'

Inside, Dr Waterman said without notes, 'Europe's current rabies epidemic started in Poland, in nineteen thirty-nine, and has advanced west at a rate of about thirty miles a year. In the mid-eighties it reached France's Channel coast. Since then Britain has been enormously at risk. Speaking as a scientist with no political axe to grind, I can say only that the risk has not been diminished by the construction of the Channel Tunnel.'

At her request Dr Waterman spoke standing in her stockinged feet on Superintendent Day's desk. She was petite and would not otherwise have been visible to everyone, or audible, what with the comings and goings and shuffling and coughing. She wore a navy skirt, white jersey, and hair coiffed very short. Twitty, film buff, thought she somewhat resembled Jean Seberg as Joan of Arc, or as the moll of Jean-Paul Belmondo in that Paris gangster movie of 1965 or thereabouts.

'She's a knockout,' whispered Twitty. Though he did not know it he had fallen as much in love with Dr Waterman's brains as with her waif's eyes and body.

'Ssh,' hissed Peckover.

·'Why's it always these gorgeous women who give us lectures?'

'Who?'

'That arts and antiques woman, remember? The one with the bronze lamps and phalluses.'

'Ssh,' Peckover hissed again.

Extra chairs had been carried into the puny office and immediately sat on by the MPs, the self-important, and the lazy. Peckover and Twitty were among the rabble standing two deep against the walls.

The best treatment for rabies, or hydrophobia, was unquestionably preventive treatment, lectured Dr Waterman. This meant the most draconian quarantine measures and the slaughter of all animals bitten by or even coming in contact with a rabid dog. Rabies was highly infectious. A dog with rabies could pass on the virus merely by licking. Vaccination of pets was essential.

'West Germany and France in the mid-seventies had close on eight thousand cases of rabies, and by nineteen eighty-one, twenty thousand, seventy per cent in the red fox. The scourge is horrendously on the increase.'

Superintendent Day checked his watch again. Lunchtime. This time he wouldn't phone, he would turn up on the doorstep. He edged from his office.

'Deaths from rabies number some fifteen thousand annually, mainly in India. All that can be done for a person who develops rabies is to keep the patient as comfortable as possible by subduing the convulsions with intravenous injections of a tranquilliser.'

To Twitty's disappointment Dr Waterman stepped down from the desk. Had he been close enough he would have assisted her.

A young lawyer, male, awed by the occasion, and thin on top – many more such occasions and he would be bald as glass – took Dr Waterman's place, though beside the desk, not on it. He unintelligibly introduced himself. Midgeley? Fudgeley? He was not a practised speaker. Where, wondered Peckover, were these people wheeled in from and did they receive a fee?

'Under the nineteen seventy-five Rabies Act,' mumbled Sedgeley, 'all animals imported into Britain must come through designated sea ports – Dover, Harwich, Hull, Liverpool, Southampton, and Ramsgate – Folkestone is not so designated – or through seven specified airports, which are not relevant to the matter in hand, the dog, or fox, as we're given to believe, having arrived by sea.' The balding legal eagle held an open law book which he kept consulting. 'The animal must have an import licence and be quarantined for six months. No exceptions. Animals imported illegally may be destroyed on the spot.' He looked up from his law book. 'Certain Hollywood stars, among others, have from time to time attempted to smuggle in their pets and been apprehended.'

He blinked, startled by his digression. He's too young to remember, Peckover mused, but he's right. Someone had stepped off a flight from the United States with a chihuahua squirming under her mink coat. Zsa Zsa Gabor? Elizabeth Taylor? He could not recall what became of the dog but he doubted it had been destroyed on the spot.

'The offender may be fined an unlimited amount and sentenced to one year's imprisonment,' said Budgeley. 'Should rabies be confirmed, the government is empowered to destroy all foxes, control the movement of house pets, put down strays, and ban hunts and cat and dog shows. Thank you.'

Smarter than he looked, the lawyer side-stepped into the mob and evaporated like ectoplasm, leaving the MPs calling out their questions and waving their order papers in vain.

Into the breach stepped, to applause, celebrity Jocelyn Bicker-staffe, his lower face obscured by familiar untrimmed whiskers and much of the upper area by overhanging eyebrows. A former director of Chessington Zoo, he had retired to Folkestone, grown mouldy with boredom, and had started firing off quirky nature notes to the press. He had become a pundit. He now had a column in a Sunday newspaper, his own radio programme, and frequently spouted on the box. He had cultivated a regional accent of intense rusticity, though it was not easy to say which region, and when excited he would revert to the staccato Eton and Balliol vowels of his youth. His fans saw him as a breath of fresh air. Others considered him a self-promoting pain in the arse.

'Urrgh, g'day,' he began regionally. 'Our friend Mister Reynard then, is it? Old pointy snout and bushy tail? "John, John, the grey goose is gone, and the fox is on the town O!" Symbol of craftiness is our Mister Reynard. Excuse me, and Mrs Reynard, too. They don't hunt by running as dogs do. Mister Reynard and his lady stalk and pounce. Gotcha! Grey goose, look out!'

Peckover's mind wandered. Were the smuggled fox and Eleanor connected? He could not see how but he believed it probable.

Someone had laid his plans with care. For the sake of argument, say McCurdle. The plans had gone a little awry. The murder of Eleanor had led to the choir's premature return home. Probably he had intended collecting the rabid animal ten days later, after Gap and Bra, so he'd had to telephone to expedite matters. Telephone who? Bahama had heard him telephoning. A farmer friend? A bent vet? Perhaps he really had visited a veterinary college in Calais, taking with him his suitcase and inside it an empty music case with airholes. At Ostend he'd extracted the music case and put it with the others. If Customs opened it, nothing connected it with McCurdle. Fingerprints? He was an amateur but he wouldn't be as amateurish as that. Customs hadn't opened it and heads would roll. McCurdle the planner had a Marks and Spencer bag, or a Prisunic bag, into which to slide and hide the music case at journey's end, Sealeigh. He wasn't an instrumentalist, he couldn't be seen swanning off with a music case.

But why kill Eleanor? She knew about the fox?

Someone had said (Twitty?) that someone had said (Eleanor?) that the most dangerous anti-Tunnel extremists didn't belong to SCAT. Bob Day didn't think so. He was off looking for SCAT's chairman, the mayor. He might be right too.

How could anyone be so insane as to bring rabies into the Kent countryside? What had the woman on the desk said? – thirty miles a year? Not many years before rabies would be everywhere in Britain, Land's End to John o' Groats. The uproar would be such – farmers, parents, pet owners, everyone except Channel Tunnel shareholders – there'd be no need for a bomb to shut the Tunnel down. A Royal Commission would be appointed, and co-opt Alderman Green for his local knowledge, if he wasn't in gaol. There'd be nothing the French could do because all Britain needed do would be to pour concrete into the Brit end of the Tunnel.

If the Chunnel was evil, this was expunging one evil with a far greater evil.

'Mister Reynard hunts the grey goose and any other colour goose for food. Also chickens, birds, eggs, rabbits, and mice. We hunt Mister Reynard for sport. Tally-ho! D'ye ken John Peel? "The unspeakable in pursuit of the uneatable." Wilde. But is the farmer who hunts the fox that gorges on his chickens unspeakable? By George, that same fox is a boon in keeping down rats and rodents, what? These are weighty matters, urrgh!'

Jocelyn Bickerstaffe, realising he might have been lapsing into Etonian, threw in another couple of urrghs.

'Has anyone here known a rabid dog?' In case someone had and would want to tell him about it, the whiskery media man hurried on. 'I 'ave, urrgh. They be fearless, arrgh. Their senses leave 'em. If they're caged they'll break their teeth biting the wire of the cage. If they're loose, and you make a noise, they'll attack the noise. Ferocious and fearless is Mister Reynard, ladies and gen'lemen, and Right Honourable Members of Parliament.' Peckover suspected that Jocelyn Bickerstaffe would not have said no to a seat in the House of Commons, or better, the Lords, because he'd not have had to shake hands and kiss babies. 'They'll attack cattle, trees, carpets, cars – as apparently this one has. Urrgh!' The whiskers quivered. 'But your rabid dog biting anything that moves, or doesn't move, is equally likely to be lethargic. He is just as lethal. He may slink off and hide, or seem affectionate and want to fawn and lick. Don't allow it! Rabid animals act funny. Why?' He hurried on before anyone else could answer. 'The rabies virus inflames the brain. The dog's throat is paralysed, it cannot swallow, it becomes frantic and dehydrated, craving water. Hydrophobia, fear of water, is a misnomer, no longer used by those of us who know, yarrrgh!' He scanned the audience for anyone so pathetically ignorant as to misuse the term hydrophobia. 'Rabid dogs must be destroyed!'

Jocelyn Bickerstaffe switched to rabies victims. Peckover thought at first that he was saying the bitten victims too must be destroyed. He was in fact saying, with unconcealed sadism, that they might prefer to be destroyed, so agonising was the treatment. First came the probing of the fanged punctures with smoking, dripping swab-sticks of nitric acid. Then vaccine therapy. We were lucky, though. The new vaccine therapy developed in the United States was bearable. Six injections over ninety days of antiserum and immunoglobulin. Up to recently the old Pasteur vaccine treatment meant twenty-one injections in the abdomen, plus side-effects, a searing pain, yaargh! Today the inoculations were in the upper arm except that . . .

Peckover nudged Twitty. 'Pubs are open. My treat. Pineapple juice?'

'Took you long enough. Go, Guv.'

They sidled nervously for the door.

A rabid dog was missing. Angus McCurdle was missing. To have listed Alderman Green as missing would have been premature, but he was not nor had been at the Town Hall, the SCAT office, the

Channel Ferry and Hovercraft office, and he didn't look to be at home. The swing-up garage door was up and the garage empty. Perhaps he had taken Gladys out to lunch.

Superintendent Day pressed again the bell of the big pebbledash house with the bay windows and carriage lamps. The lawn would need cutting before long. Who cut it? They would have a gardener. Apart from getting on in years, Phil Green hadn't time, being the most occupied and valued man in Sealeigh, in Phil Green's opinion. The sons couldn't cut it. They were at opposite ends of the world.

Day pressed again. *Are you going to arrest him?* Why would she think he might? What link was he missing?

The door opened and there was Gladys in a flowery housecoat, holding a handbag, hair in place, a smudge of lipstick, not looking any younger, but smiling, or attempting to, and nodding her head a good deal as if nodding were easier for her than speaking and might serve in place of speaking. Somewhere in the house someone was speaking. He could hear voices and whistling.

'How nice,' she eventually said. 'Do come in. You must be tired.'

Why must he? He was pretty tired, as it happened, but he didn't believe he looked it so why would she imagine he was? She'd been listening to the news and supposed he'd spent the morning sprinting about after a rabid dog? He followed her through the hall, saying, 'I was hoping for a word with Phil. How are you?'

He guessed she hadn't heard him. She led the way into a living room which smelled of cigarette smoke. The talk burbled on the TV screen, a video of a familiar face in a familiar place.

'We of SCAT are a peaceful protest,' rumbled SCAT's chairman, 'and shall win by peaceful methods as have others before us. Jesus Christ, Gandhi, Martin—'

Gladys switched him off. 'Philip left it on again. He's growing so forgetful.'

'He's at home?'

'Dear me, no. Out and about, you know. Here, there, and everywhere. I call him my lodger.'

You left it on, Gladys. You're the forgetful one.

Gladys said, 'Very well, thank you. I have been under the weather but I'm better now.'

This sounded like an answer to an earlier question. They shared a chilly leather sofa. The living room seemed a little bleak and out of character. Much of the furniture was contemporary and recently bought, as if a decision had been made to be daring, or at any rate different, and be shot of the overstuffed accretions with chintzy slipcovers that had seen decades of use, and start afresh. There were framed family photographs but no flowers. A white cat prowled in, sat on the rug, and stared at him. Gladys was not offering tea. If she remembered, he would decline it.

He said, 'I'm not stopping. Phil should soon be back for lunch, you think?'

'I doubt it. He's watching his weight.'

'Ah.'

'Ghent took a lot out of him, you see. He thought the world of Eleanor.'

'We all did.'

'A candlestick, I believe. So silly of her taking those madonnas and everything, but she rather was one for drawing attention to herself, don't you think? In the nicest way, you understand.'

'Of course.'

'You won't be hard on Philip. He's a softy, you know. He wouldn't hurt a fly.'

'He's been talking to you?'

'I can tell you I will never betray Philip. A wife is not obliged to give evidence against her husband, did you know that? I believe I read it somewhere. Perhaps it was on the radio. Dear me, it's hard to keep track.'

Superintendent Day was finding it impossible to keep track. He wished he had his tape recorder. Had Gladys said something important or was she loopy? She might not want to betray her husband but she was making a terrible job of not doing so. Her head might be a swamp of drugs. Whatever her ailment, whatever she said, she was visibly not better. She had taken from her handbag a cigarette and was lighting it with shaking hands. He had not known she smoked. If anyone had asked him he would have said he knew that she didn't smoke.

'Gladys, why d'you imagine I would be hard on Philip?'

'Why, SCAT. He's so devoted. It's all so futile, the way he goes about it, but he's never happier than when making his speeches. I can assure you he would never smuggle in a fox with rabies.'

'Where did you hear this?'

'Hear what?'

'Philip?'

'He's not like other men, you know. He needs taking care of.'

Day turned his face away from a cloud of smoke. She might have heard of the fox on the radio. The media had had the news for over an hour. Not the smuggling, though.

'Has Philip been in touch with Mr McCurdle?' he asked.

'Who is Mr McCurdle?'

'Angus McCurdle. In the choir.'

'Oh, that Mr McCurdle.' Not inhaling, Gladys puffed out rapid little balls of smoke as if in a smoke-puffing contest. The smoke puffed most rapidly wins the jackpot. 'He's in London.'

'May I ask how you know?'

'He's very fond of the opera.'

'He's at an opera in London?'

'Absolutely. Something Greek and Roman, I expect. Handel? Let me emphasise that we have no knowledge of Mr McCurdle in this house. Tibby-ibby-ibby.'

Tibby-ibby-ibby was evidently the white cat. With the hand not engaged with the cigarette Gladys patted her lap. The cat sprang on to it.

'She'll have to be vaccinated, Gladys. Take her this afternoon before the rush.'

'She's a he, aren't you, Mr Tibbles, and you've had your vaccinations.'

'When?'

'At the proper time.'

'The Pet Centre?'

'Dr Hartley, we wouldn't go anywhere else, would we, Tibbly-ibbly-oo.' She patted and nuzzled between puffs of smoke. 'Tibbles-the-wibbles-the-pibbly-poo.'

'Gladys, this is rabies.'

'Rabies?' Her voice became hushed, imparting a secret. 'I don't have rabies. I did have myasthenia gravis but really very mild.' She rose slowly to her feet. 'You must come and see us again, Bob. It is

Bob? Philip will be so sorry he missed you.' She held Mr Tibbles and the little that remained of the cigarette: a smouldering glow with a half inch of ash about to fall to the floor or onto Mr Tibbles. 'You will excuse me, I have to take my treatment. Reginald will see you out.'

'Reginald?'

'The footman.'

She dropped the cat on the floor and walked grandly from the room holding the glow, which would scorch her if she did not quickly find somewhere to drop that too.

In his car Day wrote down every word Gladys had said as best he remembered it. He remembered a good deal. Much of it was loopy. Some made horrendous sense. He radioed the police station and ordered that the mayor, Alderman Green, be found and detained for questioning. Dr Hartley at the Pet Centre should be asked when and for what she last treated the Greens' cat, Mr Tibbles.

Now that the media had trumpeted forth the news of a rabid dog or fox on the loose, the nation – the south-east, at any rate – was put on an alert unprecedented since the Blitz, or such was the comparison made by the greybeards.

Not only from the Sealeigh area but from the West Country, Wales, and the Midlands, came blizzards of sightings.

One such was in Grantham, Lincolnshire, by a pensioner who had seen what she believed to be a foaming red fox biting the almond tree in her garden, then running off. Police cars with flashing lights and camouflaged army vehicles moved in. Nobody notable ever having hailed from Grantham except Mrs Thatcher, rumour spread that it was the former prime minister, retired under an assumed name to her childhood roots, who had spotted the beast. She appeared immediately on ITN in London to allay fears that she had been bitten by anything rabid, other than by certain of her former cabinet colleagues, and to urge the nation to stay calm.

Caught by cameras outside Sealeigh police station, Detective Chief Inspector Peckover gave his opinion that, never mind a fox, relays of greyhounds setting out from Scaleigh at eight o'clock that morning, going full tilt, and each with the stamina of a canine Phidippides, if he'd got the bloke's name right, would have been

199

pushed to have made it to Grantham by afternoon. Twitty, eager to be on television, assembling his thoughts, was pre-empted by whiskers which insinuated themselves in front of the camera. The interviewer failed to notice Twitty and pounced with glee on Jocelyn Bickerstaffe, rustic motormouth.

More than a sighting occurred at 4.05 p.m. on Beach Terrace, Sealeigh. Unprovoked, a fox arrived out of nowhere and bit the hand of Denise Khan.

Denise, aged thirteen, was leaving the Mad Hatter carrying a two quid sombrero. Smashing it was, the crown with a little patch that wasn't really there, like it was just frayed, really small, you didn't see it unless you looked. Though she screamed when the fox sank its fangs into her hand, it didn't really hurt, she explained later. More the surprise, like, and the blood and sort of bubbly, snotty stuff on her hand.

First arrived squad cars, then an ambulance which took Denise to Sealeigh Royal Infirmary, next strays such as Peckover, Twitty, and Superintendent Day, and, soon after, Chief Constable Semper Fidelis with, in tow, Commissaire Mouton and Sergeant Pépin.

'Good day, sir, is good you see again,' the commissaire told Peckover, shaking his hand.

'*Enchanté*,' Peckover said, and threw in what he remembered of how the over-the-top French end letters. '*Je vous prie d'agréer, Monsieur, l'expression de mes sentiments les plus distingués.*'

Twitty, sooner than find himself expected to present his sentiments to Sergeant Pépin, drifted along Beach Terrace in search of the fox. Two dozen police were already searching and cordoning off the area.

He could not help wondering why the fox, being rabid, therefore fearless, according to Jocelyn Bickerstaffe, kept running away. He paused in front of the glass door of Curiouser and Curiouser. A notice penned with a flourish read Closed Until 16th April. He peered in at the three-legged rocking horse, the dented helmet, damp books, broken radios and typewriters, oil paintings that were all night and fog in gilt frames, and the moth-ravaged wapiti's head. The shop didn't have to stay closed until April 16th. The tour was kaput and they were back, Clemency and Fleur. They could re-open tomorrow.

Twitty presented his warrant card to a copper who stepped in front of him and said, 'Where d'you think you're going, mate?' He wasn't sure. A turn round the block, a sniff of the briny. He stepped over a ribbon into a street peopled by shoppers. Why were they not indoors? Didn't they know the treatment, if bitten, was six injections over ninety days? Agreed, less searing than the old Pasteur treatment in the abdomen. Still.

Which way to Kimberley Terrace, the messy flat with dust? Coppers were so thick on the ground he'd not be missed. If he were missed he'd be disembowelled.

Who, advancing towards him carrying a loaded shopping bag – no – it couldn't, it wasn't! What's more, if one of them didn't chassé into the gutter they would collide. She was genteelly permed, powdered, looking through him, and not stepping aside but allowing him the privilege of the gutter.

He knew what was in the shopping bag. Port.

He said, 'Hello. *Enchanté.*' For gallantry's sake.

She slowed sufficiently to say, 'I don't know you, young man. Kindly do not molest me.'

Mrs Lemon swept past with her port.

Sounds of sirens filled the air as more police and ambulances converged on the area. Unintelligible voices began to crackle through loudhailers. The chief constable had evidently decided that the streets must be cleared. Sensible decision. Less than thirty minutes ago Mister Reynard had been here, Beach Terrace, rabid and biting.

The concentration of police cars included the one from Rivermere Farm which had waited and watched for McCurdle, should he return. Nobody disputed that the rabid fox constituted anything less than a three-alarm, red-alert emergency. All cars had been radioed in. However, abandoning Rivermere Farm to its own devices turned out to be an error.

TWENTY

Wally Harvey, farm manager, found the body.

Unaware that the fuzz had been called away to join the hunt for the fox, Wally drove to Rivermere Farm with a brainwave for them. Wherever Mr McCurdle was, it might be to do with Brighton Pavilion. Mr McCurdle was a perfectionist who built his matchstick edifices from his own photographs. Since the fire at the Pavilion, parts of it were still under wraps, but perhaps some part or another had been unwrapped. He could be in Brighton with his camera.

In front of the house was parked a Volvo Estate with a label in the rear window, Penny-Wise Self-Drive Rental, UK. Wally let himself in to the house with his key, and toured, calling out, 'Mr McCurdle? It's Wally!' He visited the outbuildings.

The pigs rose up squealing. He had fed them already. 'Shurrup, you fat buggers,' he told them. The boss's Jaguar was in the garage where he had left it before going off on the Continent with the singers.

Wally found Mr McCurdle impaled on a hayfork in the storage barn. Dead by a hand or hands unknown was how Wally thought he had heard this sort of situation described. He looked behind him warily, and up at the loft. Not that anyone was dead these days until pronounced dead by a practitioner in such matters, he had heard or read somewhere else.

Whatever the practitioners might say, Mr McCurdle was dead. So much for the Brighton Pavilion brainwave.

A detective constable ran the mayor to earth in the reference room of Sealeigh Public Library, writing a speech, and escorted him to the police station. 'The rabies business, is it?' the mayor said. 'I wouldn't be surprised, sir,' said the detective constable, who had not been told what the business was. 'You don't have to say anything.'

'So do whatever you do,' said Semper Fidelis, testy and unhappy. Was this something he could have prevented? Dammit, he'd been in Sealeigh only half a day. 'Why don't you turn him on his back? Take out that damn pitchfork?'

'Why don't you leave it to me,' said Dr Hood, pathologist.

Superintendent Day said, 'Strictly, sir, it's a hayfork, I believe. Just the two prongs or tines. A pitchfork has four, usually, for digging and manure.'

McCurdle lay among sacks of Robinson's Prime Cattle Feed. The hayfork's prongs had gone through his chest and come out of his back.

Dr Hood, kneeling beside the body, jotted a note and shifted on his knees, examining and jotting. He wore one of his four working suits, two of which were usually at the cleaners. This one had a brazen silver and yellow weave and a trampled look from visits to woods and thickets, along river banks, and on one occasion into a pothole. He turned McCurdle's head sideways, prised open the mouth, and foraged with rubber-gloved fingers. With scissors ten inches long he cut away sections of clothing.

'Someone move this stuff, would you?' he asked, impeded in his journey round the body by sacks of cattle feed.

Peckover helped shift smelly sacks aside. Twitty slowly backed to the doors out of the barn, hoping to escape the bloody mess with nobody noticing. Sergeant Hall stepped round the body taking photographs. A civilian laboratory assistant powdered the haft of the hayfork. Constable Mole, plainish in her own opinion, but not without offers, measured distances with a springy metal rule, asking whoever was to hand to please catch hold of the other end.

A dozen police, among them two marksmen who with a single shot at a hundred metres could blow away a fox, and hoped they might yet have a chance to do so, searched the impacted earth floor and felt queasy. Outside the barn another dozen searched the mud, pleased not only to be outside but to have been summoned from fox duty. All well, the fox would have been caught and destroyed before they were finished here.

The laboratory assistant took Wally Harvey's prints. 'To eliminate you from the inquiry,' Superintendent Day told Wally.

As far as Day was concerned, Wally Harvey was already eliminated, and Peckover seemed to agree, if grudgingly. Any prints on the hayfork were going to be his right worshipful the mayor's. Latest on the short-wave was that the mayor had been in the library only twenty minutes before being seen and taken to the station. Previous to that he had taken an hour's walk on the seafront and read the newspaper over coffee in the Atlantic Hotel. So he claimed. All very well for Gladys to blithely say her husband was out and about, here, there, and everywhere. Not that she was to have known he aimed to visit Rivermere Farm.

An example of villains falling out, Day guessed. A little surprisingly the older mayor had bested the younger McCurdle. Over exactly what the falling out had been – the Tunnel, relics, rabies? – the mayor would speak out. If not today, tomorrow. He spoke out about everything else.

Dr Hood stood up and announced, 'Subject dead by hayfork or whatever the implement is named.' His manner was inappropriately breezy. 'Between two and three hours ago. I can't be more precise yet.' He peeled off his gloves. 'I can be precise about the entry wounds, which are in my experience unprecedentedly ragged, and the exit wounds which are even more so. Velocity of impact considerable, is what I'm saying. See for yourselves. The higher prong must have shredded the heart. I'll confirm that in the report. Otherwise he's in reasonable shape. A little dusty from striking the ground, but the hands are impeccable, like a pianist's. No sign of a struggle. End of the haft coated in earth, and here's the hole it made in the ground. He killed himself. He stood up there on the edge of the loft' – everyone looked up – 'positioned the two prongs against his chest, pointed the haft, handle, whatever you call it, at the floor – twenty, twenty-five feet, would you say? – and fell. We may now remove the implement. Would one of you hold him down? He's firmly skewered.'

The search for a suicide note began. 'Sarge, what about this?' called a constable when he found on a manure pile by the cow byre the ashes of a matchstick model of the Royal Pavilion, Brighton. An onion-shaped dome and some sections of wall had collapsed inward but survived. Perhaps rain had prevented further damage.

Zipped in a bag, Angus McCurdle left his farm for the last time. Peckover thought that when the time came the remains of the matchstick Pavilion should be buried with McCurdle, as personal treasures had been buried with the pharaohs. He would not suggest it himself. He had enough question marks on his record sheet without inviting more, such as soppy, flaky, and morbid.

'I blew it,' Bob Day said.

'Forget about it,' Peckover said from the back seat. 'I'd 'ave done the same.'

'The mayor, of all people.' Day braked for a rabbit. 'Public figure, repository of civic virtues, hauled off for questioning, and innocent as a lamb.'

'We don't know that, sir,' Twitty said.

'Question is, is he going to raise a stink?'

'No,' said the chief constable. 'I'll talk to him.'

Day had radioed Sealeigh police station to release Alderman Green and give him a lift home or to anywhere he asked. He drove fast along country roads to Sealeigh. Beside him the chief constable tuned the short-wave in and out. The last sighting of the fox had been in a garden in Dean Street, behind the Regis Hotel, where it had attacked a poodle then run off.

'French fox bites French poodle,' the chief constable said. 'Serve 'em both right.'

Another chauvinist, Peckover thought. He passed Twitty the transcript of Day's conversation with Gladys Green. Day drove through Stonebridge crossroads where that morning a dewy music case had been found. Sealeigh 6, said a signpost. The desk sergeant at Sealeigh police station cracklingly offered an item fresh from the Pet Centre. Mr Tibbles, white neutered male cat, property of Alderman and Mrs Green, had been inoculated against rabies on 3 April, Tuesday, four o'clock appointment.

'We were on our way to Ghent.'

'Sorry, Super. What?'

'Who brought him in?'

'Who?'

'Tibbles!'

'Mrs Green.'

'Find that horrible fox!'

Day turned down the desk sergeant's crackling to minimum audibility and pressed the accelerator. Twitty leaned forward.

He said, 'Mr Day, Gladys Green told you Eleanor was one for drawing attention to herself?'

'Right.'

'Eleanor wasn't drawing attention to herself when she stole the relics,' Twitty said. 'Last thing she wanted. She didn't draw attention to herself until she died. What she was trying to do was draw attention to the choir.'

'This a theory, young fellow?' said the chief constable.

'I don't know what it is, sir, but it doesn't go away. How about Eleanor was sending out a message that the choir had in its ranks a villain, McCurdle, who hoped to close the Tunnel by bringing in rabies? She got the message through to the police by nicking relics everywhere the choir stopped to give a concert. Not the rabies bit, but that something was rotten in the Sealeigh choir. Why she didn't simply come forward and tell us is something I haven't yet fathomed.'

'She was frightened for her life,' Peckover said. 'With good reason, as it turned out.'

Day said, 'She could have written to us. Not put her name on it.'

'Or phoned in a funny Irish accent?' Peckover said. 'You'd have taken it seriously?'

'Quiet, all of you,' said the chief constable. 'Young fellow, you're suggesting Eleanor Sandwich stole the relics deliberately to draw police attention to the choir?'

'Just floating it, sir. I'm not—'

'Peckover, you agree?'

'It's spot on. McCurdle was a Little England, anti-Tunnel fanatic. He probably had accomplices, one, anyway, and now we know who.' Peckover leaned forward, the better to be heard. 'McCurdle guesses Eleanor might be a closet activist, and useful, but he's wrong. He tries to recruit 'er and fails. Eleanor's so alarmed by what she's learned McCurdle is plotting that she has to do something, she

206

can't pretend these people don't exist. Why doesn't she simply go to you, Bob? What she's learned is McCurdle and his partner are dangerous and she's terrified. So she keeps 'erself out of it – almost – and involves us by nicking relics. All credit to 'er. Enter the Yard dutifully singing, one bass, one tenor. She isn't aware the new boys are from the Yard, and neither is McCurdle, but when 'e finds her eyeing the candlesticks the light dawns. Perhaps it doesn't, but either way here's Eleanor making trouble. What he doesn't need is Eleanor or anyone bringing the choir to the attention of the plods. So he disposes of 'er. A big mistake. If anything's going to bring in John Law it's a murder in the cathedral. Not that I know what else 'e should have done. He kills Eleanor, swipes 'er handbag, hoping it'll look like a routine mugging, and collects his rabid fox in Calais. But he's fouled it up. We're on to him and he knows it. We give him a fair grilling on the ferry. We're all over his farm. He was probably skulking in the orchard waiting for us to leave. When he has the farm to himself he destroys his Pavilion and why not? It's never going to be finished, not with what he has in mind. He finishes 'imself because he can't live with what he's done. Eleanor, rabies. Some could live with it but not McCurdle. Farmer, scholar, unhinged, but with a conscience. He's still a puzzle. He must have known easier ways to end it. Gawd, can you imagine?'

'Easily,' Twitty said.

'Oh yer?'

'Like you said, Guv, he was a scholar, a Classicist. He dishonoured himself. Nothing to live for. He ended it the Roman way. He fell on his sword.'

Twilight in the Kent countryside. Passably unpolluted country roads with sparse traffic and hedgerows dappled with the pinks and whites of spring flowers. In pernickety gardens such flowers would have been cast out as weeds, but here they were flowers.

The chief constable addressed himself to the short-wave. 'No further sightings, sorry sir,' responded the fox control room at Sealeigh police station. The desk sergeant reported that the French contingent, the Commissaire Mouton and his Sergeant Whatsit – Parbleu? Perisher? – were restless and feeling left out. Should he send them to Rivermere Farm? 'Give them some absinthe with a snail in it and tell 'em we'll be there directly,' the chief constable said.

Day said, 'What do we do about Gladys? I pulled in her husband. I'm not going to fall on my sword but it wasn't my brightest moment. I'd like to be sure about Gladys.'

'She sounds pretty vague and out of it, am I right?' If not downright loony, Peckover thought. 'She thinks we suspect her 'usband?'

'She does.'

'Strike you as suicidal?'

'Who knows?'

'I'd leave her at 'ome,' Peckover said. 'Why don't we visit her right away? We've only to ask why she had her cat inoculated days before anyone knew we'd have a rabies scare. If she says her husband advised it we'll have to look at the mayor again, but I doubt she will.'

'Mrs Green, the mayor's wife?' queried the chief constable. He sounded as if he were playing Happy Families. 'You realise what you're saying?' He swivelled round, came nose to nose with Peckover, whose chin rested on the back of the chief constable's seat, and recoiled. 'Mrs Green is respected and ill, from what I understand.'

Day had decanted out of rusticity into a redbrick suburbia of terraced houses and bus routes. North Sealeigh. Herein on this day's rosy morn had Chirpy Charlie the Whistling Postman, he of unerring aim, a veritable David, let fly the Granny Smith that did smite the fox on the hind leg.

'Mrs Green,' Peckover said, 'may have wanted to bring down the Tunnel because she's as paranoid as her partner in all this, McCurdle, but I doubt that too. My opinion, what it's worth, is Gladys Green was trying to do her 'usband a favour. She loves that big pompous bladder of gas.'

'We can do without that kind of talk,' said the chief constable.

'Pardon,' Peckover said. 'Gladys loves her shy, retiring—'

'I don't care for your tone,' growled the chief constable.

'Gladys is well aware that shutting down the Tunnel will mean huge kudos for her husband. I mean, chairman of SCAT? Closing the Tunnel is what he's forever sounding off about. But let him march and posture and make speeches until he's blue in the face, he's accomplishing nothing. The Tunnel is there and it's going to happen. Still, if anything shuts it down, rabies might, and Gladys knows that. The mayor will be on television puffing himself up and telling us "I told you so", and she'll have put him there, not that he'll ever know. 'Ow about rabies rampant through the English shires as the loving bequest of a devoted wife who's had a sudden glimpse of 'er mortality?'

'Glimpse of what from who?' demanded the chief constable.

'Myasthenia gravis, from her doctor,' Superintendent Day said, and was about to add how mournful this was when the radio's cracklings crackled more insistently and he raised the volume.

The fox, crackled the item from the fox control room, was on Wycliffe Way. All cars, all cars . . .

'Where's Wycliffe Way?' said the chief constable.

'Two minutes,' said Day.

'Get there! Stop dawdling, fellow! Use your siren! What d'you think the damn thing's for!'

TWENTY-ONE

Theirs was not the first police car to arrive in Wycliffe Way, but it was prompt. Superintendent Day came close to demolishing a bobby setting up a wooden barrier. Instead of hopping out of the way, the constable, recognising the super behind the wheel, came to attention and saluted. The car left a mud smear on his tunic.

Outside Sealeigh Presbyterian Church three police cars were parked every which way. Two more with caterwauling sirens barrelled in from the direction of the seafront. Though darkness was an hour away the street lights had come on. Now was a time when tennis was a matter of finishing the set rather than of pleasure. The evening was chilly but OK. Only foreigners would have complained. Along Wycliffe Way wafted a mix of lilac and exhaust fumes.

The chief constable slammed the car door. He advanced on the nearest policeman, a chubby young man with a two-way radio to his ear. 'Who's in charge?' he demanded.

'You are, cock,' muttered Day.

The greatest concentration of police, fifteen or sixteen so far, was in the churchyard. One cradled a twelve-bore. Several carried big sticks, putting Peckover in mind of grouse-beating ghillies in the Scottish heather. Where, wondered Peckover, had they found these staffs or staves? Were they police issue? The Yard, as far as he knew, possessed no such staves. Those who carried them tapped them gingerly on headstones as they trod line-abreast through the churchyard, as if the fox might be hiding behind a headstone and tapping would lure it out. Police dogs tugged on their leashes. At the side door used by the choir for rehearsal more police had assembled. One of them held binoculars to his eyes like Lawrence of Arabia. The door was shut, sensibly in Peckover's opinion. If the fox slid unnoticed into the church, and stayed there, the havoc at Sunday's 11 a.m. service would be memorable.

Sirens pierced the seaside calm and sneered to silence outside the church. The first television crew arrived. Residents watched from behind parlour windows and from their front steps, the door open, ready to scuttle behind and bolt and chain at the first glimpse of the fox. Police patrolling the road had no difficulty discouraging sorties into the outdoors.

Followed by Day, Peckover, and Twitty, the chief constable breezed through the gate into the churchyard, bore down on an inspector, and said, 'Semple-Field, Chief Constable.'

'I know, sir. Roy Barrington. It'd be nice to say we have it cornered and it won't escape this time.'

'We're sure it's here?'

'Not any more.'

'But it was?'

'It was and still might be.'

'Who saw it?'

'I did for one.'

'Where?'

'Where you're standing.'

In spite of himself, and his medals from the Falklands, the chief constable gave a little sideways shuffle.

'Then what?' he said.

'It ran that way.' Inspector Barrington pointed. 'It's a big cemetery. We're looking.'

'Thought they weren't supposed to run away. Thought they were supposed to attack and bite.'

'Perhaps it doesn't know that.'

The chief constable glowered. 'Tactics?' he said.

'Sir?'

'Your procedure if we see it?'

'Destroy it.'

The chief constable headed off between graves. Inspector Barrington winked at Superintendent Day. Day frowned. He spied Sergeant Ripon, beery but serious, a very present help in time of trouble. He went to join him.

'Company, Guv,' Twitty said, looking back towards the gate.

211

'What do you say we search the far end of the churchyard? The commissaire's all right but I'm sorry, the sergeant bloke gets on my wick.'

Commissaire Mouton and Sergeant Pépin were among a group coming through the gate. Peckover spotted Alderman Green, a vivid SCAT button on his lapel, mouth moving in a non-stop talkathon. He was clearly none the worse for his spell at the police station. He had probably supposed he had been invited there to advise on the Christmas Ball. A car had been despatched to his home to watch that Gladys did not leave, but he had not been told and wouldn't have understood anyway.

'Suits me, lad. Forward.'

'You first, Guv.'

'Not at all. Youth before beauty.'

Ahead was the churchyard, a slowly advancing line of police, and possibly a crazy fox.

'No, no, Guv, after you. You're the leader, you lead.'

'Into the jaws of death.'

'That's a bit melodramatic.'

'You realise, mate, this Mister Reynard doesn't necessarily come charging head-on. He's crafty, remember? Stealth's his forte. Why wouldn't he attack from behind? I'm telling you for your own good. All I can say, watch your arse.' Peckover set off, Twitty in his wake, away from mayors and French flics. 'You might not feel much, not right off. He'll take a small mouthful – won't do your cavalry twill a lot of good – and next you know you'll be on your back with a red-faced St John Ambulance geezer pinning you down and pumping immunoglobulin into you, not to mention the nitric acid. May not be as agonising as the old Pasteur treatment but it won't be any 'oliday. Place like Sealeigh might not 'ave caught up with state-of-the-art developments. Don't bank on 'em having much beyond aspirin and calamine lotion. Keep an eye on Jesse James there with the shotgun. When 'e starts blasting throw yourself flat. He doesn't look too steady to me. That bulge in his pocket, it's a pint of Smirnoff. Can't say I blame 'im.'

'Slow down, Guv. No rush.'

'You're right.'

They slowed. Here where the tapping coppers had gone before

was fox-free. To overtake would be to become the vanguard in untapped territory. Peckover headed for the cover of the church wall. He was damned if he was going to lead the hunt, or, come to that, join in. He had a wife and children. He had no gloves. What if the fox nipped his hand? He should at least have had gloves of the kind sheiks wore for hawks to stand on when they flew back with a sheep. He had nothing, no stave, no mountaineering boots, no binoculars. It wasn't as if he were a zoologist. He was a copper, a London copper at that, he shouldn't even have been in Sealeigh. He should have been in the Feathers enjoying a pint and a celebratory knees-up with Frank and some of the lads, anyone who cared to show up, except Frank's dread Mrs Coulter, she with the computers and disapproving mien. The mission was accomplished, the holy relics recovered, one villain dead, the other unwell in her home. Let the Sealeigh boyos chase the fox. Let Twitty. He had long legs.

Best of all, let Jocelyn Bickerstaff. He knew all about foxes. There he was, old hedge-face, poncing about with recommendations. There again was Alderman Green, blowing his nose, at sixes and sevens over the whiskery celebrity, a rival for the limelight. Come camera-time, hedge-face versus the mayor, their pinching and hair-pulling would be heard across the Channel in the auberges of Le Touquet-Paris-Plage.

For the present the sounds were of yet more police sirens and the ragtime rapping of staves on gravestones. No one seriously believed this would flush out the fox. However, the search was thorough, it would be recorded as such, and nobody had a better plan. Set out bait? A saucer of milk and a dead hen? Where did you find a hen, dead or alive, at this hour?

'Close that gap, you fairies, you 'orrible chorus line!' shouted a sergeant. 'Yes, Jefferson, you!'

'Ladies and gentlemen, your attention, please!' called out Alderman Green.

For whatever reason, that was all. Heart attack? A true-blue citizen and a democrat, he had at last stuffed an orange in his mouth? Or had he suddenly realised, after seven decades, that he had nothing to say? A step ahead of Twitty, Peckover reached the east end of the church. The chorus line on their left flank would have to wheel right. In spite of his dawdle he had overtaken them, just. He peered round the brick corner. Grassy churchyard stretched unkemptly on. A dozen paces away sat the fox.

Its eyes were closed, or half-closed. Droopy-lidded, anyway. The mouth hung open, the tongue lolled over white teeth. It sat panting, reddish and smallish, pointed snout, black ears and legs. *Vulpes vulpes.* The brushy red-brown tail switched to the left and lay still. Then to the right. The tail had a white tip and looked to be as long as the body. From the beast's chops hung a glittering thread of drool.

Peckover assumed that this was Angus McCurdle's diseased fox from Calais, smuggled occupant of a music case, apple-struck by Chirpy Charlie, biter of car wheels, trees, a poodle, the hand of Denise Khan, and a threat to the Tunnel, the government, not that the government would be any great loss, and to life, animal and human. How many foxes did genteel Sealeigh have? Unlikely there would be a duplicate fox in the churchyard, routine and healthy. Jolting its snouty face towards the grass, the fox emitted throaty, watery sounds.

Poor little bugger.

'Lad?'

'It's it. Guv, don't move. What do we do?'

They did not have to decide. 'There!' cried one of the chorus line, raggedly wheeling, tapping, rapping, through the grass and graves at the east end of Sir Blaze-Away's edifice. 'Fox!' shouted someone with decent if unexceptional vision. Someone else, an idiot, bawled 'Haaagh!' and rushed towards the fox, slashing the air with his stick. Peckover guessed he was a Highlander, possibly an Irishman. Not because he believed Highlanders and Irishmen to be idiots, though some would be, purely on the law of averages, but from the bloodcurdling 'Haaagh!' and the flailing of the shillelagh, which the idiot copper hurled at the fox, missing by a mile, the sensible fox having already launched a counter-attack with a sprint towards the chorus line, no longer apathetic but charged with energy and rabies. Always there was an idiot and sometimes he received a medal. This particular idiot (Constable Paul Woods, b. 1964, Dover), charged by the fox, fled retribution (and all chance of a medal) with an athletic dash through the cemetery and over the privet hedge on the north perimeter. The fox careered blindly on.

'Head it off!'

Confusion.

'Head it off where?' Twitty said.

'Head it off how?' Peckover said.

They viewed the turmoil of running policemen. The fox about-turned and ran in the direction it had come from, scattering its pursuers. Staves were flung. They missed and fell in uncut grass.

'Into the church! Herd it into the church!' cried a tenor voice.

Bob Day? The mayor? The chief constable?

Peckover stood by a gravestone, aware of his uselessness. Had he heard 'Herd it into the church' or 'Head it into the church'? You couldn't herd one fox. Perhaps you could. Closing the fox in the church sounded reasonable, but how? Was the plot to chase it in or lure it? Not that it mattered. The fox was nowhere to be seen.

Gone, the fox.

Peckover observed through encroaching dark only gravestones and milling mobs of coppers. He who fights and runs away lives to fight another day. He shouldn't, couldn't applaud the fox. Worse than anti-social, that would be sentimental. All the same, in his head he offered a small cheer.

Where was Twitty? There was the Amiens albino in his leather jacket, arms folded in the rejection position. *Ma foi, les rosbifs!* he would be thinking. There the mayor brandishing his arms and failing to impose order on chaos. With the fox vanished, the chaos was considerably less than it had been. Now was head-scratching time and the recovering of flung staves. The door where the choir entered for Schütz and 'April Is In My Mistress' Face' now stood open. At the foot of the steps up to the door had formed a straggly cordon of coppers as if for a military wedding.

'Everyone stay calm!' somebody called.

Semper Fidelis? Peckover could not locate the chief constable but it was the voice of brigadierdom (retd.) commanding calm where adequate calm already existed. Certainly there was no panic, only a residue of thrill, a thinning of adrenalin, a mix of let-down and relief that the fox was no longer on the town.

'Ho!' yelled someone in terror. 'Ho!'

Twitty.

He came out of the dusk in a galloping blur of tweed and cavalry twill, the fox foaming at his heels, returned, and very much on the town.

Constable Twitty would relate later, and set down in his report, that when he had spied the fox sitting in the shadow of the perimeter hedge, and stolen close and barked at it, he had not been wholly sure what he was doing. Nobody had trouble believing that. The only suggestion he had heard which made sense, Twitty would insist, was the church. If the fox could be driven or enticed into the church, and the doors shut, it would all soon be over and everyone could go home.

Whether the fox would have attacked him if he hadn't barked at it, Twitty didn't know. The expert with the beard, Bickerstaffe, had said a rabid fox would attack a noise. Whatever, it had attacked, and he had run like the clappers for the church.

He ran through the gloom as he had never run. He hurdled over a gravestone, admittedly not a high one, then a second gravestone. He thought he heard the Guv shouting. Others too shouted, though he could not have said who, or what they shouted. If the Froggies were shouting they would be telling him '*Allez!*' and '*Maillot jaune!*' Neither did he know if the fox were still in pursuit, though he knew enough not to look back. A right prat he'd be if he were running for his life and the fox had sheered off and gone to the beach.

'Lad! Jason!'

The police at the foot of the steps had melted away, or at any rate made ample room for him. Twitty took the steps in a single stride. Two strides brought him through the vestibule, nine more along the aisle's mothy red carpet to the last pew. He jumped on to the pew. Now he looked back.

The fox's tail disappeared into a pew halfway along the aisle.

'There it goes!' shouted a uniformed policeman who had lost his helmet.

Tumbling into the church came a dozen police. Twitty recognised only the guv. Then Bob Day, stalking bravely into the centre aisle as if to make amends for earlier errors. The policeman with the twelve-bore vaulted on to the stage and stood there with legs apart like a terrorist.

'There!' called a copper carrying a stave.

Twitty heard the door to the outside slam shut. He stayed on the pew, hopping from one foot to the other in case the fox should pop up and decide to join him. Vigilant, breathing hard, he looked upward. He might be better off in the gallery, but he had never been up there and wasn't sure where the stairs were. He would have been happy to depart from the church announcing, 'Right, you men take over,' but he didn't. He lacked the rank.

'There!' Day cried. 'That window! Fan out!'

Twitty saw nothing by the window Day appeared to be pointing at, or by any window. They were gloomy coloured glass, perhaps bright when the sun shone, but where was the fox? The police were treading cautiously towards a window with a sill and a vase of daffodils on the far side of the church. The copper with the shotgun came down from the stage.

'Slow and easy!' the guv was saying. 'Those with staves first!'

'Staves?' said the policeman who had lost his helmet.

'Some of us don't 'ave a stave,' wheezed another policeman, freckled and staveless, big as a Sumo wrestler.

Peckover, also without a stave, none the less started along the centre aisle. He proceeded one pace at a time, pausing just before each pew and bending forward to peer into it, because who could trust a fox? Mister Reynard, Bickerstaffe had said, stalked and pounced – gotcha! He entered a pew and moved crablike along it in the direction of the window.

When he stepped into the side aisle the fox darted at him from who knew where, a mere yard away, two at most, and bit his ankle. For good measure it then bit his hand.

217

TWENTY-TWO

Sealeigh Royal Infirmary, an artistic statement in polychromatic reflective glass and fine prestressed concrete, was opened by the Queen Mother in 1972, replacing the town's Albert Hospital, which looks like a prison and is today the Sealeigh School of Mechanical Engineering. The infirmary is equipped for open heart surgery, possesses a heart catheterisation laboratory, a CAT scan unit in the radiology department, an adjacent MRI unit, and a solid reputation in general surgery, paediatrics, orthopaedics, intensive care, urology, and more. The lawns have a sprinkler system (seldom required), the cafeteria serves energy-giving stews, chips, and steamed puddings. Sea views from the fifth, topmost floor (psychiatric).

However, the infirmary had no anti-rabies vaccine, or did not have on the night Detective Chief Inspector Henry Peckover was admitted to the emergency room. Urgent telephone calls on behalf of bitten Denise Khan, holding on to her sombrero from the shop on Beach Terrace, had earlier revealed that Brighton, Eastbourne, Dover, Tunbridge Wells, Canterbury, and Maidstone had none either.

Sergeant Pépin argued that the vaccine should be flown in from Calais, or better still, the victims flown there. What Twitty found odd about this suggestion was that it came from Sergeant Pépin, who was not, Twitty would have thought, someone to be too concerned if the fox had sunk its teeth into a score of perfidious rosbifs. He revised his opinion of the sergeant upwards a little, cautiously.

Peckover did not in fact have long to wait. The vaccine and plenty to spare was by now on its way from Guy's Hospital for Denise Khan. He told the charge nurse he would like to see Denise.

A constable guarded the door against invasion by the press and pests such as Jocelyn Bickerstaffe. Denise was a large girl who lay on the bed holding her sombrero in her bandaged hand. Her larger

218

mother lay beside her, crooning an Asian dirge and clamping her down protectively. The father was kneeling on the floor engrossed in a jigsaw. Smaller Khans, none small by normal child standards, lolled around, bored.

Peckover introduced himself. He showed Denise his own bandaged hand. They were both going to be fine because of a new vaccine developed in the United States, it wouldn't even hurt, he told her. They would be in tomorrow's newspapers. They might be the subject of an article in the *British Medical Journal*, not to mention the *Guinness Book of Records*. He hitched up his trouser leg, disclosing a bandaged ankle.

'Bloody hell,' Denise said, and with impressive agility squirmed from under her mother and put her sombrero on her head. 'Where's the fox, then?'

Peckover hesitated. What did she want to hear? That the fox had been peacefully put down? That it had suffered anguished retribution before being erased from the face of the earth? Neither version was strictly accurate. The fox had still had its fangs in his hand when a helmeted constable had broken its back with a stave. Then the bloke with the twelve-bore had blasted it, peppering at the same time a swatch of red carpet and many pews.

'The fox is dead,' Peckover said.

Denise Khan burst into tears.

Gladys Green, puffing on a cigarette, showed disappointment but little remorse as she told Superintendent Day and Chief Constable Semple-Field of her and Angus McCurdle's role in a chronicle of conspiracy, murder, and the smuggling into Britain of the rabid fox.

She couldn't speak for poor Mr McCurdle, of course. She supposed nobody could now. But he had seemed especially angry about the rail link crossing his land. He used to call it rape.

For her part, it would have been so nice for Philip if the Tunnel had had to close. He campaigned so hard and to no avail.

Then she had fallen asleep. Day retrieved the cigarette before it set her on fire.

Alderman Green was more bemused than broken by the arrest of his wife. Though he did not quite realise it, or ever would, the Tunnel had never been a burning issue for him. Rather, it was a hobby to keep him out of the house and in the public eye. He wondered if he should offer to resign as chairman of SCAT. He thought perhaps he should. The offer would be certain to be refused.

Naturally he would carry on as mayor. Sealeigh needed him.

First some pulse taking, the thermometer under the tongue, and questions on his medical history, though not 'Have you been bitten by a rabid fox before?' Next the swabbing of the bites, at which point Twitty left the room.

The room was in obstetrics and gynaecology, only here and psychiatric having a spare bed. Dr Desmond Culpepper was eager that the patient stay overnight. For observation. And because you never knew.

This last remark did nothing to reassure Peckover.

Dr Culpepper had qualified two years earlier. He was enthusiastic, overworked, and, tonight, nervous. He had never had a rabies case before. Nobody had. Now he had two. Platoons of media people were assembled outside on the lawns.

As Dr Culpepper understood it, all that had to be done was administer the vaccine. All the same. He knew that he should not have said, 'You never know.' There and there he resolved never to say it again.

Peckover would have preferred someone with more years on him than Dr Culpepper. On the other hand, the older the doctor the more likely he'd be to find at the back of his medicine chest some of the antiquated Pasteur stuff (waste not, want not) that made you feel you were being burned at the stake.

Peckover's room in obstetrics and gynaecology had two beds but the other was unoccupied. So far. No telephone. Perhaps because a ringing telephone would have frightened the babies. He was going to be incommunicado.

Fact was, he could leave after the injection, they were not going to strap him down. Miriam, though, a believer in doctor's orders, would have had a fit. On the phone in admissions he'd had trouble enough persuading her not to snatch up Sam and Mary and drive to Sealeigh.

Whether for disinfecting or incinerating, his clothes had been carried off. He had been handed a distressing, faded pink gown for imminent mothers. The gown stopped short at his hairy knees and tied with ribbons at the back. As he couldn't tie the gown one-handed, and untied it kept falling open, even open and off, on to the floor, the nurse had tied it for him. The whole hospital experience was embarrassing and the nurse didn't help, no matter she was a nurse and therefore had seen everything.

Here in maternity she would have some function such as midwife or wet nurse. She looked like every male patient's dream nurse, if you liked your nurse tall, flaxen-haired, and suntanned silly either from sun lamps or a fortnight in Tangier. He'd have said she was Norwegian, from Trondheimsfjorden or similar, and named Hedda or Sigrid, but for her Liverpool accent. Not that she said a lot. He needed pen and paper. His well-being would be very much in the hands of Sigrid.

To Sigrid

Bereft are the fjords and fjorests of Norway
Since Sigrid the flaxen Norse nurse travelled our way;
'Sigrid!' cry the patients, and I cry the hoarsest,
'Of all the world's nurses, 'tis Sigrid's the Norsest!'

Oscar Thomas visited, dutifully in and out. Squeamish in the corridor were Witherspoon and Twitty. Bahama brought him two pounds of apples (how long did she think he was going to be stuck here?) and stayed twenty minutes. Audrey Belcher and Sydney Crisp put their heads round the door, nodded encouragingly, whispered to each other, waved, and withdrew. Why were they with each other, not with their spouses? Had no one told them the tour was over? Peckover assumed they had spouses. Perhaps the spouses didn't know the tour was over.

Sigrid swabbed his arm. Dr Culpepper hovered with the needle. The fellow was sweating! Peckover would have recoiled had there been anywhere to recoil to. He turned his head to the door, wanting to call out to Twitty. Was there still time for a second opinion, which was to say, a different doctor? He felt something on his arm, near the shoulder.

'It won't take a moment,' said perspiring Dr Culpepper.

'You've not finished? Wasn't that it?'

Peckover almost asked if it would hurt but the question was not one a grown man asked. Of course it would hurt.

'Just a little prick,' the doctor said.

Aah! Nng.

Over. Sigrid applied a plaster. Dr Culpepper, consulting a calendar, said, 'Five to go. The next you can have in London. Or anywhere. It doesn't need to be here.' The thought visibly cheered him. They departed, Dr Culpepper to write the rabies entry for his memoirs, Sigrid to weigh babies.

Twitty loped beamingly in. 'Congratulations, Guv! It's a boy!'

'Ho bloody ho. Do they feed us in 'ere? Bring me my wallet. Over there. What you do, you fetch ample bottles of Bass, your mango cordial, and pizza or whatever. You choose. What's the matter, then? Got a previous engagement? Gawd, I should 'ave guessed. Bahama, right?'

'We thought we'd share a light supper. A few shrimp, a little toast, candles.'

'While I'm stuck 'ere with sodding television and the corridors alive with the sound of babies.'

'You'll have visitors, Guv. Except you probably won't, it's after visiting hours. But you're getting phone calls. You're in people's hearts.'

'You sound like a Get Well card. Whose hearts?'

'Joe Golightly and Clemency Axelrod. They phoned. They're announcing their engagement.'

'High time. Indecent, the way those two have been carrying on.'

'Nothing compared with Helen Willis and Robin Goodfellow. They've gone to Brighton in a chauffeured limousine.'

'Stop leering. It'll be a bridge tournament. Soul of a gossip columinist, that's what you've got. Who else?'

'Archy Newby and Fleur Whistler. You'll be getting flowers. Must be an on-off thing, those two. Now it's on.'

'Who're they?'

'Archy, as I recall, was your first suspect in a matter of some stolen relics.'

'Balls. He was your suspect. You kept on about how he was an

222

earl and you were at school together, diddling each other behind the bicycle shed. Bathing in the reflected glory, you were.'

'Bollocks. With respect. You were the one was fascinated. Toffs and class, the national obsession.'

'I don't want to hear any more. I'm weak. I've got rabies.'

'Commissaire Mouton has invited us to lunch tomorrow. Far as I can make out he likes singing the old songs and we're singers. Two hours of "La vie en rose" and Beaujolais in the Cricketers' Arms.'

'Bloody 'ell. The sergeant bloke too?'

'Pépin? Ask him. He's down the passage chatting up your nurse.'

'Sigrid?'

'Who?'

'The Norse.'

'Not Norse. Nurse.'

'All you know.'

'Wouldn't surprise me. They look as if they might have some Aryan thing going.'

Peckover's hand, arm, and ankle throbbed somewhat, not too much. Dr Culpepper had warned him that that was what they might do.

Pink-gowned in bed, he brooded on musical, passionate Sealeigh Choral Society, a pulsating hive of yin and yang all coupling off in a horny gavotte. Perhaps that's what choirs did. Perhaps in the cultural compartment of the brain, or in the gonads, bubbled a hot meld of lust and alleluias. Now Pépin too, contaminated by exposure to the Sealeigh rosbifs. The Viking nurse might be just his cup of aquavit. Ironic if she were Jewish.

'The good news, Guv, is Mr Veal phoned and you're to give him a buzz, soon as you're well.'

'I'm well, dammit. What's 'e want?'

'Best it come from him.'

'Don't mess about, lad.'

'The BBC's going to do us live, the whole concert, Schütz and Mo and April and the sisters and the cousins and the aunts—'

'Good luck to them.'

'Not them, Guv. Us. The choir.'

'I 'appen to be taking Sam and Mary to the zoo that day.'

223

'Orders from the assistant commissioner. He's very keen. Great public relations, shows that coppers are cultured, the Factory's finest as repository of Western civilisation's musical heritage. Look, Henry, you'll be on the back row. No one will see you.'

'True.'

All the same, he wasn't going to sleep well. In the first place there'd be the wailing of new-born babes. Worse, chorister's melody malady syndrome would be back. His head would be howling with lobets and coelis, rehearsing for the cameras.

'The cameras can zoom in, of course,' Twitty said. 'Big close-ups of Our 'Enry with his mouth open as a jam jar and chirruping forth the lobets and herring to a million amazed viewers.'

'Bring me my beer, you 'orrible man!'